FRANKLIN HORTON

NO TIME FOR MOURNING

BOOK FOUR IN THE BORROWED WORLD SERIES

NO TIME FOR MOURNING

1

The Valley

ARIEL STALKED TOWARD THE BROOK, parting thick late-summer grass that rose nearly to her waist. It was the determined walk of a head-strong child, a walk intended both to reach a destination and to put distance between her and her mother.

"Don't go too far," Ellen, her mother, warned, slinging the tactical shotgun over her shoulder. She picked blackberries and dropped them into a plastic bucket, each berry making a soft thud against the bottom of the empty bucket.

"I won't. I'm exploring," Ariel said. "I used to play here all the time. You always let me."

"Things were different then," Ellen said.

Ariel rolled her eyes and continued to the edge of the creek. She picked up a sliver of limestone the size of her palm and tried to skip it, but the creek was too narrow for that. The rock bounced once off the surface of the creek and then lodged itself in the soft mud of the opposite bank with a solid *thwack*.

"Stupid creek," Ariel said, kicking at the grass which yielded in a completely unsatisfying manner.

She noticed the exposed roots of a Sycamore tree, the soil having been washed away by decades of water. A crusty snapping turtle sunned on the gnarled roots looking like some prehistoric revenant. Ariel crept toward it, intent on grabbing it by the tail and showing it to her mother. She knew it could bite her if she wasn't careful. She was the type of child who had to pick up every frog, every snake, and every lizard she saw. Her parents didn't discourage it – they wanted a brave, inquisitive child.

As she reached toward the leathery stub of a tail, the turtle lurched into the water, having sensed the child approaching.

"Stupid turtle," Ariel said, stomping her foot.

She collapsed against the trunk of the tree, brushing a strand of hair from her face and sighing dramatically. She looked back at her mother. Ellen was still focused on picking berries so the dramatic sigh and collapse had been completely wasted.

Ariel returned to scanning the creek and movement caught her eye. A Blue Heron was moving up the creek. It approached with such stealth, such grace. The head moved from side to side in an eerily robotic manner, scanning the water for anything that might make a meal. Ariel admired the bird for a moment, then a sneaky smile spread across her face and she began looking for another rock.

She found one within arm's reach as big as a dinner plate. She slid it into her lap, trying to move as slowly as the Heron so she wouldn't startle it. When it was within a dozen feet, she grunted and slung the rock toward it with both hands. The rock didn't reach the bird but landed close enough to splash it with a sheet of water.

Startled, the bird stumbled a few awkward steps, then took to flight, shrieking its primitive squawking cry. Ariel sat back beneath the tree, a broad grin of pleasure on her face. She wondered why such a pretty bird made such an ugly sound. She thought it sounded like a pterodactyl from dinosaur movies.

"Ariel!"

She jerked and turned, looking up to see her mother standing beside her.

"Did you try to hit that heron with a rock?"

Ariel thought quickly. She knew her mother loved birds, particularly herons. "No, Mommy, I was trying to keep it from eating a frog. I have a frog here that I'm friends with and I didn't want the heron to eat him. I had to scare it off." Ariel concentrated on making herself appear as innocent and sincere as she could. She was the hero here, not the villain.

Ellen frowned, unslung the shotgun, and dropped to the ground beside her daughter. She put her arm around Ariel and pulled her close. "What's the matter with you, baby? Why are you in a bad mood?"

Ariel debated her response, then decided to be honest. "I heard you and Dad talking this morning. You said it would be almost time for us to start school but you didn't know if they'd be having it or not. Then Dad said probably they wouldn't and it made me sad."

Ellen hugged her little girl tighter. "I'm sorry, sweetie."

"You know what my favorite time of year is?" Ariel asked.

"Going back to school?"

"Yes!" Ariel said. "And you know what my favorite thing to do before school starts is?"

"Buying school supplies," Ellen responded, recalling how much her daughter had always loved buying her supplies and new clothes for the school year. She would lay everything out and organize them, packing and re-packing them until the first day.

"Yes," Ariel said. "And am I getting to buy school supplies this year? No! All because of this stupid apocalypse. This is the worst summer *ever*."

Ellen couldn't help but smile, which riled Ariel even further.

"It's not funny," Ariel whined.

"I know it's not funny. I'm not laughing at you. I'm laughing because you keep calling it the apocalypse. This isn't the end of the world, sweetie. Things will get back to normal one day."

"That's not what Dad says," Ariel said. She lowered her voice and adopted her dad, Jim's, serious tone. "You know, Ellen, things may never be the same again. Not in our lifetime anyway."

Ellen cracked up again. Ariel mocked Jim enough in jest that she was pretty good at it.

Ariel smiled at her mom's laughter, her eyes filling with tears. It was one of those complicated childhood emotions – wanting to laugh with her mother but unable to stop the tears from flowing at the same time. "I want things to be normal again. I want to go to school and see my friends. I want to be able to watch kid shows on cable TV. I want the power to come back on. I want to see a movie. We didn't even get to have a vacation this summer. We didn't get to go camping or to the beach or anything."

Ellen sighed. "I want things to be normal again too, but you have to be a big girl and accept that things are different now and might be for a while. You are not the only one feeling bad right now. Some people have had worse things happen to them. Lloyd lost his parents. Buddy lost his daughter. Gary's family lost a son-in-law. None of them has even had time to sit around and be sad about it. We've all been too busy."

"They haven't even had time to be sad?" Ariel asked. "It sure doesn't seem that way to me. *Everyone* is sad and serious *all* the time. I don't like it."

"No, honey, they haven't had time to mourn because they've been busy trying to help everyone else stay safe. Everyone is worried about their families."

Ariel mulled this over, staring off at the creek. She hadn't really thought about the bad things happening to other people.

"It's not only our town, Ariel. The whole country is going through this right now. You should be glad that your daddy loved us enough to prepare ahead for bad times. Some people didn't have those extra things. Some people didn't think this would ever happen. That's why things are scary right now."

"Buddy said his little girl was buried at the cemetery in town," Ariel said. The world and all its people were too big a thing to think about. She couldn't comprehend that. She could comprehend her friend Buddy and his loss.

Ellen nodded. "I think she is."

"I'd like to go visit her with him one day," Ariel said.

Ellen's heart melted at this, that her daughter could be throwing rocks at water birds one moment and then be so sweet the next. "I think he'd like that."

"I'd like it too," Ariel said.

Ellen disentangled herself and stood. "Now I need you to help me pick some berries so we can get back to the house. We have work to do."

They worked together to fill the bucket, Ellen's mind not on the job. They'd been so busy lately with all the requirements of this new way of life. Although they were managing better than most, it was easy in the summer. In a few weeks the nights would start getting cooler. Their dwindling fuel supply would likely be gone completely. Some people would be starving to death already. Others, who had never been prone to violence in their previous lives, would be gazing upon their hungry families and contemplating things they'd never imagined.

"Not everyone feels bad, Mommy," Ariel said as they walked toward home.

"What do you mean, sweetie? Who doesn't feel bad?"

"I don't think Daddy feels bad," Ariel said. "You remember how grumpy he was in the mornings when he was going to work? He's not like that now. He's happy in the morning."

Ariel was right. Jim did spring out of bed each day with a sense of purpose.

"I don't think he's happy about what happened, Ariel. I think he's just pleased that he's been able to take care of us. I think he gets up each day with a plan of what he can do to make our lives better right now." She was finding it hard to explain *sense of purpose* to a child, but that's what it seemed like to her. They'd never discussed it, though Jim did seem to have a new sense of himself. He was more confident. He had more energy. As much as she didn't want to admit it, perhaps he even was happier.

2

_____

Jim

JIM AND POPS were working on the farm's water system when Ellen and Ariel returned to the house. Jim was relieved they were back. They'd been less than five minutes away the whole time and they had a radio with them. Still, it worried him when they were out of his sight. He imagined that this was the same feeling homesteaders experienced in that same valley two hundred years before when residents lived in fear of Chief Benge's band of Cherokee who frequently slipped in to kill farmers and kidnap their wives and children.

The family's small farm had a good supply of drinkable spring water, a creek, and a pond. Even though he was grateful for the multiple sources of water, there was no denying that hauling water from those sources was a laborious chore that no one enjoyed. The lack of working plumbing was also an inconvenience. Jim had never minded an outhouse, however he was apparently the only one. Everyone else complained constantly. Although they were adapting to the lack of electricity, the lack of indoor plumbing was a more difficult hardship to overcome.

He'd made plans for an off-grid water system several years back and bought all of the components. Unfortunately, his daily schedule was the same as that of most people he knew in that there was never enough time to do everything that needed to be done. Something else was always broken and needing repair, so projects he simply *wanted* to do were usually pushed to the side by projects he *had* to do.

The basis of his water system was simple. He had a nine hundred gallon plastic water tank that he'd painted black. The black color would help it absorb heat and keep the water from freezing. He wasn't yet sure what he was going to do about the coldest months of winter. Water from the home's gutters would go through a series of screens, filters, and settlement barrels before being stored in the big tank. A garden hose ran from a fitting on the big tank to a twelve-volt RV water pump. From the pump, another hose was connected to an outside spigot of the house.

When Jim closed the main shut-off valve to his home's plumbing, the valve between his well pump and pressure tank, he created a closed system that was fed from his nine hundred gallon tank instead of from the well. The RV pump ran off of a boat battery that was charged by a solar charger Jim built from parts on the internet. The RV pump had cost less than fifty dollars and was designed to start running when it sensed a loss in pressure. If someone in the house flushed a toilet, the pump started running and recharged the water system. Once it reached a certain pressure, the pump would quit running until someone used the water again. It was a simple system that would make life in the off-grid home much more convenient. It would be a small step back toward the normality of their old life. A very small step.

Jim was mounting the solar panel when Ellen and Ariel approached.

"Can you take these inside and set them on the counter?" Ellen asked Ariel, handing her the basket of blackberries.

Ariel nodded and pranced off with the bucket, humming a song.

"Bye, sweetie," Jim called after her.

"Oh yeah," she said. "Bye, Dad."

When Ariel was out of earshot, Ellen told him what had happened with their daughter while they were picking berries.

"I try to be conscious of what I say in front of her," Jim said. "At the same time, I want her to understand the gravity of the situation. I'm afraid if she's not a little scared she may take unsafe risks, like wandering off from the house or talking to folks she doesn't know."

Ellen nodded. "I know and I agree, but I want her to have a childhood too. How do we balance it all? I want to get her out of the funk she's in. I want her to be happy and playful again."

Jim's radio chirped and he groped for the black pouch he carried it in. It was always on his side, now part of his expanded set of everyday carry items.

"*Groundhog to Roadrunner,*" came Pete's voice. He'd insisted on call signs, taking his duty at his outpost ever more seriously.

"Go ahead, Groundhog."

"*You guys out of sight of the road?*" Pete asked.

"Affirmative."

"*Can you see the road from where you are?*"

"Negative, Groundhog. Do I need to?"

"*Maybe. There's a truck with a cattle trailer coming down the road. I don't recognize the truck.*"

"Coming from which way?" Jim asked.

"*From the direction of town.*"

"Until we're certain what this is, arm up and get in the house," Jim said. He took off at a jog, heading for a vantage point where he could observe the road.

He thumbed the mike on the radio. "This is Jim. Everyone east of me, we have visitors. A truck with a cattle trailer. While it may be nothing, Pete doesn't recognize the vehicle. Keep an eye out."

He ran around to the front of the house and took a position behind a vehicle. From there, he was able to see the paved road running through the valley. He could now hear the growl of a Cummins diesel engine headed his way. You didn't live in farm country and not learn to recognize the sound of the different engines.

When Jim saw the banged-up Dodge dually he immediately had an idea who was in it. He didn't know the pair by name but he knew that they were farmhands who worked at Rockdell Farms at the far end of the valley. When times were normal, he passed these men nearly every day at the big barn that served as the base of operations for this end of the massive cattle operation.

Rockdell Farms was one of the oldest continually operating businesses in the United States, having been established before the Revolutionary War. The original deed to the property was signed by Patrick Henry. It was one of the largest cattle operations east of the Mississippi River. At one point it had been nearly a hundred thousand acres, though the size had been greatly reduced over the years. Still, they raised tens of thousands of cattle and sheep every year.

When Jim had gated off the road between the valley and town, he and the other residents accepted that there would still be some people who needed to come and go, which was why he'd used a gate instead of sawing a tree down across the road. He didn't have a problem with residents of the valley coming in and out. He hadn't thought about the folks working Rockdell Farms because the farm had its own network of roads and those folks rarely passed through his valley to get there. He wondered why they opted to come in by a different road. There had to be a reason. Anything that didn't make sense was a reason for concern. It might mean you had a problem that you didn't even know about yet.

Jim's radio chirped.

"What's up, Jim?"

It was Gary, who was now living in Jim's valley after having been run out of his home in a nearby town. The guy had made many of the same preparations as Jim had, then his location proved unsustainable. Too many neighbors. Too many scumbags.

"I got eyes on the truck. There are some guys I recognize. Don't really know them. Maybe if I recognized them, they'll recognize me. They work at the big farm as you come into the valley the back way. I used to pass these same guys every day driving to work and we'd throw a hand up at each other. I want to talk to them about why they came in from this side of the valley. They never do that. They have their own road system."

"Is that a problem?" Gary asked.

"Just being cautious. If there's some kind of trouble on the other side of the valley that kept them from coming in the normal way I want to know about it. I'd hate to be totally oblivious to some developing threat right in our backyard. We're kind of operating in the dark here and any information is helpful."

"You think it's safe to go talk to them?"

"As safe as anything these days, I guess. I'll be armed."

"They may be too," Gary replied.

"I'll be careful," Jim assured him. "If I follow the creek that feeds the pond, it will bring me out at one of the bridges near that farm. I'm hoping that's about where I'll find them."

"How about I go with you? I could hang back and provide a little backup."

"That'll work," Jim said. "But hopefully I won't need you."

"You never know when shit will get crazy. If we've learned anything these past weeks, we've learned that."

Jim smiled. Gary didn't use much foul language, though curse words were occasionally slipping out now. The state of the world was rubbing off on him. It was a barometer of the times.

Jim walked the woods to Gary's house, the scenery as peaceful as any on Earth. The house that Gary was staying in had belonged to Jim's good friend Henry, now dead along with his wife and son. They'd been killed by a scumbag named Charlie Rakes who had been released prematurely from jail when the county couldn't feed the inmates anymore.

Gary was waiting on him with an AR-15 and a vest of gear. They set off without a word, following a creek that ran through the inner recesses of undisturbed farmland. There were no houses, or any signs of man visible for most of the walk, save for the occasional strand of rusty barbed wire embedded in a tree. Jim imagined it looked much

like it had when Daniel Boone passed through the area on his way to the Cumberland Gap.

Eventually, they reached a fence, a concrete bridge, and the road that exited through the back of the valley. Beyond that, in the distance, they could see an open gate and the dually truck pulled just inside. The two men he'd seen in the cab of the truck were pushing a four-wheeler down the ramp at the back of the cattle trailer.

"You stay here," Jim said. "You'll have cover if you need to fire."

"Got it," Gary said. "Be careful."

Jim climbed up the bank and walked in their direction, his M4 rifle in front of him on a single-point sling. He didn't hold it at a ready position, but he did keep a hand on it, which was necessary to keep it from bouncing off his body. While he didn't want to appear threatening, at the same time he didn't want to appear defenseless. He had to be ready.

One man swung onto the ATV and started it. He shot off down the pasture, headed for a cluster of cattle at the far end of the fenced meadow. The remaining man pulled some steel gate panels off the trailer and quickly set up a temporary loading chute to funnel the cattle onto the trailer. He pulled a pint liquor bottle from his back pocket and watched the other man round up cattle. He unscrewed the cap and was taking a swig when Jim called to him.

"Hello!"

The man jumped, sputtering, and nearly dropping his bottle.

"Easy now," Jim said, holding a hand up in front of him. "Didn't mean to startle you."

The man threw a quick glance to the ATV, checking to see if his buddy knew they had company. He quickly screwed the cap on the bottle and shoved it back in his pocket, like Jim might take it from him.

"Glad you didn't spill that," Jim said. "That would have been tragic."

The man nodded and cracked a wary smile. He could appreciate a joke about liquor. He was missing most of his teeth, except for a few scattered in his lower jaw. He looked like a human Jack-O-Lantern. "Ain't so easy to get right now."

"That's a fact. What's your name?"

The man hesitated. "Hodge."

"I'm Jim. I live back in here. I pass you guys here every day working this farm," Jim said. "You usually see me in a dark blue Chevy with a cap on the back."

"I recall the truck," Hodge replied, the familiarity not putting him at ease. "You needing something?"

"Not really. Like I said, I live here in the valley and I noticed you guys coming through. We haven't seen much traffic at all," Jim said. "I wondered if there was some reason you drove in through my end of the valley instead of this end. I want to make sure there's nothing out there that I need to be worried about, other than the obvious shit." Jim was trying to keep it friendly and conversational, hoping to put Hodge at ease.

It appeared to be working. Hodge relaxed a little. "You the ones put the gate up back yonder?"

Jim nodded. "We did. There were too many people coming through just looking for trouble or looking to steal. We wanted to let them know they weren't welcome. Thought the gate might at least slow them down."

"You might have to replace the lock then," Hodge said. "We had to cut the son-of-a-bitch off."

Jim ignored that even though it irritated him. He gestured toward the small herd of cattle. "Patrick selling some cows or just moving them?"

Patrick was a descendant of the original owner of Rockdell Farms and the one currently running things. He was in his sixties and had grown up in the operation. Jim didn't know him well. They were just acquaintances.

"Why you give a shit?" Hodge asked. He looked a Jim warily, then turned back to watch the ATV again. He pulled the bottle from his pocket, took a quick nip, and tucked it back.

"I'm asking because I know some folks who might be in the

market for buying a few cows if they're for sale. I ain't trying to stick my nose in anybody's business."

Hodge looked satisfied by this. "Patrick ain't likely to be selling no cows anymore," the man said. "He's dead."

Jim was surprised for a second, then realized it was a purely old-world reaction. People were dropping like flies in the current state of the world. There wasn't any reason to be shocked that someone had died. There were a lot of things a man could die from these days.

"What happened?"

"Caught some people breaking into this house and tried to run them off. They was a better shot than he was. Killed him and his wife both."

Jim nodded, letting this sink in. "So who's running the farm?"

Hodge shrugged. "Ain't no one running it. Patrick only had the one son and he's out west. He ain't likely to make it back here anytime soon."

Jim had never been able to hide what he was thinking and feeling very well. He never had much of a poker face. His looks always gave him away. Right now his look was saying that he understood this man didn't have any right to the cattle he was taking. At least no more right than anyone else. Although he didn't intend it to be accusing, apparently the man took it that way.

"Look, we got to do something with the cattle," Hodge said defensively. "We won't be able to get feed this winter. They ain't no more hay or silage being put up. They'll starve and die off. Our families will probably starve and die off too if we don't get some food coming in."

"You have a point," Jim said.

The sound of the ATV grew louder and Jim could see that it was headed in their direction, slaloming back and forth to steer a herd of cows in this direction. Hodge noticed too, and he looked nervous.

"I reckon I'm going to have to get back to work," Hodge said.

"I'll get out of your way then," Jim said. "I was just wondering how you guys were set for fuel. If you have enough fuel to be hauling cattle, maybe you have enough to trade?"

"What's in this truck is all the fuel we got between us, but word is that Wallace County is buying cattle," Hodge said. "They got a lot of hungry people over there and some of them have a lot of damn money. You know that big subdivision over by the golf course? They took up a collection and they're paying people to haul in cattle plus they'll provide all the fuel. They even got their own security guarding the place."

"Really?"

"Yep. This is the first load but we heard they'll buy whatever you bring them."

When the ATV reached them, the driver kept a wary eye on Jim, though he couldn't stop what he was doing without the cattle scattering. Hodge jumped into action, yelling at the cows and tapping them on the back with a long stick. After a few minutes of tapping and hollering, the cattle were all loaded. The ATV was loaded up too, the cattle panels propped up against the fence so they'd have them for the next load.

The man from the ATV wiped his forehead with his shirttail and pulled a jug of water from the cab of the truck. He'd yet to acknowledge Jim. He drank from the water jug, now staring at Jim. When he'd finished, he wiped his mouth on the back of his hand. "Who the fuck are you?"

"I'm a neighbor," Jim said, trying to take the high road for a change. "I used to pass you guys every day on my way to work. Just thought I'd stop in and see if you'd heard any news."

"Ain't heard a damn thing," the man said. He looked at the other man. "Hodge, you hear any news?"

Hodge shook his head. "Nary a bit."

"Then there you go," the other man said. "Nothing to tell."

Jim had tried to be friendly throughout the conversation even though that wasn't natural for him. He did it because he was trying to put them at ease and gain some information. Being dismissed like this was pissing him off, though.

"With times being what they are, a fellow should be friendly to his neighbors. You never know when you might need one of them."

"I'll take my chances," he said. "Get in the truck, Hodge. We got places to go."

The driver started the truck and drove out the gate, maneuvering the long trailer between the posts. Jim followed along behind them. When the truck was through, Hodge leaned out the window. "You mind getting that gate for me, buddy?"

"Shut your own fucking gate," Jim told him and walked off.

3

Randi

WHEN RANDI WALKED INTO HER PARENTS' kitchen that morning, she went straight to the coffee pot out of habit. It was clean and empty. Her head dropped. She'd survived quitting cigarettes, but the lack of coffee was going to be the death of her. "Shit!"

"We're out," her dad, Ernie, said from behind her. "Coffee's all gone now."

He was sitting there at the kitchen table, a cigarette in one hand, his favorite coffee cup in the other. He took a sip from the mug.

"Then what's that?" she asked.

"Hot water," he replied. "I'm pretending."

"How's that working for you?"

"It ain't."

"Going to be out of those things soon," she said, nodding at his cigarette. "You might as well go ahead and quit like I did."

Her dad took a drag on the cigarette and shook his head. "Ain't gonna."

"When that carton runs dry, you'll be quitting whether you like it or not."

"Got a tobacco patch," her dad said. "I'll be rolling my own by winter."

"I thought you sold your allotment?" Randi asked.

Farmers had been growing tobacco on a quota system since around the Great Depression. Although the crop was a labor-intensive effort, it brought in more cash than most other crops a farmer could raise. Around 2004, the government started buying those allotments back from farmers, essentially paying them to not raise tobacco.

"I did sell my allotment, but I always liked having a little 'baccy patch. Selling the allotment didn't mean you couldn't grow any. It just meant you couldn't sell it. I had a little patch this year, and I'll grow more next year. Can you imagine what people will pay for tobacco if they can't buy cigarettes at the store?"

"A lot," Randi said. "If you can hang on to it."

Her dad shrugged. "We'll hang onto it. Between me and your brothers, we'll keep it."

"I wish you could grow coffee," she said, casting another forlorn glance at the empty drip coffeemaker.

"Reckon I wish I could too."

Randi sat down at the table and rested her face in her hands, staring at her dad.

"What's wrong, honey?" he asked.

"What isn't wrong? I quit smoking and there's no coffee. I don't know what to do with myself in the morning now. This keeps up I might have to take up jogging or something."

Her dad grinned and let out a low, steady laugh.

"I might," she said, mildly offended.

He shook his head and kept laughing, sounding like the struggling starter on a car with a low battery.

The sound of footsteps coming through the house made them turn. Randi's daughters came in. When Randi looked at them, she saw teenagers, though both were in their mid-twenties now. It was hard for her to comprehend that it had been so long since they were born, since they were children. Where had the time gone?

The fact that they were together now and that they were both looking at her made it clear that they had something on their minds. They were conspiring, just as they'd done their entire lives.

"What is it?" Randi asked, already suspicious.

"We want to go see Dad," said Carla, the youngest. She was always the spokesperson – or mastermind – for whatever schemes the two developed.

Randi dropped her head to the table, allowing it to thump off the surface several times. "No coffee, no cigarette, and now I have to hear about your dad."

"We haven't heard from him," Carla said, her sister nodding in agreement. "We'd at least like to know if our dad is still alive. You'd want to know your daddy was safe, wouldn't you?"

"My daddy isn't an assh—"

"Randi Ward!" her dad said, cutting her off. "It's too early in the morning for cussing. I can accept it at the dinner table but not at breakfast."

"I haven't had breakfast," Randi reminded him. "Nor coffee."

"Well, I'm having mine," he said, nodding at his cup of hot water and his cigarette.

Randi sighed. "Look, girls, he hasn't made the first effort to check on you two," Randi said, turning her head sideways to look at her daughters while still not lifting it from the table. It was obvious that talking about her ex-husband was not her favorite subject.

"He could be hurt or injured," Carla pleaded. "He could need us."

"Or he could be drunk and laid up with some floozy," Randi said, then shook her head. "Oh, sorry, that was when we were married and you girls were babies."

Her daughters frowned at her.

"That's ancient history, Mom," Sherry spoke up. "You've got to move on. It's been, like, fifteen years or something."

Randi lifted her head from the table and looked at her father. "Give me some help here, Dad."

Earl tamped his cigarette out in a blue glass ashtray. "Can't blame the girls for wanting to see their dad," he said. "Even if *you* hate him, he's still their daddy."

Randi turned to her daughters. "You know we're completely out of gas now and it's probably a two-hour walk each way."

"We know," they said in harmony.

"When's the last time either of you walked that far?" Randi asked.

The girls looked at each other, then back at their mom. The answer was *never* but they weren't going to give her the satisfaction of admitting it.

"We can do it," Carla insisted.

"Oh, I know you can do it," Randi admitted. "Sherry can do it too. I hope you know, though, that those grandkids cannot do it."

"They want to see their grandfather," Sherry protested. "It's been weeks."

"They've gone weeks without seeing him before. It was some-times weeks between his visits when the world was normal," Randi said. "Those kids can't walk it and we can't carry them the whole way."

Sherry had three children from her ex-husband. No one even knew where he was anymore. He'd disappeared from the picture over a year ago. Sherry had no idea that he'd only disappeared because Randi had paid him to. She'd used a bonus check from work to bribe him into signing away his parental rights and disappearing forever. He'd been hesitant until Randi explained that if he didn't take the money, she'd give it to a couple of shady country boys she knew and they'd *make* him disappear. Either way, the result would be the same. The choice was his and he chose wisely.

"She's right," Randi's dad pitched in. "The grandkids will stay here with us if you want to go. Your grandmother and I can look out for them. Tommy can go with you and Jeff will stay here with us."

He was referring to Randi's older brothers. Randi resented being assigned a babysitter. "I'm a grown woman, Daddy. I do not need someone to go with me. I am perfectly capable of getting my girls to their dad's house and back home alive. Do I need to remind you that I walked all the way from Richmond? We'll carry guns and stay off the main road."

Her father studied her. They'd butted heads more times than he could recall. Randi won some. He won some. Sometimes no one could be declared winner and they avoided each other for a few days until the smoke cleared. "How about if you just do it for my peace of mind," he finally said. "Let Tommy go with you as an extra gun in case you need it. Jeff's already out hunting this morning anyway, so he can't go."

Randi looked around the room at all the eyes on her. She didn't have the energy to fight them off this morning. She lowered her head back to the table. "Okay," she conceded. "We can go. Tommy can go."

Her daughters looked at each other, sharing some sister telepathy. They weren't done with their mother yet.

"Maybe we could go with Tommy, Mom, and you could stay home. We don't need you to go if he's going," Carla offered. "You don't even want to go anyway."

Randi laughed. "Not a chance."

"Why not?" Sherry asked, knowing that her mother would be complaining about their father for the entire trip.

"'Cause if we find him dead, I don't want to miss the opportunity to spit on his dead body."

Randi's daughters frowned and walked off.

"She's joking," their grandfather called after them.

"The hell I am," Randi said.

4

Jeff

RANDI'S BROTHER Jeff spent more time in the woods than he did in the house. He was always camping, hunting, or fishing. Like many of the people in the remote area where they lived, Jeff observed his own hunting seasons. If game was moving around it was hunting season. If game was laying low it was fishing season. While his family was always worried that he'd get in trouble with the game wardens, it was hard to call Jeff a poacher. He didn't hunt for trophies, but for subsistence. He ate everything he killed. That he lived in an era and location where subsistence hunting had fallen out of favor was an injustice in his eyes – a much greater injustice than him killing a deer out of season.

Jeff had a variety of tree stands and semi-permanent blinds built around the family farm. He planted food plots that would draw game near those locations. On this morning, Jeff had not had any luck. There had been a lot of does on the property lately and he wanted to harvest one. They could have a nice dinner and then his mother could can the rest. Of course, with their special senses, the deer seemed to know he was out hunting today. On the days that he was working the fields or riding around on a four-wheeler, they paid no attention to him at all. They would barely even look up at him as they grazed in plain sight. Not today.

He had started to climb out of his tree stand several times but kept thinking he heard something. Then he heard it again—the snapping of a tree branch. Jeff held his breath and listened carefully. It could be a deer, yet it sounded different, like the snapping of the branch was muffled by a foot on top of it. That was more likely a bear.

Or a man.

Jeff cocked his head and finally got an inkling of where the sound was coming from. He raised his rifle, sighting through the scope. He caught a flash of movement. It was not an animal unless they'd taken to wearing plaid flannel shirts. Jeff felt an immediate flush of anger. This was his family's farm. Anyone from around here would know that. Whoever this was had to know that this wasn't their own property and was willfully trespassing. It wasn't just the crime that angered Jeff, it was the bold affront to his home, his sovereign territory.

The figure in flannel left the trees and entered a clearing. Through his scope, Jeff could recognize the figure now. It was Kyle Cross, a man of about Jeff's own age who lived with his parents on a farm down the road. Kyle and Jeff had never gotten along. They'd fought on the school bus, on the playground, at parties, and at high school football games. They'd fought over words, over women, and over the way one man looked at the other. If Jeff had any enemies in this world, he was looking at one of them right now. Kyle was indeed a man with no respect for boundaries, whether legal or social. It was nothing to him to cross a fence and hunt another man's game.

It irritated Jeff that Kyle had land of his own he could hunt, and instead chose to poach off a neighbor. He had brothers and a sister that often ran with him but Jeff couldn't see anyone with him now. Maybe the brothers were hunting their own land and Kyle wanted to venture out and see if he could bring home some meat when they couldn't. He'd made the wrong call here. This could be a fatal mistake.

With the crosshairs of his scope centered on Kyle's head, Jeff touched the trigger lightly and made the sound of an explosion with his mouth. He smiled. "Got you, you bastard."

He continued to watch Kyle. The man stopped, leaned his gun against a tree, and unzipped his fly. Jeff's anger rose again. Kyle obviously felt so confident in his trespassing that he could take a comfortable piss there in the open as if he didn't have a concern in the world.

Jeff lowered his crosshairs to the open fly and snapped the safety off. "Now that would give them something to talk about, wouldn't it?" he muttered.

He considered the shot, considered the implications. The man had two brothers, a sister, and parents who were as mean as any people had ever been. They were a family that the police only visited when things got so bad they could not be ignored. They stole, they sold drugs, and they sometimes burned down houses. They'd once beaten a man so badly that his brain nearly came loose from its moorings and his head swelled so bad it threatened to push his eyeballs out. The man's crime? Breaking up with their daughter.

Still, in this part of the country, allowing a man to take this liberty with your property would only be the first step. Once he saw that he could get away with trespassing, he'd come back. He'd try something else the next time. Maybe he'd steal something. This could only end one way. A family like Kyle's only understood one thing.

As Jeff considered all this – safety off, finger on the trigger – Kyle zipped up and deprived Jeff of what would have been a shot of legendary acclaim. Kyle dropped down to the ground and took a rest against the base of a tree. He removed a water bottle from his pants pocket, took a drink, then lit up a cigarette.

Jeff remembered being at a party a year or so ago at a run-down trailer way back in the woods. The man who owned the trailer was a hunting buddy of Jeff's, a friend from high school. His name was Red Lawson and he worked as a diesel mechanic. His trailer was old, with power and little else. No phone, no TV, and barely even a road going in, only a trail through tall grass that stopped at a clearing. There sat the trailer, covered in peeling green paint and shedding parts like it was frozen in the early stages of an explosion.

As Jeff pulled up, he could hear loud Lynyrd Skynyrd. There was a keg in the yard and lots of people sitting around on coolers and logs. There was a fire, which was one of the better things about living in the country. If you wanted to have a bonfire in your front yard you just did it. Jeff parked his old Ford, grabbed his twelve-pack of Milwaukee's Best, and joined the party. He knew everyone and everyone knew him.

They were all having a good time until Kyle Cross showed up with a rough-looking crew comprised of one of his brothers, Tim, and his sister Lisa. They'd been into meth a lot lately and it appeared that they'd been into it that night. Their eyes were red and crazy. They were sucking down straight liquor and kept laughing like they shared some private joke.

Lisa's nose was running and she was constantly sucking at her scabby lips. The other women kept looking at her. She was universally hated by nearly everyone except her brothers. Most men were afraid of her and most women skirted around her like she was a chained Rottweiler. She knew how other women felt about her and she lived up to their expectations, antagonizing other women and starting fights. Everyone at the party thought they knew how the night would end. They would be wrong.

When the group of ruffians tried to mingle no one would interact with them. For most, it was out of fear. The Cross family took it as an insult and began antagonizing the other guests. Lisa Cross thought another girl was looking at her funny and threw a beer at her, catching the girl square in the face. The host of the party had enough and approached Jeff to see if he would back him up in asking the Crosses to leave. Jeff had no problem with it. He sucked down his beer, flipped his cigarette into the fire, and said, "By God, let's do it."

They found Tim and Lisa Cross sitting on the tailgate of their truck passing a bottle of Jack Daniels between them.

"That bitch started it," Lisa said when she saw them approaching.

She'd been thrown out of enough places in her life to know what was coming.

"I don't care who started it," Red said. "It's my house and you all need to go."

"My brother's taking a piss," Tim said. "When he gets back we'll talk about it. We don't care much for people telling us what to do. It kinda pisses us off."

Red shrugged. "There ain't nothing to talk about. You all got to go. Get your ass in that truck and get the hell out of here."

"Who's going to make us?" Lisa asked. "You?"

Jeff was standing behind Red in case he needed him. He didn't hear Kyle come up behind him. He didn't know anyone was there until a pain exploded in the back of his head and he lurched forward. As he fell to the ground, he saw Tim and Lisa lunge for Red. Although Red was a big boy, nearly two hundred and sixty pounds of muscle, the Crosses fought like each fight was their last, showing no mercy and fighting utterly without rules. While those two were engaging Red and keeping him distracted, Kyle lashed out at Red with the same weapon he'd used on Jeff, a pair of homemade brass knuckles. He caught him in the back of the head. Red grunted and staggered.

Jeff was on the ground beneath the tailgate of the Cross' pickup. He was trying to clear his head to get back in the fight but the pain was blinding. He was afraid they'd cracked his skull. He willed his arms to work, to lift his body so that he could help his friend. He had a pistol in the truck. A pistol would be the only thing that would stop this fight if he could focus enough to retrieve it.

He rolled to his hands and knees and tried to get up. Tim Cross turned from punching Red and kicked Jeff in the ribs, then again in the head. Jeff fell over, his synapses misfiring and his signals crossing. He lay beneath the tailgate watching his friend being kicked and punched by the three siblings, completely unable to do anything about it.

In the periphery of his vision, he saw a gun come out of Kyle Cross' waistband. It seemed like it was happening in slow motion.

"Noooooooooo," Jeff slurred. "Noooooooooo!"

He tried to crawl, tried to yell for help. He looked for others at the party who could stop what was about to happen but he couldn't see that far. He knew that no one would get in the way of the sociopaths. They were all probably running for their cars about now. Jeff focused on the face above the gun. Kyle was grinning as if he were in the midst of telling a joke and wanting to make sure that everyone was following along.

Kyle dropped, his knee landing on Red's chest. Jeff saw his friend's face – red, swollen, bleeding. Jeff tried to raise his head, tried to find words. A tooth rolled from Red's mouth and stuck in his beard.

Kyle lay the pistol flat against the side of Red's head and pulled the trigger. There was a flash and a concussion. Dust blew up from the ground. Red's eyes flew open, bulging. His mouth gaped and sucked air, trying to scream, unable to gain enough wind to make a sound. Kyle had fired into the ground, missing Red, but in placing the pistol against his ear, he'd blown out his eardrum.

Kyle grinned at the suffering man, raising himself back up to stand over him. Lisa was standing beside Tim, her hand resting on his shoulder.

"Damn," she said, shaking her head. "That shit was cold."

"Let's get out of here," Tim said.

The family clambered into their truck, unhurried, as if they were leaving a convenience store after a run for cigarettes and beer. Several men from the party ran over and dragged the two injured men clear of the truck. The Cross family had made no effort. They would have backed over them with no more regard than they held for roadkill.

Although Jeff had never gotten even, not a night passed that he didn't think about it. Maybe now, in a world with no rules, it was time. If he took his revenge, what consequences could there be? It wasn't like the sheriff would come. It wasn't like anyone would even care about the death of this piece of shit.

His buddy Red could no longer hunt with him, unable to hear the sounds of the woods above the permanent ringing in his one good ear. He wasn't the same man anymore. He didn't even like to leave the house. While the Crosses hadn't killed him, Jeff had still lost his best friend. He watched Kyle Cross sitting beneath the tree and finishing his cigarette without a care in the world. Kyle flipped the butt into the grass, unconcerned with whether it might start a fire in the last summer grass. He raised his water bottle to his lips again. Jeff centered his crosshairs on the bottom of that plastic bottle and fired a round right through it.

The round exploded the bottle and shattered Kyle's teeth before slicing through the brain stem in a less than surgical manner. A spray the color of roses wrapped the front of the tree. Kyle remained propped there a moment before he tipped over, sagging lifelessly into the grass.

Jeff walked casually down to the body and regarded it. The ruined head and face would have nauseated him had it not pleased him so much. On anyone else, the devastation would have been off-putting. On Kyle, it was deserved and fitting. Jeff picked up the man's rifle and slung it over his shoulder. He saw the butt of a pistol exposed beneath the tail of Kyle's flannel shirt. His knuckles brushed the still-warm flesh as he pulled a Springfield Operator 1911 from the belt. It was too expensive a pistol for trash like this, and Jeff knew it had to be stolen.

He leaned over to start patting Kyle's pockets then heard voices. He froze and listened. There were people coming. Kyle's family must have been close and heard the shot. They wanted to see if he'd killed anything and needed help dragging it out. As Jeff jogged off, he thought of the surprise those Crosses were in store for. He couldn't help but smile. About damn time somebody killed one of those lowlifes.

5

Jeff

WHEN HE GOT BACK HOME Jeff found Randi, his brother Tommy, and Randi's girls had already left to go track down the girls' father. Sherry's three kids were awake and running around the house, yelling and chasing each other. When he walked in the door, the children altered their course and mobbed him. Jeff toppled over playfully, letting the kids wrestle him to the floor.

"Hungry?" his mother, Vergie, called from the kitchen.

"Starving," he replied. Despite the violence of his morning, he felt no apprehension at all. It was like a gnawing pain had been removed from him. All he felt was a sense of satisfaction that made him want to tell people what he'd done, yet he knew he couldn't. His brother and sister would understand though they'd be the only ones. His parents would never approve. They'd raised him to be better than that.

"I got pancakes," his mother said. "Didn't think the kids would leave you any but I managed to squirrel away a few. There's no syrup. We have some good honey butter, though."

"That sounds fine," he said. "If I can get up."

"We're not letting you up," the children chorused, launching into a new effort to pin him to the floor.

"If you don't let me up, your mamaw is going to give you all baths," he whispered.

The oldest screamed and took off running, her young siblings not far behind. Jeff got up from the floor, brushed off, and strode to the kitchen.

"I told those young'uns you'd bathe them if they didn't let me go," he said, seating himself before a plate of pancakes.

"They need it," his mother said. "They're all dirty as a hoe handle. I can't recall the last bath any of them had."

"I saw them playing in the watering trough yesterday," Jeff said, shoving a forkful of pancakes into his mouth. They were delicious. The honey butter was as good as any syrup.

"That ain't nothing but a festering stew of cow poop and slobber," his mother said. "Ain't nothing clean about that."

"If it makes you feel better, I'll bring up a couple of buckets of spring water after breakfast and dump them in a washtub. Maybe it'll warm up enough by afternoon that Sherry can give those babies a good scrubbing later."

His mother nodded. "That would make me feel better," she said. "You might as well bring up enough for several baths. We're all getting ripe."

Jeff devoured his pancakes, lamenting that they were gone.

"It'll be like when I was a kid," his mother said. "Everyone shared the same water, washing in order from oldest to youngest. My daddy was the only one that ever had clean bath water. Sounds nasty now but that's the way things were."

Jeff frowned at his now empty plate.

"Swallow them whole?" his mother asked.

"No, just hungry I reckon," he said, carrying his plate to the sink. He leaned over and kissed his mother on the head. "I'll go carry that water."

His mother took his plate and washed it in the pot of water

warming on the camping stove. Jeff went outside and grabbed a galvanized washtub from where it hung on the wall of the barn. He found a nice spot in the yard that got lots of sun, affording about as much privacy as could be expected when bathing in the yard.

He grabbed two five-gallon buckets used for watering livestock and carried them toward the spring box. It was only about a hundred or more feet from the house, though at forty pounds each when full, the two buckets made it seem like a lot farther. When he reached the spring, Jeff stopped and lit one of his few remaining cigarettes. After this, he would be using toilet paper to roll up scraps of tobacco from the barn where his family had cured tobacco for fifty years. If you got a handful of old stuff it tasted like dirt. The thought made him relish the last of his store-bought ones all the more.

Cigarette dangling from his lips, he walked to the overflow pipe that constantly poured numbingly cold water from the spring box. He dropped the bucket and nudged it with his toe until it was centered under the stream of water. He stepped back from the mud and took another draw from his cigarette. He was preparing to exhale when the cold ring of a pistol barrel pressed against his neck.

A lot of thoughts raced through Jeff's mind at that moment. First, he recalled that he'd placed his pistol high on a cabinet in the living room when the kids mobbed him. He didn't want to be wearing it while they wrestled around. He'd left it off while he ate, and in fetching water for his mother, he'd gone off without it.

There was no doubt who held the gun on him. While he didn't know which Cross it was, it was most certainly one of them. He guessed it didn't much matter. If they'd found his handiwork in the woods, which he assumed they had, it was probable that they all hated him equally at this point. They were going to kill him. There was no doubt about that. If he knew anything about the way their addled brains worked, he suspected that they would lead him off somewhere to kill him slowly and painfully. After they'd accomplished that, they'd return for the rest of his family.

Jeff was not scared to die. He was not scared of pain. He was, however, scared of those things being inflicted on the few people he loved in this world. He did not want this family of mad dogs to kill his parents. He did not want them to kill Sherry's children.

How could he warn them? He could yell, but would they hear him over the chattering and squealing of the children? He'd only have time for one attempt before the Crosses would try to knock him out and drag him off. He suspected the only thing that would alert his parents and get their attention would be a gunshot. With no gun of his own, it would have to be a shot from one of the Crosses. The only reason they would fire one this close to the house, giving away their presence, would be if they were trying to kill him. He would have to provoke that and make them fire a shot.

Jeff spun to the left, sweeping back with his left arm and pushing the gun off him. He trapped Tim Cross' gun hand in his armpit and drew the Buck skinning knife from his belt, shoving it up under Tim's ribs. Jeff pulled the knife out and was going to stab Tim a second time when an explosion rang out.

Jeff flinched as the rifle round caught him below the left shoulder blade. He tried to catch his breath, but he couldn't. There was another BOOM and he sagged to the ground, landing atop Tim Cross.

The Cross patriarch stared at the bodies, smoke rising from the barrel of his rifle. Behind him, Lisa Cross and her uncle stood soundlessly. The uncle walked forward, nudging each body with his foot.

"They both dead," the uncle said, spitting into the grass.

"Well shit," Lisa said.

6

Vergie

VERGIE WAS DRYING dishes when she heard the gunshot. It startled her and she nearly dropped a soup bowl. Jeff would never hunt that close to the house. Something had to be wrong. She set down the plate she was drying and hurried into the living room. The children were all sitting on the floor coloring.

There was a clambering of someone on the basement steps and her husband burst through the door, his eyes wide. "What was that?"

"I don't know," she said. "Jeff went to get water. It sounded like it might have come from that direction. I don't know." She was breathing hard, her nerves getting the better of her.

"He's not come back?" he asked.

She shook her head, her lips tight, her eyes wide with fear.

"You kids get up!" Ernie said, rushing to them. "You all got on shoes?"

The youngest one did not and Vergie flew into action, finding a pair of tennis shoes beneath her husband's recliner. She helped the child put them on.

Ernie ran off to the bedroom and returned with a shotgun.

"What's going on?" Vergie asked. "What are you doing?"

Ernie shook his head. "I got no idea," he said. "I want you and the kids to go hide in the coal bin. Just in case."

"Why?"

"Just go," he said. "*Now*. If it ain't nothing I'll come get you in a few minutes." He shoved a worn revolver into her hands.

"You really think I need this?"

Ernie leaned forward and kissed her. "I hope not. I really hope not. Now get out of here. Don't waste no more time."

Vergie gathered the children and they ran out the back door, down the steps, and toward the coal bin. Vergie hadn't run in years but she loped along, apron gathered in her hands. The coal bin was an ancient, sagging shed with tendrils of Virginia creeper working its way up the back and sides. Although they hadn't used coal in twenty years, occasionally someone would use the shed for storage, despite the filth.

When they reached the shed, Vergie grabbed the old poplar door and pulled. The stiff, rusty strap hinges squealed. She looked around nervously, the pistol in her hand. "Get in kids," she said. "Don't make any noise. We have to be very quiet. Do you understand?"

They all nodded seriously, sensing her urgency, slipping into the dark, low-ceilinged structure. Vergie joined them, pulling the door shut tightly behind her. The siding was made of vertical boards and gaps had opened up between them as the boards dried over the years. Sunlight came in through the cracks, creating narrow shafts in the black dust stirred by their movement. Vergie took them to the very back. There was nowhere to sit except in the fine black dust, so that's what they did. The children huddled around her. She pointed the gun in the direction of the door and waited, her heart racing.

The coal bin was as filthy as filthy got. There were spider webs with wolf spiders as large as biscuits. Her hip ached from sitting on the ground and she could feel it all the way to the top of her head.

"How long we got to stay here?" one of the kids whispered.

Vergie held a finger to her lips and shook her head.

A burst of gunfire startled her and her body lurched. Small hands clutched at her, feeling like pinches all along her arm. The children whimpered. She could tell that it was on the other side of the house. She was sure that at least one of the shots had been from her husband's shotgun. Not all of them, though. Someone had shot back and there was no more shooting going on now.

Her leg spasmed. A deep cramp gripped her leg and hip. She felt like she needed to get up to move around. She tried to get up and the children clutched her tighter, holding her in place.

"I need to check on your Gramps," she whispered. "I need to make sure he's okay."

"You can't leave us," Linda, the oldest whispered. She was six.

"Honey, I can't stay in here. I've got to go check. I want you all to stay put. You do *not* come out of this coal bin until your mama or grandma comes for you, okay?"

There was no response.

"Okay?" she said more forcefully.

"Okay," Linda said, her voice cracking from fear.

"That's a big girl," Vergie said. She turned awkwardly to her side and pushed herself up with difficulty. There was a sharp twinge in her back that made her straighten up and hit her head on one of the low rafters.

"Bless it," she hissed.

"You okay?" Linda asked.

"I'm fine," Vergie whispered. "Don't worry about me. You take care of your brother and sister."

The other two children snuggled tightly against Linda, who wiped tears from her eyes, smudging her face with the greasy coal dust.

Vergie crept toward the door, pushed it open, and struggled out. She straightened her stiff back, the revolver hanging loosely in her hand. When the spasm eased enough that she could walk, she hobbled toward the edge of the house.

The kids all moved to the front of the coal bin, pressing their eyes against the vertical cracks, watching their great-grandmother hobble across the yard. When she reached the edge of the house and peered around into the front yard, she emitted a loud groan of pain, her hand flying up across her mouth. She took one step and there was another gunshot. She dropped into the yard, the revolver flying from her grasp. She took a few wet breaths, stiffened, kicked, and died under the dispassionate gaze of the Cross family.

The children sucked in a collective gasp at the death of the woman who'd practically raised them, receding back into the darkness of the coalbin and huddling together, too scared to cry. They tried to shut their ears against the sounds of laughter and breaking glass. Then they smelled smoke and heard the crackling of a rising fire. They could do nothing but stare at one another in sheer terror.

7

Randi

IT TOOK RANDI, her brother, and her daughters nearly three hours to reach her ex-husband's community. It should have taken two. They kept running into people they knew who either wanted information or wanted to share stories about how inconvenienced they were. Tommy knew everyone and liked to talk. That had cost the group nearly an hour of travel time. Randi and the girls had to drag him along when he got into conversations or he would talk all day.

Eventually, they reached the community of Neon, where Randi's ex-husband lived. The story went that the daily train that passed through the community would never completely stop because there were so few people living there, but it would slow down enough for anyone wanting to board to get a "knee on."

Randi had no interest in seeing her ex unless she were blessed enough to find him dead. She made Tommy promise that, if that were the case, he'd come back and get her. She had not been joking in her threat to spit upon his corpse. She still held a few hard feelings about the way their marriage had gone.

Perhaps more than a few.

"I'm going to wait here," Randi said, gesturing to the railroad tracks.

Tommy cast a wary eye around them. The road was empty and there was no one about anywhere. "I don't know if I should leave you here," he said. "You'd be sitting out in the open."

Randi rolled her eyes. "I'll be fine. I'm going to sit down on the tracks and rest a while. You stay with the girls. I've got a gun and I don't mind to use it if I need to."

"Right," Carla joked, not used to seeing her mother as a woman capable of violence unless it was directed at Carla's dad.

Randi cut her a sharp look. "You think I got home to you without having to spill a little blood? I still have nightmares about the shit I saw. The shit I *did*."

"Geez, Mom, I didn't know," Carla said sheepishly. "You never said anything. You don't have to get all...*intense*."

Randi walked toward the tracks. "Let me know what you find."

Tommy looked at the girls and smiled. "Let's go find the son-of-a-bitch that knocked my sister up."

"Please," Sherry said. "I'd rather you refer to him as my dad."

"Same damn thing," Tommy said.

Sherry sighed and walked off. "Let's just go look for him, okay?"

Tommy took a quick sip of water and stuffed the bottle into the back pocket of his jeans. He winked at Randi, who was sitting on the tracks and wishing for several things she didn't have at the moment – a cigarette, a cup of coffee, even a beer.

After Tommy and her daughters walked off down the dirt road, Randi looked around her. There were probably a dozen houses in the little community, old company houses. There'd once been a sawmill here that cut support timbers for the coal mines and the mill built these homes for the managers. Now the houses were peeling and the yards were fighting back kudzu. The place didn't look any different than it had forty years ago. She couldn't tell if the houses were still occupied or not. Maybe the folks living there had moved on or perhaps they stood in the dark watching her. As long as the residents left her alone, she didn't care what they were doing. Still, it was creepy to think of them watching her from their dark homes.

She had a hard time believing she'd once lived here in this little cluster of ramshackle dwellings. She'd been seventeen and pregnant when she arrived in a blue 1973 Nova. The car was loud, rusting, and had mismatched tires that made it steer funny. They moved into a tiny trailer in his parents' backyard. It was unbearably hot in the summer and impossible to heat in the winter. Her ex had ended up being less than she'd expected, and she hadn't expected much. He had no intention of giving up drinking and chasing women even when they were living under the same roof. He'd also been a hitter.

She hadn't told many people the story of how their marriage ended, although she had told Gary when they were walking home from Richmond. She probably wouldn't have told him had she not been so exhausted that her veneer was worn thin and her emotions playing closer to the surface than she usually allowed. Sherry had been around ten when her daddy slapped her because Randi had the audacity to take her girls to church. It had turned uglier, with him hitting the girl again and challenging God to come and stop it.

He did stop it. His fiery sword of justice arrived in the form of Randi, who beat her husband into unconsciousness with a log from the firewood stack. She thought she'd killed him. After the mistake of marrying him in the first place, letting him live was the second biggest mistake of her life. To this day, she did not want to lay eyes on him for the fear that she might be unable to resist the temptation to finish the job she'd started.

She'd called the law and confessed to killing her husband. Two deputies arrived shortly in brown Plymouths. They examined the body carefully before one of the officers approached her. It was not the first time he'd been to their home. He knew the deal. Randi extended her arms toward him, waiting on the handcuffs.

"Ma'am, your husband isn't dead," he said. "Would you like us to drive back down the road and come back in a few minutes?"

At first, she didn't believe she'd heard him right. When she looked in his eyes she knew she had. He was making her an offer. They could go down the road, wait a few minutes, and then come back. They were offering to give her time to finish the job.

She didn't take them up on it. She packed a bag for her and the kids and the deputies drove her to her dad's house. She'd been there ever since. For their parts, neither Sherry nor Carla seemed to recall that experience at all. While in some ways it was a blessing that they didn't have a memory of that horrible day, Randi did wish they had more recollection of the horrible husband and father he had been. In the absence of those memories, the girls unfairly laid much of the blame for the failed marriage at Randi's feet. No doubt at the insistence of her ex-husband.

Wading through the mire of her past agitated her to the point that she rose from her seat on the warm metal train tracks. She began pacing, kicking at rocks, wishing they were his head. Fifteen feet from where she started pacing, she came to the spot where the dirt road crossed the train tracks. There, she found a couple of empty beer cans and a small heap of debris where someone had stopped their vehicle to dump the contents of their ashtray onto the ground.

She stared at the contents of the ashtray. She sank to her knees and dragged a finger through the ashes, the gum wrappers, and the crumpled cigarette butts. She pulled one of the butts from the ashes and raised it to her nose. It smelled like she expected it to smell but she didn't care. She slung her pack off and dug in the slash pocket for a lighter. When she found it, she delicately placed the short butt into her mouth, pleasantly surprised to find that it tasted no worse than expected. While it didn't taste good by any means, it was tolerable.

She struck her lighter and lit up, sucking the stale smoke into the deepest recesses of her lungs. She felt like she was breathing for the first time in days. When she exhaled, her entire body relaxed and she felt at peace with the world.

She tried to avoid thinking about the original owner of that cigarette, the first person to saturate that same filter with saliva, just as she was doing now. In the end, she found that she didn't care. If the filter had once sat in the toothless gap of an alcoholic's smile, she didn't care. If it had dangled from the scabby lip of a herpes-infected meth-head, she didn't care. If it hung from the painted lip of a pre-teen headed down the wrong path, she still didn't care.

She was on her fourth butt before she began to feel like she'd almost had a full cigarette's worth of tobacco. She was still huddled there over the contents of the ashtray when she heard her brother and daughters returning earlier than expected.

"What the hell are you doing, Sissy?" Tommy asked in his booming voice.

"Nothing," she said, looking up at them.

"Mom, your lips are black," Carla said.

"And you've got black streaks across your forehead," Sherry added.

Randi remembered wiping a hand across her face several times. She must have smeared ashes there.

"Sissy, are you smoking butts off the road?" Tommy asked.

Randi hesitated, not sure that she could lie her way out of this. Her delayed response answered the question for them.

"God help us," Carla announced. "Our mom has turned into a hobo."

Randi stood and shouldered her pack. "I am *not* a hobo!"

"Yeah, Mom, do you have a bottle of Wild Irish Rose in your pack?" Sherry piped in, joking, though with an edge of the anger she always carried.

"I brought you girls into this world and I can take you out of it," Randi warned.

The girls laughed and shook their heads.

"I don't think you all should be pushing her," Tommy said. "Now that you're too big to spank, your momma will probably have to kick your asses, and she'd do it. She's tough too. She's kicked mine once or twice."

The girls grumbled and started walking off in the direction of home.

Tommy walked over to Randi and slung a concerned arm over her shoulder. He was probably a foot and a half taller than her. "Honey, do we need to get you some counseling?"

"No, damn it!" Randi spat. "It's just that being here is stressing me out." She emphasized *here* by stabbing an angry finger at the cluster of houses.

"Well, why didn't you say so?" Tommy said. He reached into his back pocket, pulled out a flask, and held it out to her. "Southern Comfort."

She frowned but took it, tossing back a swig before returning the bottle to him. "Thanks. I needed that."

"At least it will wash the taste of bum slobber out of your mouth." He grinned and patted her on the back. "Any time, little sister. Now let's catch up with them girls."

"What about their dad?" she asked as they started walking.

"Gone," Tommy said, taking his own swig off the bottle before replacing it in his back pocket. "Neighbor woman said that he took off about three days ago with some of his drinking buddies. They said they were going to someone's hunting cabin over in Bland County."

"Walking?" Randi asked.

"Nope. Had a pickup truck full of shit."

Randi had nothing to say to that.

"You still sweet on him?" Tommy teased.

Randi stared coldly at her brother, then raised the tail of her shirt, exposing the wooden grip of an Old Hickory butcher knife shoved into her belt. "I grabbed this out of the kitchen this morning. If I could have gotten him alone, out of the sight of those girls, I was going to end it. I was going to stick it in his belly and watch him die slow."

Tommy resumed walking, Randi falling back into step beside him. "You were always a tough woman, Randi. Now you're a hard woman too."

"It's the only way to survive," she said. "This isn't the same world anymore. It's just not."

8

Randi

RANDI and her companions were exhausted by the time they neared her dad's farm. They'd finished what water they had and were parched. The day had been hot and everything they drank had leached back out through their pores. Randi's exhilaration at her nicotine relapse had turned to nausea when she realized that she'd probably sucked down a few too many of the old stale butts while sitting on the tracks. That feeling, along with the tiredness and dehydration had put her in a nasty mood.

"I hope Dad's okay," Carla said. The remark was aimed at her sister. They were walking ahead of Randi and Tommy though within earshot. Conversation had ground to a halt a while back. Everyone was too tired to talk.

"He's fine," Sherry assured her. "He's tough. He'll be okay."

"Yeah, he's like a fucking cockroach, girls," Randi said. "He'll be fine. No matter what he does he lands on his feet. Wrecks homes, wrecks marriages, leaves other people to clean up all the damage, and he still comes out smelling like a rose."

"Don't be bitter, Mom," Carla said.

"Oh, honey, I am bitter," Randi said sarcastically. "Let me give you an example of how bitter I am. There are times that I wish I could turn into a zombie so I could watch the look of terror in your dad's eyes while I ate him alive. I know being a zombie would suck in every other way, but that one thing would make it all worthwhile."

"Hell hath no fury," Tommy said, shaking his head in amusement.

"Clearly," Sherry agreed.

They hadn't got much further when Carla started sniffing the air. "Smells like smoke."

"It's probably Mom," Sherry said.

Randi frowned. "It's not me. It's probably somebody cooking."

"I don't think so," Tommy said. "You can smell plastic in it. Smells like burning trash."

No one wanted to voice the obvious concern. They were getting close to their own home now and there weren't many houses around them. It made them all nervous and they picked up the pace.

In a few minutes they went around a bend in the road and the narrow valley opened up some. They could see sky. They could see smoke. The smoke was clearly coming from their farm.

"Son-of-a-bitch," Tommy said, taking off running.

The girls and Randi were not far behind. Sherry was crying already. Randi was kicking into mommy-mode, assuring her that it would be okay, that everyone would be fine.

They reached the gate to their road. Tommy had cleared it already, dropping his pack as he ran toward their home, now fully engulfed in flames. Sherry screamed. Carla burst into tears. They all climbed the locked gate and took off running after Tommy.

Sherry was screaming the names of her children. She and Carla were pulling ahead of Randi, who was cursing her age, her condition, and her years of smoking. She still thought everything would be okay. Somehow someone had *accidentally* set the house on fire. Maybe it was cooking on the camping stove. Maybe it was a candle. They were okay, though. She knew it. Until she heard Tommy's howl of pain and rage.

"NOOOOOOOOOO!!!!"

Randi ran faster. Carla was yelling now, Sherry screaming. Carla was pulling at her sister and tried to run toward the house, run *into* the house.

Randi reached the yard, saw her children struggling with each other. Saw Tommy holding their mother in his arms. She was covered in blood. It didn't make sense. Burns didn't kill you from blood loss. Why was there so much blood?

Something snapped in Randi's overloaded brain. She had to take control. She had to calm down. She reached her daughters as Sherry broke loose from Carla and lunged toward the burning house. Randi grabbed her daughter by the arm and pulled her around facing her. Sherry was hysterical.

"Shut the hell up," Randi hissed.

Sherry tried to pull loose again and Randi slapped her this time. "Look *around* the house. You can't go in there. No one could be alive in there. They could be around back."

Randi turned to Carla. "Take her! You two look around the other side of the house."

She ran to Tommy, still holding their mother. When she got closer she saw the ragged holes in her mother's face and neck.

"Fucking shotgun!" he said. "Somebody shot Mommy!"

"We've got to find everyone else," she said. "We can't help her. Get up and help."

There was another scream. Carla or Sherry. Randi took off running. Tommy lay his mother gently on the ground, pulling his shirt off and draping it over her face. Then he was on the run.

In the side yard, Randi found her daughters on their knees beside another body. Her father. Her *father*. She couldn't let that inside now.

No grandbabies, she kept telling herself. *They could still be alive.*

She crouched over her father, clinically touched his neck, and detected no pulse. Her poor daddy was a ragged thing. Bloody and shot multiple times with a shotgun too.

"He's dead," she said. "Keep looking."

Her daughters looked at her in disbelief.

"Keep *looking!*" she yelled.

Tommy came around the corner just then, sliding in the grass. "Jesus no!"

"You go that way!" Randi yelled to her brother, pointing down the trail to the spring. It was a trail the children traveled often enough that they might be comfortable running in that direction if they'd had the opportunity to flee.

Randi pointed at Sherry and Carla. "You check the barn. Go!"

The girls took off running, wiping tears from their cheeks, smearing their grandparents' blood on their faces. Randi pulled her pistol from her waistband and began circling the house. She made a complete circle and found no more bodies. She looked at the burning house, trying to imagine what might have happened.

She went back to her father's body, trying not to look at it. He was in the side yard, where the trail came from the spring. If someone had come to the house this way, he would have confronted them. What would her mom have done? She wouldn't have come outside to fight. She wouldn't have left the kids, would she?

She went back to her mother's body. She looked at the house. Through the flames she could tell that the back door was open. Maybe her mother had run? Randi got as close to the house as she could. In the distance, she could hear the faint sounds of her daughters calling for her grandchildren. With her back to the house, she imagined her mother running out the door and looked for places she might have gone.

The barn may have been too far if there were people near the house. They might have bushwacked their way up the hillside, scrambling through the weeds, though that would not be easy going. There were too many blackberry vines and wild rose bushes. Then in the weeds, she noticed the old coal bin nearly overgrown with kudzu. It had been there so long that it had become part of the landscape. She'd seen it so many times that she didn't even notice it anymore. With the vines engulfing it, perhaps no one else would have noticed it either.

She checked the chamber of her pistol and verified there was a round ready. She raised the pistol in front of her, gripping it with both hands in the manner that Gary had shown her on their way home from Richmond. She walked softly through the tall grass.

The coal bin was made of old poplar boards, assembled when they were still green. The roof was rusty tin. A door made of boards covered the entrance, hanging from strap hinges.

Randi stood at that door, her heart pounding. She took her left hand from the gun and grasped the wooden door handle. She pulled gently, her finger easing into the trigger guard of the pistol and resting lightly on the trigger. The hinges groaned and it took some effort to pull the door open. She swung it to the side, letting it open completely until it rested against the siding of the coal bin.

It was too dark inside to see anything, especially with her eyes adjusted to the bright daylight. She stuck her head in and still couldn't see. She raised a foot and stepped into the high opening. The ceiling was low and she could not stand upright. She waited for her eyes to adjust. There was more light closer to the door. In the far recesses, the boards blackened by decades of coal blended seamlessly with the shadows. Then she saw a pale disturbance in the darkness.

It was still. There was no movement at all. Her heart froze. She lowered the gun, tucked it into her back pocket, and sank to her knees. She reached out, touched the body, and found it warm. Feeling around, she found that it was not just one body but three small ones. They stirred.

Randi sobbed involuntarily. She took the children into her arms and tried to crawl out with them. She couldn't carry them all at one time, so she lifted them one at a time, walked on her knees, and deposited each grimy child into the blinding sunlight. They were still waking up, shading their eyes.

She carried the last child out the door and then crawled out herself. Her brother and daughters were there and they all wept, cradling the grimy children.

Tommy met her eye. "They killed Jeff too."

With a surge of pain, all of the loss hit Randi, but she had no tears left. All she felt was a burning rage. They would figure out who did this and she would make them pay.

9

Wallace County

Don, the driver of the truck, and his co-pilot Hodge knew where the Glenwall golf course was even though neither had ever been there before. There would have been no conceivable reason the two would have ever ventured onto its grounds prior to the terror attacks. It was a completely alien place full of alien people with concerns that would have sounded ridiculous to the two farm hands. It wasn't that the two men felt inferior; in fact, it was the opposite. They didn't think the people there knew much about the real world and that was to their detriment. The fact that they were relying on men like the two of them for something so basic as a delivery of food further demonstrated that point in their eyes.

"You add up everything you and I have ever earned and we still couldn't afford the cheapest house in this damn place," Don commented. "Ain't that some shit?"

Hodge slept most of the way over, a consequence of drinking so early in the day. He was hoping to find a way to get some more booze because he was nearly out. If things got really bad, he had a bottle of

Lysol tucked away in his bedroom closet. He hated to resort to it because it burned his stomach something awful. If he mixed it with water in a gallon jug it would hopefully keep the shakes away until he could find something better.

Although he hadn't paid a lot of attention to what Don was saying he nodded anyway. That was what he usually did. Besides staying drunk, agreeing with Don was one of his primary responsibilities during the day.

"They're welcome to the damn place," Hodge said. "Not sure I'd live here if they was to give me a house for free."

"I might," Don said. "I'd do it just to keep them all pissed off. I'd run up a rebel flag and keep chickens and goats. I'd pee wherever I felt like and I'd keep at least two junk cars parked in the yard. They'd fucking hate me."

Hodge chuckled, low and slow.

Don maneuvered the big rig onto the entrance road and was forced to stop. Two Wallace County Sheriff's Department cruisers were parked nose-to-nose blocking the road. Four men were visible behind the cars. They wore civilian clothing, jeans and t-shirts, and had on body armor. Their black pistol belts were packed with utility pouches and other gear. The men all had military-style rifles that Don couldn't identify though that wasn't as important as the fact that they were all leveled at him.

He put the truck in park and killed the loud diesel engine. It was nearly impossible to talk over. He kept his hands on the wheel in plain sight and leaned out the window. "Got a load of cattle," he called out. "Supposed to see a fellow named Baxter."

One of the group spoke to the other three, then came around the vehicles. He kept his rifle leveled on the cab of the truck as he passed. He looked in the trailer and saw that it was indeed packed with cattle.

"They're good," the man called to his buddies.

Another, still behind the vehicles, spoke into his radio, then listened to the response. "Mr. Baxter is on his way," he called out.

The man who'd checked the trailer approached the cab. "If you gentlemen have weapons, you'll have to leave them here at the gate."

"We ain't got nothing," Don said.

He looked surprised by that. "Well, if you're going to be making this trip very often you may want to carry something," he said. "You wouldn't catch me on the road without a gun. It ain't safe out there anymore. People are crazy."

"I'll keep that in mind," Don said.

A golf cart came zipping up to the roadblock driven by an over-weight man in black military fatigues wearing dark sunglasses. There was a patch on the shoulder of his jacket that read *Campus Security*. In the passenger seat was a taller man wearing a tan safari jacket and a black cap with the letters WCEM on it. When the golf cart lurched to a stop, the man in the safari jacket swung out and approached the truck. Another in black fatigues got out too and stood by the cart. He was tall and had a shaved head.

Don opened the door, climbed out, and stuck out a hand. "My name's Don. I was told you was buying cattle."

The man in the safari jacket eagerly shook hands with Don. "I'm John Baxter, Director of Wallace County Emergency Management. We're glad to see you."

"I heard from a buddy that you all were buying cattle. My friend and I have access to quite a few. We thought we'd come over and see if what we heard was true."

"Oh, it's true," Baxter said. "I've got folks willing to pay top dollar for beef and about any other food in quantity. We can provide fuel and pay you in cash."

"That's what I heard. How much a head for the cattle?" Don asked.

Baxter named a figure. Don couldn't conceal his grin.

"I think we can do business," Don said. "Where do you want the cattle?"

Baxter said to one of the security men working the gate, "Can you escort our new friend to the tennis courts?"

The guard ran around to the passenger side of Don's truck. He pulled open the door and climbed in beside a frowning Hodge. He and Don rode in this truck together all day every day and he wasn't used to having to share it. The seat was molded to him. It seemed to have some special magnetic properties that held him in place no matter how tired or drunk he was.

"I'll get your cash and meet you at the tennis courts," Baxter said.

Don climbed into the truck and started the engine. The remaining security guards backed the cars out of the way and Don drove through the roadblock. He turned to the guard riding shotgun to ask him what direction to take and noticed the odd look on his face.

"Something wrong?" Don asked.

"Damn right," he spat. "This old fucker stinks."

"Reckon I've got used to it," Don said. "Which way?"

He gestured toward a side street and the tennis courts beyond where there was a lone cow wandering the tennis courts, corralled by the high fences. "That's good thinking right there. They ain't got no grass though."

"We have grain but they don't stay alive long enough to worry too much about it," the guard replied.

"Go through a lot of beef?" Don asked.

"There's a lot of folks here. A lot of people like my buddies and I that work here. They probably go through a cow a day. What they don't eat they can trade for other things they need."

"Like what?" Don asked.

"Vegetables, fruit, liquor, or cigarettes to name a few things."

Hodge perked up. "They got liquor?"

The guard stared at Hodge. "You *should* be asking about soap. When's the last time you bathed?"

Hodge shrugged. "Reckon it woulda been last time I got real dirty."

"Hell, I feel like I'm going to need a bath just from riding beside you," the guard grumbled. "I may even have to burn these clothes."

"Easy now," Don said. "He's got feelings too."

"I'm surprised he can still feel anything under all that dirt," the guard snapped.

While Don was thinking of a reply, the guard jumped out and

directed him where to turn. He guided Don while he backed up to the tennis court, getting close enough that they could open the gates on the trailer and there would be nowhere for the cattle to go but onto the tennis courts. While they prodded the cattle out of the trailer, Baxter drove up in the golf cart.

"You boys want cash or is there anything you need to trade for?" Baxter asked.

Don looked at Hodge like he wasn't so sure about how to respond. "What kind of things do you have?"

"We got about everything," Baxter said. "This is a community of folks with good resources. They're compiling those resources for the good of the community."

"By resources, you're meaning money, right?" Don asked.

Baxter nodded. "That's right. The money that these folks have invested in their community goes toward these cattle, security, fuel, and other resources."

"You got liquor?" Hodge asked. "That feller there said there might be liquor." He gestured at the guard.

"There might be some spirits available," Baxter said. "Do you have a preference?"

"His preference is cheap and strong," Don said.

Hodge nodded.

Baxter got on his radio. "Debbie, I need you to bring a quart of liquor to the tennis courts. The gentlemen requested something cheap and strong."

While Baxter was counting crisp green bills into Don's hand, another golf cart arrived and a young woman brought Baxter a bottle of liquor, leaving it in the seat of his golf cart. When he finished counting money, he took the bottle and presented it to Hodge.

"How much you take out for the liquor?" he asked.

"Not a cent," Baxter replied. "Consider this bottle a gift from me. It's a gesture of goodwill. I'm hoping you boys can come back in another day or two with more cattle."

"We can if we have the fuel," Don said.

"The guard that brought you in will take you to the maintenance shed and refill your vehicle," Baxter said. "You come back in a day or two with another load of cattle and we can do this whole transaction over again. Anything in particular I can be on the lookout for? A particular food? Cigarettes?"

Don's eyes lit up. "I don't need any cigarettes. I'm about out of chewing tobacco, though. A carton or two of Red Man would be a welcome sight."

Baxter smiled. "I'll have it waiting on you."

"We'll be back, Mr. Baxter. You can count on it," Don assured him.

"Good. You gentlemen get your vehicle fueled up and I'll see you back here day after tomorrow."

Everyone shook hands again and the two men got back in their vehicle. The security guard chose to walk rather than sit by Hodge again.

"I really smell that bad?" he asked Don.

"Some days you're riper than a melon," Don replied.

Hodge pulled the collar out of his shirt out, buried his nose in it, and inhaled deeply. "I don't smell it."

"You're a fortunate man," Don said.

10

Baxter

BAXTER WAS WELL aware that he was in over his head. Everyone had been turning to him for answers since the shit hit the fan, like he was some kind of expert. He didn't have any answers. Being an Emergency Management Coordinator was about being a liaison between agencies. It was being the person that communicated with FEMA, talked to the media, applied for aid for disasters that had already occurred, and applied for grants to prepare for those that had not yet occurred.

Although he'd gone to a lot of trainings, none of them were worth a damn as far as preparing him for the current situation. He'd sat through a lot of PowerPoint presentations in his position. He'd learned about continuity of operations, setting up a command center, resource management, and interagency coordination. What was happening now was not like anything he'd trained for.

Things had fallen apart. Everyone had their own opinion about what was happening in the world and what it meant. No one wanted to listen to him and before long he was being elbowed out of the picture. Emergency resources that were supposed to be under his control started disappearing. He kept reverting back to his training, trying to hold daily briefings, while fewer and fewer people were attending.

He felt like everyone could see that he was an unqualified phony. There were so many people around who were used to functioning in real emergencies. There were veterans, cops, EMTs, and National Guard folks all giving him the same look. He tried to maintain control but he was a *phony*. He was a bureaucrat who was in this job because he'd screwed up everything else he tried to do. He'd been a teacher, a banker, a real estate agent, and nothing had worked. He'd been fired or forced to resign from all those positions. If there were anyone around to fire him now, he was sure he'd be gone from this position as well.

A family friend who'd felt sorry for him had pulled some political strings to get him this job. Everyone saw it as the kind of position that every county was required to have though it served no purpose most of the time. He had come into it with enthusiasm, anxious to learn the new job and see what he could do to help his community.

After developing a local emergency plan—a key part of the position—the county administrator called him to his office.

"Look, Baxter, we're glad to have you aboard. Don't be trying to change the world," he said.

"Excuse me?"

"I'll be blunt with you," the administrator replied. "You're here as a favor. We get grant money for your position. I'll be determining how those funds are spent. Your biggest job is to not rock the boat and not fuck anything up. Are we clear?"

While Baxter was shocked, he completely understood. He rose from his chair, shook the administrator's hand, and backed out of the office. For the last two years he'd gone to all the trainings they asked him to go to and signed where they asked him to sign. He spent no money and issued no memos. He simply did the minimum that the position required, which was exactly what the county wanted.

He was completely taken off guard on the day of the terror attacks when the county administrator came to him and asked what they—specifically Baxter—were planning in terms of a coordinated local response.

Baxter shrugged. "I don't have a clue."

The county administrator had gotten very angry, slamming his fist on Baxter's desk. "What the hell do you mean you don't have a clue? This is your job."

"You told me my job was to stay out of everyone's way and not fuck things up," Baxter reminded him. "You never allowed me to do my job."

"You're a damn liar," the administrator said. "I never said that. You repeat that and I'll deny it."

"Look, I'm not trying to get anyone in trouble," Baxter said.

"You're not in any position to get anyone in trouble," the administrator exploded. "Remember there are a lot of eyes on you right now. You screw this up and they'll hang you from the rafters. You wrote an emergency plan. I suggest you reacquaint yourself with it and start carrying it out immediately."

That was when Baxter knew they were going to make him a scapegoat. If there were any shortcomings in the county's response, they would be pinned on him. Any deaths would be pinned on him. Any misappropriated resources would be pinned on him. He had everything to lose and nothing to gain. There was no way that anything they did would be adequate in the face of the pending disaster they faced in the wake of the terror attacks.

That very day he set up a daily briefing for the community and began sharing what limited information he had. He hoped that if he could get his face out there, if he could be seen as being active in the disaster response, it would be hard for them to paint him as a failure. That was his hope, anyway.

The only practical thing he had to offer was basic instruction to the community on water filtration and hygiene. While most of his training was in keeping communities stable until aid arrived, every indication was that there would be no aid arriving in this disaster. He was lying to the community around him. He was a fraud.

It was after one of his less than mediocre briefings that a contingent from Glenwall Country Club approached him. He did not know the men that introduced themselves to him though he recognized their names. He knew them as wealthy, powerful men who were at the epicenter of local society. They were men who understood that being successful in business wasn't always about your own abilities. Sometimes it was about identifying a problem and being able to put the right person on that problem.

In this case, the problem was the societal collapse and the failure of the infrastructure. Somehow these men had come across his name as being the person to bring onto their team to help them face this problem. More likely they'd merely seen his title and assumed that he brought some skill and training to the table. While Baxter felt like a fraud and felt vastly underequipped to deal with this problem, there was no way he was telling these men that. He could have a new future at Glenwall. They could provide him with a level of insurance against the pending collapse. If what they said was true, all he would have to do was identify what they needed and they would work toward gathering those resources.

Above all, they respected him. At least they respected what they thought he was. He'd never been respected in this position before. He was treated like a child and basically told to sit down and shut up unless spoken to. He now had the opportunity to change that. How could he not take that opportunity?

11

Randi

SHERRY AND CARLA took the kids to the spring and tried to clean them up as best they could. It was difficult. Cold spring water with no soap didn't have much effect on ground-in coal dirt. While they were gone, Randi and Tommy buried their parents in the yard. They'd already siphoned all the gas out of the tractor. Tommy was able to start it anyway, using it to dig until the fuel was exhausted. Then it was shovel and mattock. At four feet, they could go no further and squeezed their parents in side-by-side, covering them up with rich black dirt. It was as emotionally exhausting as it was physical, with Randi and Tommy alternating between tears and rage.

When their work was done, they returned to the barn with their arms and backs aching. They found the girls still trying to clean up the children, this time using some glass cleaner they found on a shelf. Tommy took the digging tools and returned them to their proper place. Carla got up from where she was scrubbing a child and gestured for her mom to follow her outside. From the look on her face, she had something to say, and her daughter was so hot-headed Randi didn't know what to expect.

"Linda says that she saw one of the people that set the house on fire," Carla said. She was the oldest of the children and probably the only one capable of verbalizing what she saw.

"She said that after Granny got shot, a woman with long blonde hair and tattoos on her arms came around the corner and touched Granny's neck. She said the woman stayed there until someone yelled for her and then she left."

That instantly had Randi's full attention. That only described one person she knew.

"Did she hear what they called her?" Randi asked.

Carla nodded. "Lisa."

The information hit Randi like a fist. She shook her head, pacing involuntarily and trying to get her breathing under control. Tommy walked out at this point to see what was going on.

"What the hell is going on?" he asked.

Randi stopped pacing and stared at him, her eyes on fire.

"What?" he repeated.

"Lisa Cross," Randi said.

"Did this?" Tommy asked, gesturing toward the still-burning house.

Randi nodded.

"Alone?"

"No," Carla said. "Linda said there were others but she only saw the girl. Heard her called Lisa."

"She described that bitch to a tee," Randi said. "Long blonde hair and tattooed arms."

"She'd have been with her family," Tommy said. "The rest of that trash would have been with her."

"Why?" Randi asked. "Why do this?"

"I ain't got no idea, Sissy," Tommy said. "But there ain't but one way to fix it."

Randi was nodding.

"What's that?" Carla asked, certain that she knew the answer.

"Kill every fucking one of them and burn their house to the ground," Randi said.

"I still wonder why they did it," Carla said.

"It don't matter why," Tommy said. "All that matters is that we make things right."

"When do you want to do it?" Randi asked.

"Dawn," Tommy said.

"I want to go," Carla said.

"No way," Tommy and Randi said at the same time.

"Why not?" Carla asked both of them.

"Somebody's got to watch these babies," Tommy said. "You and Sherry need to stay with them in case we don't come home."

"How am I supposed to live with that?" Carla asked. "How are the rest of us supposed to go on if you all don't come home?"

"I can't live with not doing something," Randi said. "I have no choice in this. It's what every fiber of my body is ordering me to do."

"What happens if you don't come home?" Carla asked. "Seriously, what do we do?"

"You go to my friend Jim's place and you tell him what happened. Hopefully, he's in a position to help you out," Randi said. "I'll draw you a map before we go."

Carla ran the fingers of both hands through her hair, trying to grip the magnitude of the conversation. "Sherry won't be happy about this."

"Sherry can get over it," Tommy said.

12

Randi

SHERRY AND CARLA made a bed in the hayloft, putting the children between them and covering up with old horse blankets. They didn't expect to get much sleep out of fear that the children would wake during the night and wander off the edge of the loft, though they were all exhausted both physically and mentally.

Randi and Tommy stood guard. With the shock, the anger, and the sadness of the day, sleep would not have come to them anyway. They sat outside the barn in rusty metal folding chairs watching the night pass. The moon reflected on dewy grass. Owls hooted. Eventually even the crickets got tired and went to sleep.

When Randi's clothes became soaked with dew, she shivered. Nearly all their clothes had been burned in the fire. There were some things still hanging on the clothesline or scattered in vehicles, however it wasn't anything warm. It would be a long winter if they couldn't get a hold of appropriate clothes for each of them. It was but one more thing on a list of many.

She walked to the remains of her childhood home. The structure had collapsed into the basement and burned completely up by this point. All that remained was a deep bed of glowing embers radiating a wall of heat. She could not help but feel guilt for warming herself over the charred shell of her family's home. It raised a lump in her throat to think that this was the last time the old house would ever provide her comfort.

She stared into the embers, thinking about the things lost in there. Most of the guns the family-owned, with the exception of what they carried, had been in there. All of the family photographs. Everything special that any of them owned had been in there. They'd lost everything except for the people at their sides.

She heard the scuff of a step behind her. Tommy came alongside her and stared into the embers. It was like watching a lava flow cool. "I'm tired of sitting over there thinking by myself. Ain't nothing but the same thoughts swirling round and round. It's making me crazy." His voice was abrupt and alien in the stillness.

"You thinking about what I'm thinking about?" Randi asked. She already knew the answer. There was only one thing to be thinking about.

"Probably," Tommy said.

"How we kill the Cross family?"

"Yep."

"Come up with anything?"

"I've ruled out anything complicated," he said. "I'm back to the groundhog method."

"What's that?"

"We set their house on fire and shoot them as they come out. Same way you'd smoke a groundhog out of a hole."

"I like the sound of it."

She caught her brother in the corner of her vision. The glow of the coals washed his face in red and orange, colored his damp eyes.

"Momma and Daddy were good people," he said. It wasn't a statement of loss or emotion, merely a comment on the nature of the two people they'd lost.

"Being good people doesn't mean much anymore," Randi said. "Bad shit can still happen to you."

"They thought it was important to be good people. They thought if you did the right thing, everything would be fine."

"People that think that way may not be prepared for the reality of this world," Randi said. "They may be better off dead than to have to change into something they don't want to be."

"I can't believe you even said that," Tommy said. "How can they be better off dead?"

"Daddy wouldn't have had the stomach for what people are becoming," Randi said. "He's better off not seeing it. I think I'd rather that he died being the man that I remember, a good man, rather than having to become something else. I've had to become something else and there's times I'm not comfortable with it."

"Still, Sissy, that's a hard thing to say about your parents."

"It's a hard world. I've been telling you that. I've been telling the girls that. No one believes me. I've *seen* it with my own eyes."

Tommy thought about this. The hardness of the world. The things this world may require. He wasn't sure he was ready for it either. He didn't mind a good fight every once in a while but that should only be a small part of your day. The rest should be about hunting, fishing, and hanging out with your buddies. He wasn't ready for such a cold, serious world.

"I'm going to go check on my grandbabies," Randi said. "Them being in the loft scares me."

"You do that," Tommy said. "I'm going to get a drink of water. I'm feeling dehydrated from all that walking today."

"And digging a grave."

"Yeah, that too."

They went in opposite directions, Tommy to the spring and Randi back to the barn. She climbed the ladder into the loft, aware that it wasn't as easy for her as it always had been before. While she didn't like to admit she was getting older, it was apparently sneaking up on her. When she finally reached the top, she clicked on her headlamp and directed it away from the children, watching them in the reflected, ambient light.

Her three grandchildren lay there in a scattering of hay, a thick blue blanket pulled up over them. They slept so deeply, so innocently, despite the events of the day. Before the terror attacks, before society began to crumble, the sight of her grandchildren in such a state could make her heart overflow to bursting. In this world, such feelings were tempered by the practicality of survival and what it required.

The burning of their home had impacted the quality of their survival. She had known this was going to be a hard winter with no fuel, no electricity, and no law. Still, she thought her family could make it. They had the essentials of survival. They had a woodstove for heat, food put away from a large garden, they had some livestock and access to game. They were armed and hopefully had enough ammunition to defend their home, and were in a remote area that was not likely to be traveled by folks on their way somewhere. That seemed like enough to assure a decent outcome.

All of it had been taken from them in the blink of an eye. They had to rebuild their lives and they didn't have a lot of time to do it. Cold weather would be upon them before they knew it. She knew she would have to push her family. They couldn't do it without her. None of them had that *edge* that was required. Thinking of the work that was required, work that would have to start immediately, made her think about the mission that she and Tommy intended to take tomorrow.

What if she got herself killed? How would they go on?

She suspected that if she got killed, her family wouldn't make it. She was the flux that held this group together. She was the cold, hard planner that could help them focus and not get bogged down in fear and emotion. She was the driver that would push them through pain and suffering. She was willing to push them until they hated her, and that's why she could keep them alive.

It became clear to her. She *couldn't* get herself killed. It was as simple as that.

She climbed back down the ladder and found Tommy in his damp, rusty folding chair outside the sliding door. "We can't do this now."

"What?" he asked.

"Kill the Crosses."

"It's still a couple of hours until dawn," he pointed out. "We don't have to do it now."

"We can't do it at dawn, either," she said. "I need the kids to be safe. I need the grandchildren in good hands. I need to know that they'll be okay if we get killed. I can't risk my life and worry they won't be safe."

Tommy pursed his lips and looked at Randi with the utmost sincerity. "I can't live in peace knowing the Cross family is getting away with this."

"They won't get away with it," Randi promised. "We'll come back and we'll butcher them like hogs."

13

Jim

WHEN JIM WAS YOUNGER, he'd been a night owl. He preferred the world when no one else was awake. As he got older, he learned to appreciate the early morning better. It brought the same quiet, though with the renewed energy that came after a night of sleep. He'd found that staying up all night and sleeping all day put you at odds with the normal rhythm of the world.

Even in post-collapse America Jim maintained this portion of his routine when he could. He got up early and dressed, then went to the kitchen and prepared coffee. His current method to do so was the MSR Pocket Rocket and a small canister of compressed gas. Once the water was heated, he poured it through a GSI H2JO attached to the top of a Nalgene bottle.

While the coffee steeped, he checked in with the night watch, usually Buddy or Lloyd, to see if anything out of the ordinary had happened. Then he began to kit up with his EDC, or everyday carry items. This part of his gear had evolved over time. When he'd been on the road coming home from Richmond, his EDC consisted of a particular collection of survival and self-defense gear that was based on ideas he obtained from books and the internet. He had a lot more practical experience now and a lot better idea of what things he would actually use over the course of a day.

He wore a neoprene ankle holster with a .22 magnum mini revolver. It was strictly a weapon of last resort. He probably wouldn't have gone out and purchased the gun but it had been left to him by a relative who carried it in his front pocket every day. Jim had become attached to the gun and kept it in the ankle holster in case all else failed. His faithful SOG Twitch had taken a beating on the trip home. He had chipped the blade removing a screw with it. He had bent a pin prying with the knife. He'd also batoned kindling with it several times, using a small log to pound on the back of the blade until it split chunks from a larger log. The knife had done its job, and Jim had retired it from his EDC. He'd restored it with a new edge and a little oil and it lived on a shelf now, not in his pocket.

It had been replaced with a Microtech LUDT. The knife was an automatic, commonly referred to as a switchblade, and Jim had owned it for several years. He never carried it because of Virginia's prohibitive knife laws. Now he didn't figure it was an issue. The Gerber LMF fixed-blade knife that he carried home was still in his bug-out bag; his EDC fixed-blade was an ESEE 4. He had a scout-carry Kydex sheath that kept it out of the way of his pistol.

For his primary sidearm, he still carried his Beretta 92. There were newer guns and there may have been better guns, but this was his gun. He knew it inside out. He could fire it without thinking. His muscle memory was built around this gun and when he shot with it, he hit because it was a part of him. He had hundreds of hours on it.

Aside from those items, in his pockets or on his belt he carried two butane lighters, a Sawyer mini filter, a trauma kit with tourniquet and Israeli bandage, and his radio. Beyond that, he had a pack he carried daily with more gear, a load-bearing vest with ammo and tactical gear, and his M4.

Ellen came into the room as he was tucking away the last of his carry gear and preparing to pour his coffee. "Ariel's right. I've never seen you so happy."

Jim turned around in surprise and saw Ellen standing in the door to the kitchen. He looked for sarcasm, a hint that it was a joke, however, there was no such indication. "You're joking, right?"

She shook her head, a smile tinged with sadness on her lips. "Ariel brought it up the other day when we were picking berries. I hadn't thought much about it but she's right. I've never seen you so focused."

"I can't even believe you said that," Jim said, staring at her. He shook the Nalgene bottle with his coffee, unscrewed the lid, and removed the H2JO. He poured it into his favorite mug. He didn't have enough coffee to last forever, so he'd enjoy it while he could. Today it was LavAzza Crema Gusto. He'd bought a case off the internet when the price was right.

"It wasn't an accusation, Jim, only an observation." She came into the kitchen and sat down at the table.

"How could it *not* be an accusation?" he asked. "People are dying around us. Friends have lost family. We've lost neighbors. Why would I want all this bad stuff to happen?"

"I'm not talking about any of those things," she said. "I'm talking about what I see when you get up in the morning. I'm talking about your state of mind as you prepare for the day."

"It's not like I dreaded going to work every day," he said. "I never minded my job."

"You never loved it, either. You never got up in the morning and put this much attention into your preparation. I'm not saying this makes you a bad person or anything. I'm just saying that you seem to enjoy trying to stay on top of this particular situation we're in. You enjoy trying to solve the problems of the day. Whatever is going on out there seems to be matched to your skillset. That's all I'm saying."

"I prepared for times like this because I love this family, not because I wanted something bad to happen," Jim said. "I did it because I didn't want you guys to suffer. I didn't want to see my children go hungry or die of simple infections that an antibiotic would have cured."

"That doesn't make you a bad person," Ellen said.

"I know it doesn't, but I feel like it does when you say you've never seen me this happy," he countered.

"I'm sorry you feel that way. I wasn't trying to fight with you. I wasn't trying to make you be defensive."

"I'm not being defensive," he snapped, a fake smile stretched tight across his face.

Ellen smiled sweetly at him and dropped it. "Can you heat me some water for tea?"

He shrugged, sighed, and did as she asked. She watched his actions without comment.

"It's hard not to feel a sense of satisfaction when your actions—your *forethought*—pay off," he admitted. "But I feel guilty if I think about it too much. You pointing it out made me feel guilty."

"I'm sorry," Ellen said.

"I'm sorry too," he said. "I wish it could go back to the way it was. I wish I'd come home from that shitty trip to Richmond like all the times before and we'd got to go on a final camping trip of the summer. I wish a lot of things. I wish that the world would leave me the hell alone too."

She laughed. "You've always wanted that."

"I used to *have* that," he said. "I used to come down the driveway to our little farm and shut the gate behind me in the afternoons. I shut the world out and only dealt with it when I wanted to. An ideal weekend for me was when I didn't have to go anywhere or deal with anyone."

"I remember," Ellen said.

Her water started boiling. Jim carefully removed the pot and poured the water into her teacup, dropping an English Breakfast Tea teabag in.

"I'm not sure you can ever have that again," Ellen said flatly.

"I still want that," he said. "I still want to be left alone."

"If you ignore the world now, it will come after you. It will show up on your doorstep. People are depending on you to not let that happen."

"I don't want people depending on me for that," Jim said, raising his voice. "I didn't want to be responsible for the people I walked home with and I don't want to be responsible for anyone outside of this house now. The decisions are too critical. If you fuck up, someone can die. I don't want that on me."

Ellen held the string of her teabag and traced it around the cup. "Not always your choice. Sometimes we don't get to make up the rules."

14

Jim

JIM WASN'T in the best mood when he started tinkering with the water system he hadn't finished the day before. Though his conversation with Ellen didn't leave him angry, it continued to buzz around in his head like bees around a hive. It complicated his decision-making. Now, with any issue, he would have to question if his head was in the right place. He hated second-guessing himself. He knew that this hadn't been her intention; she'd simply been making a comment. Still, he couldn't stop analyzing.

Buddy came by as Jim was pitching plumbing parts around and cursing to himself. Buddy was still limping from the worst of the coyote bites on his calf but was doing significantly better. "Building an outhouse before you needed it was good thinking," he said. "You took your time and did it right."

Jim straightened from the box of fittings, sighing loudly. "Thanks, Buddy. Glad you like it."

"So, what you up to, besides cussing at a cardboard box?"

"I've got a lot on my mind, I guess," Jim admitted.

"That would be natural for a man with a family. I don't have a family so life is a little easier for me."

"You're welcome to claim Lloyd as family."

Buddy laughed. "I do kind of feel like I've adopted him."

"Then maybe you can straighten him out some. Musicians are famously weak of character and have delicate dispositions. They're prone to moodiness and emotional outbursts."

"I came along too late in life to fix him," Buddy said. "He's a lost cause. Entertaining, though."

Jim was still flipping through fittings, looking for something that would adapt half-inch threaded to PEX. He hadn't found it yet. "I'm trying to figure out if I should do something about the road into the valley."

Buddy flipped over a plastic five-gallon bucket and used it as a stool, easing himself down. "What are you thinking about doing?"

"That damn gate didn't do a thing. Some guys cut the lock and drove through yesterday to take some cattle off Rockdell Farms. They didn't bother us but they could have. They could have been anyone. If Pete hadn't been on watch and spotted them, we might have never even known they were driving through the valley."

Buddy nodded. "That's concerning, for sure. It's hard to block off an area where people are used to coming and going."

"I don't want people coming and going," Jim said. "We need to make it more difficult for people to reach us. I'm not so concerned about foot traffic because I know it's nearly impossible to block that out. Vehicles concern me more."

"I ain't arguing with you," Buddy said. "You're preaching to the choir. Let's do it."

Jim shook his head. "I've brought up blocking the road before with some of the other families in the valley and the older people start raising hell the minute I bring it up."

"Us older people can be difficult," Buddy said.

"Sorry," Jim said. "I'm talking about Mrs. Wimmer and some of her family. Some days they seem like they get it. Other times they don't. One of them asked me the other day if I'd seen the UPS truck because they were expecting a package from Amazon. Then Mrs. Wimmer told me that we couldn't block the road permanently because she had people in Florida who came up for Thanksgiving."

Buddy chuckled. "Change is hard on people. Life-altering change like the one people are going through now sometimes does funny things to the mind. People deal with it differently. Sometimes they get a little crazy. Happened to me when my daughter died."

Jim didn't know all the details though Buddy had been opening up to Lloyd a little bit about what he'd been up to when Lloyd picked him up on the road. Buddy's daughter had overdosed on drugs the day before the terror attacks. What Buddy was referring to as *going a little crazy*, according to Lloyd, meant going to the home of his daughter's drug dealer and burning him alive. Jim didn't judge him. He was a parent and he understood. It had been justice.

"I'm not sure what to do," Jim said.

Buddy shrugged. "I don't know you real well, but I'm learning a little about you. I guess what I'm having trouble understanding is why you give a shit what other people think about your plan. I hear you're more the type to ask *forgiveness* later than to ask *permission* first."

Jim laughed. "That's true. It's one thing being a hard-ass with people you work with. It's another being that way with people you have to live beside. If you piss someone off, grudges can last for generations."

"Seems like there's only two paths to choose from. One path, you spend all your damn time trying to keep everyone happy. That's proved to be a waste of time in my experience. The other path, you spend your time trying to keep everyone safe. From what I see, you have a pretty good intuition for what that requires."

"So, if I'm planning to blow up the road, I should just do it and worry about the consequences later?"

Buddy shrugged, tilted his head. "If your intuition tells you that blowing up the road is how you keep us safe, then I'd go with that and not worry about old ladies and their Amazon packages."

"You ever blown up a road?"

Buddy laughed again. "As a matter of fact I have."

Jim raised an eyebrow at him.

"Vietnam War."

15

Randi

EVERYONE WAS UP EARLY, sleeping conditions being what they were. Fighting exhaustion, Randi took it upon herself to prepare breakfast after the sky began to lighten. The family had what was referred to as a dairy, a food storage structure similar to a root cellar, a cinderblock room built into the hillside. Much of the structure was below the freeze line, allowing it to stay above freezing for most of the winter. It was where people in the country stored canning, bushels of potatoes and apples, and hung braided bundles of onions.

Using her flashlight, Randi chose some jars of homemade applesauce, cubed beef, several potatoes, and some onions. Tommy raided the henhouse and collected a dozen eggs in a rusty Folgers can. In the barn loft, Randi went through some old boxes of stuff she'd brought home when she left her husband. She found a scratched skillet with a loose handle.

There was a fire circle behind the barn where the family occasionally had gatherings. Tommy built a fire there. Once there was a bed of coals, he took a wire shelf from an old refrigerator and balanced it on rocks a few inches over the coals.

"You think anyone feels like eating?" Carla said from behind them.

"People have to eat," Randi said. "The babies will be hungry."

Carla gestured at the burnt-out house. "How can you sit here beside that and feel like eating?"

"Sit down," Randi said, gesturing at an old wooden chair nearby. "There's no use getting so upset first thing in the morning. There's nothing we can do to change anything that's happened."

"I don't feel like sitting," Carla spat. "And I sure as hell don't feel like eating."

"Sit down anyway," Randi said firmly. "Before I sit your ass down."

Carla took a seat, crossing her arms defiantly in front of her chest. Randi looked at her daughter, seeing in her both her own personality and that of the ex-husband she detested. She always had to be careful dealing with Carla. She had to make sure she didn't overreact when the girl began to too closely resemble her ex-husband. She couldn't punish the girl for something over which she had no control.

Tommy put the skillet on the fire. He poured beef chunks and some of the fat from the jar into the skillet. He sliced potatoes with his pocket knife, dropping them straight into the pan.

"I know what you think of me," Randi said to her daughter. "I know you think I'm a bitter old bitch and that the last thing you want in this world is to end up like me."

Carla started to open her mouth but Randi jabbed a finger at her.

"Don't say a word. I know you better than you know yourself. I know exactly what you think. It's exactly what I would be thinking if I were sitting there."

Carla stared off at the burned house, keeping her mouth shut.

"Do you know how I got home from Richmond?"

Carla shrugged. "You walked."

"You say it like I walked from here to town," Randi said. "It was nothing like that. How far do you think we walked yesterday?"

"Couple of miles each way," Carla replied.

"I did three times that every single *day* to get home," Randi said. "For weeks."

Carla didn't reply.

"You know why?" Randi asked.

"Duh, you wanted to get home, of course," Carla said.

"Why do you think I wanted to get home?"

"I don't know."

"Think about it," Randi urged. "You think it was only because I was worried about my mom and dad? You think I was worried about whether my flowers were getting watered?"

Carla turned up the corner of her mouth. "No."

"Then who the hell was I worried about?"

"Your grandkids, probably," Carla said.

Randi took a deep breath and eased it out. Carla's tone *challenged* her sometimes. "You think that's it?"

Carla hesitated. "No."

"Who else?"

"Maybe you missed Sherry and me," Carla admitted.

The frying pan was beginning to sizzle. They hadn't had any luck finding a spatula so Tommy was using a sharpened stick to nudge the food around the pan. The cooking beef was providing enough grease to keep things from sticking as long as Tommy didn't let the pan get too hot.

"I was *so* worried about you two," Randi said. "I couldn't get it out of my head. I lay awake at night trying to speak to you in my head and hoping you might be able to hear me. I tried to tell you that I was coming. I tried to tell you I would be there to take care of you as soon as I could."

"It's not like we didn't have anyone," Carla said. "We had grandparents. We had uncles. We were okay."

"You didn't have your mother," Randi said, standing up and staring at Carla. "You think *anyone* in this world cares for you the way I do? Even if you were okay, I wasn't!"

Carla looked at the ground. For once, she said nothing.

"I shot a boy about your age one night," Randi blurted out.

Carla stared at her mother in shock. Tommy raised his head in surprise. Even he had no idea of what his sister had been through on the way home.

"Why?" Carla asked. Her voice was not accusing, not challenging. She'd lowered her tone. She understood this was serious for her mother.

"There were two men, young men, who sneaked into our camp one night. They were trying to rob and kill us. We had reason to think they'd done the same thing to some hikers they met along the way. They set our shelter on fire thinking we were in it. I happened to be awake and some things happened. I shot him."

Randi looked at her brother and daughter. Their eyes were glued to hers. She needed to tell this story. She needed her family to know.

"Did you...kill him?" Carla asked.

Randi shook her head. "I wish I had. It would have been much better than watching him scream and cry in pain as he bled there in the dirt."

"Lord, Sissy," Tommy said. "It breaks my heart that you had to see that."

"What did you do?" Carla asked.

"I fucking threw up," Randi said.

"Did you get help for him?" Carla asked. "I mean, he could be okay, right?"

Randi gestured around her. "Where? Is there anyone helping us now?"

Carla looked away.

"There *was* no help," Randi said. "We were in the middle of the woods. Phones didn't work by this time. There was nothing we could do."

"Is that why you're... *different*?" Carla asked.

Randi frowned. "I wasn't aware I had changed."

"You've definitely changed," Tommy said.

Carla nodded. "Definitely. You were always kind of a bitch, just not so intense. It's hard to be around sometimes."

Randi looked at the fire. "I guess it did change me. Maybe the trip in general changed me. He was the first, but not the last that I either killed or played a part in killing to get home. The world out there is like what we saw here yesterday. It's just as ugly."

"That must have been hard," Carla said.

It was a big step for her to acknowledge her mother's experience. They were usually on opposite sides of the fence from each other. Maybe this was a step toward meeting in the middle.

"It was very hard," Randi acknowledged. "There were a lot of mornings like this, where all I wanted to do was forget the things I'd seen the day before. I couldn't, though. I didn't want to eat, but I had to. Those guys I came home with reminded me every day, every time I didn't want to eat, that food was fuel and I needed it to get home."

Carla looked at the pan on the fire, her stomach twisting in knots.

"So you eat the food whether you want it or not," Randi said. "You eat it because you have people you're responsible for. People who need you. You eat it because you have shit to do and that shit requires fuel. Do you understand?" She looked at her daughter.

Carla raised her eyes from the fire to her mother, then nodded. "I do, Mom. I'm sorry."

"Sorry about what?" Randi asked. "That's not something I hear from you very often."

"Sorry for everything you went through getting home to us," Carla said. "I didn't appreciate the effort it took. I didn't know what you went through."

Randi shook her head, her lips tight. "Don't be sorry. Knowing what's out there is an asset. A hard-earned asset."

16

Wallace County

VALENTINE WAS BORN in 1970 in Hell For Certain, Kentucky. He was the sixth child of Tarzan and Eliza Powers. His father was only one of the many boys named after the Johnny Weissmuller character that had captured the imagination of 1930s theater patrons. Tarzan had been a coal miner in a time when nearly every man in that region was a coal miner. When Valentine was four years old, his daddy's leg was crushed when a chunk of slate the size of a sofa dropped from the mine roof with no warning. The miner walking behind Tarzan had been completely flattened, only the toe of one boot protruding from beneath the rock. Such was the life of a coal miner.

The doctors put pins in his leg and there was a metal frame around it that was supposed to make it heal straight. Tarzan was given a gallon jug of rubbing alcohol and told to put it on the pins every day so they wouldn't get infected. Valentine had been fascinated by the way the pins disappeared into the skin of his father's leg making him look like some kind of laboratory creation.

There was no managing Tarzan's pain. He felt excruciating pain in his leg. He said it felt like it was on fire. The doctors had nothing to offer him, explaining that the pain would go away as his body healed. With no solution in sight, Tarzan eventually graduated to drinking the rubbing alcohol and totally neglecting his pins. They grew angry and inflamed, with red streaks shooting up his leg. Eventually, the doctors were forced to remove it at thigh level to keep the poisoned blood from killing him. Tarzan was a full-fledged alcoholic at this point, perhaps even slightly crazed by drinking the rubbing alcohol.

The removal of the limb did not make the pain go away. The missing leg continued to burn and throb, making Tarzan sleep restlessly and cry out. Although the phenomenon of phantom limb pain was known to the doctors, there was no solution.

Tarzan became prone to rages that could not be traced to anything in particular. The family knew it was the pain slowly driving him crazy. His anger was free-floating and seemed to emerge from nowhere, the way a thunderstorm might materialize on an otherwise beautiful day. He lashed out during these spells, pulling and beating on anyone within reach. They tried to stay out of his reach. It was not always possible.

One time Tarzan had pinned Eliza to the couch beside him, angered over some money she'd spent on the children. She got away from him before he could land a solid blow, which only angered him more. How dare she attempt to evade a beating! He rose and tried to chase her but he'd failed to properly secure his ill-fitting prosthetic and fell across the coffee table, breaking two legs from it and sending copies of *Life* magazine in all directions.

"Help me," he slurred at Valentine. "Leg."

Although Valentine was only six years old at this point, he knew that to help his father with the leg would only result in his mother getting beaten more severely. Valentine picked the leg up and stared at it.

"Gimme my leg!" his dad hollered.

Valentine ran out the front door with it, tossing it over the sagging porch rail and into the yard. A mangy coonhound came and sniffed at it, found it unworthy of further investigation, and went back under the porch.

"Get back here!" Tarzan yelled. "Bring me my leg!"

Valentine hid under the porch with the coonhound and cried until his mother came and got him for dinner. His father had passed out on the floor by that point and they stepped over him the way that folks stepped over dead snakes.

Valentine eventually grew to be a large young man, who was still terrified of his father. He understood that there would be an inevitable point in their relationship where he'd have to hand out a beating to his father. They were on a collision course that had been determined many years ago. As much as Valentine, or Val as his friends now called him, dreamed of pounding his vile, hateful father into the dirt, the idea scared him. To confront his father would be of the same magnitude as confronting the devil in the dark of night.

Fate spared Valentine that confrontation. Looking at it another way, that confrontation and the closure it might offer were stolen from him. It occurred on a gloomy January day when Valentine and his siblings were at school. His mother had taken a job as a cashier at the new discount store in town. When they got home that evening, the house was dark and cold. Tarzan was gone in the car and he'd let the coal stove burn out.

Eliza didn't call anyone that afternoon. Tarzan being gone was not an unusual thing. Drunk and unemployed, he often sought the company of like-minded individuals. He'd apparently been doing exactly that on the day he went missing. The state police found his car later that night. He'd rolled off the mountain near the Ace of Spades, a mountaintop beer joint near No Name. Although the crash in itself had not been fatal, Tarzan had sustained a deep laceration on his upper arm as the vehicle tumbled off the mountain. He lay there unconscious and bled to death before he was found.

Though stunned by his death, it could not be said that the family missed him. They adapted to his loss the way a creek adapts to the removal of a stone from the riverbed. They went on with their lives, each of them damaged in some way by their interaction with Tarzan.

Valentine eventually went to work for a company providing security guards to the coal mines. The best part of the job was pouncing on parked lovers and scaring the shit out of them. As more and more mines shut down, the need for private security dwindled and he eventually got on at the community college. It was a much better gig. He got good benefits and a state salary. He still held out hope of getting to be a real cop, but this was the next best thing. He got to meet a lot of young girls who were impressed with the badge. He got to talk tough to mouthy punks and throw them off-campus. He even got to write tickets.

It was a dream job until the terror attacks came. The school had closed down soon afterward due to the lack of power and hadn't re-opened since. There was no prospect for when that might change. He'd been lucky to cross paths with Baxter and the Glenwall folks. They were feeding him and giving him a place to stay. He hoped to be able to experiment with some new law enforcement techniques he'd been developing. He'd always thought that being campus security was too restrictive. Now there were no restrictions at all. As long as he didn't screw up the good thing he had going, he could probably get away with anything.

Perhaps *this* was the dream job he'd waited his entire life for.

17

Randi

RANDI'S FAMILY had four horses grazing the scant pastures of their hillside farm, along with the cattle. Her dad always enjoyed them, though he never showed them or participated in any of the events that control the lives of true horse people. These animals were his private pleasure. Randi joked that he liked to check his fences on horseback so he could pretend he was a cowboy and recall the western movies of his youth.

"Matt Damon ain't got a thing on Lash Larue," he'd once told her.

Those recollections brought a stab of sadness as she saddled his favorite horse. What remained of her family was going to head to Jim's valley, where she hoped they could find sanctuary and a place to outlast this bump in the road. She knew they could tough it out and survive here at her parents' place. They could rebuild. What kind of life would they have, though? They had no other heated structures besides the house, and they didn't have the time or materials to build a new one. They would never feel safe here after what had happened to her parents. Randi understood now that the luxury of feeling safe would only come from being with a group.

Tommy was saddling another of the horses. He hadn't said much all morning and she was concerned about him. Their physical exhaustion only compounded the fragility of their mental state. Without conversation to pull her out of it, she felt herself slipping into that sucking pool of emotional blackness.

Without preamble, Tommy said, "I changed my mind. I'm not going with you."

It took Randi a moment to process what he'd said and pull herself back into a place where she could form a sentence. "What the hell does that mean? Why not?"

"Can't do it," he said. "That's all there is to it. I can't let those Cross bastards think they ran us off. I'm going to stay here and be a thorn in their sides, pick them off one by one. Few weeks of that, they'll be burning their furniture and eating their dogs because they're too scared to step outside."

Randi finished cinching the saddle and walked around to where she could see her brother. He was concentrating on what he was doing, his brow furrowed. His fingers struggled with the task, exhaustion pulling at the body like quicksand. He had a deep tan and his black hair needed cutting. In his sleeveless shirt and cap, he looked exactly like the country boy he was. She felt her maternal side kick in.

"It's going to get cold soon and we don't have much of anything left. How do you plan to live? *Where* do you plan to live?"

"I've been thinking about it," he said. "I'm going to camouflage the dairy building with branches and straw. It's out of the way and it's dry. It doesn't freeze. I'll make me a bed in there. I'll do some hunting and eat what canning you don't take with you."

Randi sagged against the barn wall. "Well shit, Tommy, now I feel like I should be staying. I thought I had this all figured out. Now I'm doubting myself and I'm too fucking exhausted to rethink it."

"You had things figured out for you, Sis, not for me," he said. "I don't think I ever said I was going with you."

"I want us all to stay together."

"We can't. Like you said, you have to get these kids to safety. You don't need me to do that."

"I could come back," Randi said. "Once I've got them in a safe place. We can both be thorns in their side."

Tommy finished with his saddle and looked Randi in the eye. "That's up to you. I ain't deciding for you. I'm deciding for me and I'm staying."

Randi knew better than to argue with him. He was as hardheaded as she was. It was likely hereditary. She knew that he wasn't trying to change her mind in any way. He was simply doing what he felt like he needed to do. Everybody processed this shitty situation in their own little way. She'd learned that much.

"I want you to take the fourth horse too," he said.

"Won't you need it?"

Tommy shook his head. "No, it'll draw attention. You can use it as a packhorse. We'll load as much of the canning from the dairy onto it as we can. That way you're not showing up at your friend's place empty-handed."

"Have we got something to carry it in?" Randi asked.

"We'll pack it into the old feed sacks and tie them in pairs. Hang one over each side."

They stared at each other awkwardly. They were a loving family, yet not an affectionate one. Feelings were present while never discussed.

"Then I suppose there's not much more to do except load everyone up and get out of here," she said. "It's going to be a long day. None of us have ever ridden that far. It'll be hard on the little ones."

"How are you going?"

"We'll go out the back side of the farm and follow the river for a while. I'd like to cut across some of those big farms along the highway. If I can go across them instead of around them it will save a lot of miles."

"Just be careful," Tommy warned. "People may be pretty aggressive about how they handle trespassers."

"I will," she said.

Randi needed to get everyone saddled up, she needed to get the canning, she needed to get her Go Bag. She couldn't stop staring at the farm though. At the burned-out rubble of the home she'd grown up in. "I always thought this was the safest place in the world," she said. "No matter what happened to me in my life, this was the one place where none of it mattered. I knew I could always come home and it would be okay."

Tommy nodded. "That's why I never left."

"Bullshit," Randi said. "You never left because you were too damn sorry to cook for yourself."

Tommy grinned. "That too."

18

Wallace County

WHEN DON and Hodge pulled up to the gate of the Glenwall golf course, it was nearly dark. The two had not been out much at night, and certainly not out of their own local community. Darkness made the powerless state of the world that much more peculiar. Places like Glenwall, which had spent hundreds of thousands of dollars on accent and area lighting, were never intended to sit in the dark. The two had learned on their last visit that some of these million-dollar homes didn't even have functioning windows. It was assumed that the air would be conditioned, regardless of the time of year. There would never be a need to actually open a window and let outside air in. Some people had been forced to break their own windows out of desperation, trying to get some relief in the summer heat.

The guards at the gates were the same ones as last time and they recognized the two approaching men. One spoke into a radio. Don shifted the truck into park and killed the engine. The guard that had called out on the radio approached. Although his rifle was raised, he was not so on-edge as last time.

"You guys know the drill," he said loudly. "Any weapons?"

Don shook his head. He thought the guard's loud commands were for show. "No."

The guard laughed. "Better be getting some then. Shit is dangerous. We hear shots popping off all day long." He walked to the trailer, glanced in. "They're good! Nothing but cows!" he called to the other guard.

The same golf cart as last time whizzed up to the gate and Baxter, the Emergency Management Coordinator they'd spoken to last time, hopped out. He was accompanied again by the same menacing bald man.

"Fucker looks glad to see us," Don commented to his co-pilot. "Reckon they ate all those cows already?"

Hodge shook his head, a single thought on his mind. "Ask about the liquor?"

"Hellfire," Don said. "You either going to have to cut back or learn to make it, Hodge. You can't count on it to keep turning up."

"It don't always turn up," Hodge said.

"Yeah, no shit," Don said. "I know you were the asshole that drank my Aqua Velva aftershave."

Hodge didn't deny it. "Where you gonna wear aftershave anyway?"

"Don't matter," Don replied. "It was a gift from a lady friend. It had sentimental value. Didn't expect I'd have to be on guard against some damn boozer sucking it down his pie-hole."

"If it makes you feel any better, it tasted like shit," Hodge said. "You got to strain it through a slice of light bread before you drink it. Supposed to filter out the bad parts."

Don shook his head in disgust. "That's about the dumbest shit I've ever heard."

Don recalled that at one time Rockdell Farms had employed nearly a thousand people. Now all they could keep were alcoholics who couldn't hold another job. It was a sad state of affairs.

"Good to see you," Baxter said, approaching the vehicle and

extending a hand to Don through the window. "You had me a little worried."

"Said I'd be back," Don stated.

"You eat all them cattle already?" Hodge asked.

"They aren't simply for eating," Baxter laughed. "We trade them for medicine, fresh vegetables, ammunition, and fuel."

"Pay those guards with meat too?" Don asked.

"Sometimes. Our guards come from a variety of different backgrounds. They work under a special arrangement. Their compensation is commensurate with what they bring to the table in the way of skills and experience."

Don nodded. That sounded like some kind of boring shit he wasn't interested in sitting through. "We planned on being here hours ago except some son-of-a-bitch took it on himself to blow the road up that we used to get these cattle. We had a time backing the trailer out of there and coming around to our farm from the other side."

Baxter looked concerned. "Someone blew the road up? Who?"

Don shook his head, spat out the window. "No fucking clue. Reckon one of those people that lives back in there."

"Why would they do that?" Baxter asked.

"They got a good place to live," Don said. "Reckon they don't want any company."

"What's so good about it?" Baxter asked. "What makes it any better than what we got over here?"

"They got plenty of good water," Don said. "Springs and creeks. They got a lot of cattle and grazing land, good fields for crops, plenty of game. It's a hard spot to get into."

"Damn sight harder now," Hodge pitched in.

"How many folks even live back in there?" Baxter asked. "I don't know much about that area."

Don shrugged. "There were probably two dozen families before shit got bad. Don't know how many are left. I heard they had some trouble a while back with an escaped convict or something and a few folks got killed."

Baxter nodded, processing. "Well, we better get these cattle unloaded," he said. "When they get the gate open, you all pull through to the tennis courts, same as last time."

Don nodded and restarted the engine. Baxter stepped back, called to one of the guards to follow the truck to the tennis courts and help them unload.

Hodge leaned awkwardly across the cab and stuck his head out Don's window. "Reckon a feller could get another bottle of that liquor? I think the last one evaporated or something."

Baxter smiled. "I'll take care of it." He wanted to keep these guys coming back.

Hodge grinned. "Appreciate it, buddy."

Don pulled through the gate, giving Baxter a nod as he did. Baxter smiled and waved back, continuing to watch the truck and trailer as it wound its way toward the tennis courts.

Baxter jogged back to his golf cart where his head of security was waiting. The man's name was Valentine and he'd been on the campus security staff at the local community college until Baxter recruited him. Valentine appeared to know a lot about survival in these situations and had impressed Baxter. If he had any bad qualities, it was that he was perhaps a little too gung-ho. Baxter had to monitor him closely. There was a dark bend to him that Baxter tried not to think too much about.

He jumped in the cart and leaned toward Valentine. "I need you to drop me off at the clubhouse, then I need a favor. Don't say a word on the radio but I want you on a motorcycle ready to go in ten minutes. You'll need a compact weapon, night vision goggles, a satphone, and food for a couple of days."

Valentine nodded and sped off, Baxter holding onto his hat. He'd have to drop Baxter off at the clubhouse to get cash and it wouldn't give him much time to get ready.

19

Wallace County

DON DROVE CAREFULLY. He couldn't remember the last time he'd driven at night by headlights. In his normal life, he didn't go out much at night. He'd driven this particular road many times over the years since it led to the cattle market, and it was in the worst state he'd ever seen it. With the highway department no longer working to maintain the roads, no one cleaned up the debris that found its way onto the road. There were branches of all sizes, trash, dead animals, and disabled vehicles in abundance. Driving required a moderate speed and full attention.

He was afraid now, due to the reminders from the guard at Glenwall, about the dangerousness of being out at night. Though he'd heard stories about increasing violence, somehow it never occurred to him that he could fall victim to such a crime. He'd never been paranoid in his normal life because he wasn't the kind of person people robbed. He didn't have anything worth stealing most days. Now that was probably not the case. He had an operable vehicle with a full tank of fuel. He and Hodge both had pockets bulging with cash. If Hodge didn't drain it before they hit Rockdell Farm, they even had a decent bottle of liquor in the vehicle with them.

"I wish to hell you'd help me keep an eye out," Don said. "This drive is giving me bad nerves."

Hodge threw his hands up in frustration. "I don't know what else you think I could be doing. It ain't like I'm playing the damn ukulele. I'm staring straight ahead just like you."

"You're drunk as a boiled owl. You ain't no help at all. What I need to do is hire a new farmhand that knows how to stay sober."

"You best be thanking the Lord for drunks because when we run out there won't be nothing left but pill-heads and they don't take to farm work. They'd rather stay home and collect disability," Hodge said.

"Pretty damn sorry world when drunks represent the top tier of the labor pool," Don muttered.

Hodge laughed. "You think you're pretty fucking funny, don't you? Ain't just anybody that would put up with a bastard like you."

Don locked up the brakes on the truck. The dually truck screeched to a stop, the trailer slewing sideways. Hodge flew forward, hitting his head on the passenger window. Had he turned loose from his bottle, he might have been able to throw his hands up and lessen the impact but he didn't. It was a natural reaction for him to clutch the bottle, the same way a mother would throw her arm out to the side to brace a child seated beside her if she had to stop suddenly.

"What the *hell*?" Hodge bellowed, rubbing his head. "What did you do that for? Was it a deer?"

"Take it back," Don said, looking at Hodge with a stare cold as the February wind.

"Take what back?"

"You called me a bastard and nobody calls me that," Don said. "There's joking and there's serious. This is serious. You can take it back or take an ass whooping right here in the middle of the damn road."

Hodge threw his head back and laughed, then cringed and

grabbed his forehead. "If it didn't hurt so bad, that would be pretty fucking funny."

"How about I throw your ass out on the road here and make you walk home?" Don said. "An old drunk like you, it wouldn't take much. I could do it."

Hodge could now tell that Don wasn't joking. His smile faded. "You serious?"

"Do I look like I'm joking?" Don reached forward and turned off the key. Silence cinched tight around them. The dash lights faded and darkness filled the cab.

"This ain't right, Don. We've worked together for a long time. This how it's going to end?"

"Yeah, we've worked together a long time and I've hated every fucking minute of it," Don said. "I ask myself every day why I don't get to work with someone with a decent personality instead of a damn drunk that don't say more than five words an hour. I could prop an inflatable Santa up in that seat and get the same amount of conversation out of it."

"You know how low you are? You're so low, you have to look up to see Hell," Hodge said.

Don shook his head in disgust. "You getting out of the truck or am I coming around and pulling you out? 'Cause this is the last time I'm asking."

In the darkness, Don heard fumbling, then a distinctive metallic click. Even in blackness, he knew the sound. *Shit.* "That a gun?"

"Damn right it is," Hodge said. "And I got it pointed right at you."

"Thought we didn't have no guns on us?"

"Just because you're too stupid to carry a gun doesn't mean I am," Hodge said. "I'm a hell of a lot smarter than you are. Ain't that obvious? Now start the damn truck and drive me to the house."

Don didn't move. A fly in the cab flitted against the glass window. It wanted no part of what was going on either.

"You may be prone to repeating yourself, but I'm not," Hodge said. "This truck ain't running by the time I'm done talking I'll shoot you and take it. I know where you're taking the cattle now so I'll start making my own runs. Who needs you anyway?"

Before the words could even settle out of the air, the truck was started and lurched into motion.

Don had realized he had no choice but to give in. Still, he was angry and couldn't keep his mouth shut. "You know you're fired, right?"

The pistol shot exploded in the cab of the truck, shattering Don's window, and leaving both men with ringing ears. Don jerked and cried out. The truck swerved, then straightened.

"What the *hell*, Hodge?"

"I know you were wondering if I'd do it. You were also wondering if the gun was even loaded. I thought it best to address that before there was a misunderstanding of some sort."

"You're still fired," Don said. "You show up at my house for work tomorrow and I'll kick your ass."

Hodge laughed. "You know the gun is loaded, you know I ain't scared to pull the trigger, and you *still* won't shut up? You best remember that I'm drunk and irrational. I'm also a career alcoholic and the folks at the detox say I potentially have organic brain disease due to drinking."

Don locked his mouth in a grim line and looked straight ahead.

"That's what I thought," Hodge said. "Bastard." He laughed.

Neither man had any idea they were being followed. Had the motorcycle been using its headlight, they would surely have noticed it due to the lack of other vehicles on the road. The rider, Valentine, was operating the bike using a night vision device that attached to a helmet and pulled down over his eyes.

It was a third-generation military-grade device owned by the Wallace County sheriff's department. With some of the deputies now working for Baxter and the residents of Glenwall, Baxter had access to all sorts of law enforcement and military hardware. That included body armor, some night vision and thermal equipment, and several select-fire Law Enforcement Only weapons.

Valentine had no idea what was going on when the truck slid to a stop on the dark highway. The trailer blocked his ability to see the cab of the truck. He had been concerned that they may have somehow detected his presence so he stopped and turned off the bike. He listened carefully and no one got out of the truck. After several moments of indecision, wondering whether he should turn back, the truck started again and continued on its journey. He had no idea where they were headed, only that it was in a nearby county. He was to do a recon of the area and then call a report into Baxter tomorrow on his satellite phone.

When the gunshot blasted out the side window ahead of him, Valentine flinched, assuming they were firing at him. He swerved off the road and stayed put for a minute, but there was no follow-up shot. The truck continued on its way as if nothing had happened. Satisfied that they were not firing at him, he pulled back in behind them.

Valentine wasn't sure what he was doing out here though he knew that Baxter was always a step ahead of everyone else. Baxter had sized up the scale of this disaster and realized that there were more resources in the hands of the Glenwall folks than in hands of the county government. While not everyone knew about it, including the county administrators, Baxter didn't work for the county anymore. He'd taken a more lucrative position with the folks of Glenwall.

Baxter had been persuasive to the group that he assembled, a collection of folks he knew from his work for the county. Among the residents of Glenwall were many retired executives. Those men formed the Board of Directors of the private golf course community. They were very wealthy men who built their wealth by nature of being forward-thinking and proactive. When the disaster hit, they were quick to see the writing on the wall. They knew that this situation would be no different than a stock deal. It was critical to get in early. In this case, getting in early meant securing as many local resources as they could—food, security, fuel, and weapons. The Board of Directors was quick to point out to Baxter that the residents of Glenwall collectively had more money than the county did. Significantly more.

20

Tommy

FOR MUCH OF the morning after Randi and her brood departed, Tommy traced lines in the dirt with a stick and pondered the smoldering shell of his home. He considered various ways he might make the Cross family pay for the death of his family and the destruction of his home. His natural inclination was to rush the home and shoot everyone in sight. He worried that he wouldn't be able to kill everyone before he himself got shot. He didn't particularly worry about the dying part of getting shot. He didn't want to die while any of the Crosses remained alive. He thought of setting their house on fire and shooting anyone that ran out. Somehow he didn't find that idea...satisfying. Vengeance was about more than just killing.

It was about feeding a hunger.

Around midday, Tommy took up his guns and retrieved two jars of stewed venison from the canning in the springhouse. He went to the charred remains of his parents' home, rubbed some charcoal on his fingertips, and smudged his face with black stripes for camouflage. He walked through the woods to the property line between his land and that belonging to the Cross family. He walked with ever-increasing caution until he found himself in the woods outside their home.

His presence was quickly detected by the two short-haired curs sleeping in the patchy yard. Tommy immediately opened the venison jars. The smell reached the dogs' nostrils, stirring their hunger. Motivated by their stomachs, the dogs chose to investigate rather than start barking. When they tracked him to a shadowy clump of brush, he tossed chunks of the stewed meat in their direction. They flinched at his movement but soon realized that he was feeding them and not threatening them. They abandoned their responsibility as guardians of the Cross home and stood a safe distance from Tommy, waiting on him to throw them more chunks of meat. He'd always had a way with dogs. They both shared the simple belief that friends brought food. As a bringer of food, he was their new friend and he was welcome.

He watched the family's movements from a distance. He had no idea who lived at the house before the terror attacks. The only people he saw coming and going now were Lisa, her uncle, her dad, and his wife. They may have only been four people, but they held the collective meanness of any group of two dozen on the planet. People who knew the family said it was the matriarch, Oma Cross, who was the cold core of the family. She was bitter and scornful, having raised her children at the business end of a stick, a belt, and occasionally even a fist. The children's accomplishments went unnoticed. Transgressions were met with a fury that led to bruising and scars. In the same way that Oma Cross made her family tremble under her gaze, her family went on to do the same for the community at large. Oma sowed the seeds; the community suffered the bitter harvest.

Tommy sat in his hide with the stillness of a hunter. He sat so quietly that the wildlife came to ignore his presence. A squirrel scrabbled down the very tree that Tommy lay against, running onto his shoulder before realizing its error and fleeing. A misshapen cat of questionable genetics walked up on him as it scoured the weedy hills for rodents. The cat smelled him before it saw him and scurried away.

It was only when a snake slithered by oblivious to his presence that Tommy struck upon an idea. He'd been a young man working in the coal mines in 1989 when the UMWA went on strike against a local coal company. The strike was a long one and there was a lot of bitterness. The company hired scabs to come in and replace the striking miners. The scab wages were so high that many unemployed could not resist the tempting money. It came at the cost of being shot at, beaten up, and threatened. Tommy knew of scab truck drivers who'd had to get armed family members to ride with them as protection while they hauled coal.

While the strike had been a battle between the company and the miners, it sometimes seemed that it was a battle between the strikers and the Virginia State Police. They were the officers usually put in the position of having to arrest miners and keep the peace. Often local deputies would avoid making those arrests since they had to live in the community and didn't want to have to watch their backs all the time.

One of Tommy's favorite memories involved a picket line on a hot August day. The strikers were sitting down at the gate of a coal processing plant to block scab truckers from hauling coal in. Troopers had to pick up the miners and drag them out of the road. They were not always very gentle about it. Tommy had been part of a group selected to stay out of the protest while busloads of miners got hauled to jail.

The state troopers were parked along the road and left their windows cracked against the summer heat. Tommy and a friend moved along the road, using thick welding gloves to pull copperheads out of a sack, shoving several of the snakes through the window of each trooper car.

He never got to hear about the fruits of his effort though he often imagined the looks on their faces as the snakes slithered from beneath their seats. He wanted the Cross family to know that same fear.

21

Valentine

WHEN HE WAS WORKING as a security guard at a coal mine, Valentine lived in a rented trailer close to his job in an area known as Convict Holler. The trailer park was overcrowded, full of junk, and without a blade of grass anywhere. There were more broken down cars than running ones. Children ran like pack animals without regard for whose yard they were playing in or whose possessions they were breaking. Drinking and drugs were rampant, as was violence and abuse. Every day some child or someone's wife was getting smacked around.

As best he could tell, Valentine was the only person in the trailer park who held a job. Rather than being a mark of honor, this drew hostility from the other men in the trailer park. If he could find a job, their wives, girlfriends, and mothers would nag them harder to find one. Being employed led to him having luxuries the others couldn't afford, like a drivable car and a telephone. Rather than being conveniences, those items were more of an inconvenience to Valentine in the end. Someone was always wanting to use the phone or asking him to drive them somewhere.

Valentine had grown up rough, and the bleakness of the trailer park did not bother him. His attitude toward the undercurrent of violence was that it was not his problem as long as it didn't directly impact him. When it did, he would react. While his position as a security guard bought him no respect or deference in the neighborhood, the fact that he was six foot four inches tall and weighed nearly three hundred pounds did. He would be a hard man to fight. If you were a scrawny drunk or meth-head, he could twist you in a knot and roll you home.

Moving into an environment like Convict Holler was like joining a pack. There was always a hierarchy in place and his role within it would have to be established. The challenges began within days of moving in. He'd barely pulled in from a night shift one morning. It was around 10 a.m. and some men were out enjoying their first smokes of the day. As soon as he turned off his car, one of the men was at his car door, leaning through the open window. The man was scrawny with unkempt hair, brown from loafing in the sun all day, and had crude tattoos on his hands. Valentine could smell his rotten breath and sour body odor.

"Hey, carry me to the store," he demanded. "We're out of smokes."

"Not my fucking problem," Valentine said. "I just got off work. I'm going to bed."

"That ain't neighborly," the man said. "You might need something from me one day."

"I don't need a damn thing from you," Valentine said. "Now back up so I can get out."

"Maybe I'll borrow your car," he said, making a grab for the keys in the ignition.

Valentine latched onto the man's arm, twisted it violently, then hit the power window. The window raised against the inside of his bicep, trapping it.

He cursed and flailed, trying to jerk his arm back out. He balled up his other fist, rage contorting his face. "I'll bust this fucking window out!"

Valentine was still gripping the man's trapped arm. He changed his grip, moving it from the forearm to the hand, pointing the man's index finger at the ceiling of the car. That finger was designed for one motion – straightening and curling. Valentine wrapped his own fingers around the index finger like he was holding a butane lighter and preparing to flick it. Then he put his thumb against the tip of the finger and began pressing the joint sideways.

"Roll this fucking window down now or you're a dead man!"

Valentine pushed the joint harder, dislocating the tip of the finger until it bent sideways at an angle. The man began flopping, his face turning red. He yelled. His friends were standing up but didn't approach. Valentine met his eyes then moved to another finger.

"Nooo!"

Valentine dislocated it too. He gave his victim a small smile that was not returned. The man was nearly screaming at this point, trying to jerk his arm from the window. Valentine unlocked his door and shoved it open, the arm still trapped in the window. He jerked a .357 magnum from his console and unfolded his body from the low vehicle. He shoved the pistol into the man's face and thumbed back the hammer.

"Shut the fuck up!"

He shut up, though he trembled, his eyes bulging and his face red from the pain. Valentine thought he might pass out.

"You don't ever look at me again," Valentine said. "You don't ever talk to me again. You got it?"

"I got it," he said in a high voice. "I got it!"

Valentine swung the gun onto the onlookers, who threw up their hands. "Same goes for you all. Don't look. Don't speak. We clear?"

No one replied.

"We *clear*?" he yelled.

There were mumbles of agreement. Valentine dropped a finger to the window button and lowered it, and the man dropped onto the dirt driveway. He lay there for a moment, his injured hand cradled to his chest. Valentine started to yank him to his feet and send him on his way when his rage got the better of him. He drew back his polished black patrol shoe and kicked him in the side several times. Then he locked his car and started toward his trailer.

He whipped back suddenly, pointing his gun at the man on the ground. "One more thing. Anything happens to my car, even a scratch, and I'm taking it out of your ass!"

He went inside and watched from the window as the man's buddies retrieved him. He made sure they left his car alone. Maybe they had some sense after all.

Valentine ended up living there for about two years before his job ran out. There were some tight months before he applied at the community college and got that position. To be less than seventy-five miles from home, he hadn't expected it to be very different but it was. It was entirely unlike any place he'd ever been before. Valentine was a hillbilly. He didn't realize that until he left the company of other hillbillies. He was not only a hillbilly, he was a hard, violent hillbilly, and they didn't always settle well into the world of civilized men, despite their best efforts.

Not long after reaching Wallace County and moving into an apartment, Valentine began dating a waitress at Pizza Hut. Her name was Molly and she was a hillbilly too. He'd asked her about her accent, embarrassing her until she caught enough of his own to realize their roots were similar. It turned out that she was from Dismal, a community near where he'd grown up. She'd had a baby with a man who'd turned into a jerk and had moved over to Wallace County to hide from him and his family. Finding someone from home, someone who spoke her language and didn't tease her about it, was like a dream come true. She and Valentine began spending more time together.

Her son was six and Valentine tried to like the boy. He found him to be soft, a sissy. He understood that without a man in the boy's life it would be hard for him to toughen up the way he needed to. It wasn't the kid's fault. Valentine felt like it was his duty to toughen the boy up. He tried it in front of Molly, correcting the boy and offering recommendations on parenting until Molly eventually drew the line. She felt Valentine was too harsh and told him that they couldn't continue dating unless he accepted that her son was her responsibility, not his.

Valentine publicly accepted that. There was an issue once at the local K-Mart. The boy had wanted a guinea pig. Molly had told her son no and Valentine had agreed that was best. The animals were noisy, smelly, and disgusting. The boy had responded with a crying fit and Valentine had not been able to contain himself. He'd never have been allowed to act like that. No one when he was a child would have. He couldn't tolerate it.

"I'll whoop your little ass!" he told the child, drawing offended stares from other patrons. The comment drew an icy response from Molly, who then conceded and bought the pet to try and make the child forget the terrible way Valentine had spoken to him.

Valentine had pouted all afternoon. The child responded by gloating, practically rubbing it in Valentine's face that he'd ended up with the guinea pig despite Valentine's best efforts. While Valentine wasn't very talkative that evening, he stayed over that night at Molly's request. It seemed like she was trying to smooth things over with him.

The next morning, Valentine was fixing breakfast for Molly and her son when they got up. Molly was pouring herself a cup of coffee when her son came in and asked where his guinea pig was. It was then that Molly noticed the bloody cutting board on the kitchen counter. The small pieces.

She met Valentine's cold eyes and knew.

Molly told her son to go look in his room and she would look through the rest of the house. When he was gone, she tried to find words to ask the question she already knew the answer to. She never did find the words.

"I think you should leave," she said. "I'm probably going to call the police."

Aware that he would lose his job if she did, Valentine shook his head. "You tell anyone and I'll call your husband's family in Dismal. I'll tell them where you're at. I'll bring them to your fucking work."

"Then go," she said. "Don't ever call me again."

Valentine picked up his coat and left without a word.

Molly took the frying pan from the stove and walked it out to the trash dumpster, dropping it inside with a hollow thud.

22

Randi

RANDI FULLY INTENDED on reaching the valley where Jim lived in one long day on horseback. Although in her plans it had seemed completely possible, it was not working out that way. While she had never looked at it on a map, she had an imaginary overview of how she thought her local fields, woods, rivers, and private property all fit together, the day was proving her wrong.

For example, she knew from years of driving that the Clinch River passed under a particular bridge, and then a few miles down the road passed underneath another bridge. In her head, that meant that traveling along the river for the purpose of staying off-road and low-key shouldn't be a very significant detour. What she would have found if she'd actually studied a map was that the river took long, meandering routes through farmland before returning to cross under that second bridge. Following along the river hadn't added only another half-mile to the trip, it had added seven miserable and bug-infested miles.

She assumed that cutting across a farm of several hundred acres would bring her out along the main four-lane highway that traversed the area. However, she navigated without a compass, relying on feeling more than bearing, and brought her family out on a dirt road several miles from where she had intended. By this time, it was getting very late and the sun was setting.

The children were now becoming fussy and exhausted. They were hungry, bug-bitten, and not interested in the traveling provisions that Randi had packed for them from the meager selection in the dairy. They were asking for things that Randi's mother could have fixed them had she still been alive and had a house to cook them in. It was a sobering and saddening realization for all of them, the little things they would no longer experience.

At Carla and Sherry's insistence, Randi threw caution to the wind. They traveled in plain sight on the dirt road, knowing it would eventually lead to the four-lane road that stood between them and what they referred to as Jim's valley. There were occasional ranch-style houses of brick or aluminum siding. Some people came to windows and doors and watched them pass. No one raised a hand in greeting and no one spoke. How quickly the civility and friendly nature of rural America was changing. For Randi, that was fine. She was just glad that no one was trying to steal their horses or pointing guns at them. She didn't expect *friendly* from the world anymore. She expected anger and violence.

The world was proving her right.

It was twilight when they finally crossed the four-lane highway. It felt like a significant waypoint, like the barrier between one world and another more promising one. Between one life and another. On the positive side, they were standing at the abandoned stretch that Randi had been shooting for all day, they were simply reaching it six hours later than she intended. There were no cars visible either moving or stalled. There were no homes or businesses on this section, either, only vast fields on both sides. Randi urged her horse forward and it walked across the pavement, its shoes on asphalt sounding very loud to her, like the ringing of a bell or the honking of a horn.

They plodded across the median, across the next lane, then off the gravel shoulder on the other side. There was a sagging gate fastened to a rotting post with a rusty chain. There was a new padlock on it. Randi got off and checked it because sometimes padlocks were left hanging in a manner that made them appear locked. There was no such luck in this case.

Randi had bolt cutters on her saddle and she used those to cut the lock. She led her horse through and waited for her family to pass, then closed the gate. She arranged the chain and the lock to look like they had not been tampered with, then remounted her horse.

"Can we stay in that barn?" Carla asked, pointing to a large red hay barn off the highway.

Randi shook her head. "No way. Too close to the road. It's not safe."

"Well, I hope there's a place we can stop soon," Carla said. "My ass is killing me."

"It's only about a few more miles," Randi said. "And we're *all* tired."

The grandchildren pitched in at this point, a chorus of whining and crying that tugged at Randi's heart. Obviously, they wanted to stop.

"If we don't get to Jim's tonight then we're going to have to sleep outside and all we have is the horse blankets and a tarp. No tents or anything. We need to keep moving while there's still light."

"It's already getting dark, Mom," Carla said, her voice rising. "I don't like horses anyway. I don't want it stepping in a hole and killing me."

"Carla, honey, this is Rockdell Farms. This farm goes all the way to the valley where Jim lives. Let's follow this farm road a little longer and get clear of the highway. Then we'll figure it out. It's not safe to stay this close to the road."

"Better listen to your mother," came a voice from behind them.

Randi spun and found a haggard-looking man approaching them, having walked out of the barn door. She held up a hand. "Stop right there!"

The man held his hands up in a gesture of innocence. "What?" he asked. "I'm just being friendly."

"Mom?" Carla said fearfully.

The horses, sensing the wave of anxiety in their riders, stomped their feet and pulled at their reins.

"Nice horses," he said. "Where did you get them?" He continued walking toward them. He was less than twenty feet away, his hand raised as if to calm the horses, or perhaps to make her *think* that was his only intention.

Randi yanked the automatic from her belt. Without warning she fired a round to the side of the man, then raised the pistol, letting it fall level with his chest. "I told you to stay back." Her horse skittered and she held him tight.

He continued to smile that same used car salesman smile but stopped moving toward them. "I don't mean you any harm," he said. "I'm passing through and stopped off for the night."

Something about the man sent shivers down Randi's spine. His tone made her skin crawl. People didn't make conversation anymore. They avoided each other. They kept to themselves if they knew what was good for them. This man was lying.

"On the fucking ground," she said.

"Wait a minute," he said. "You're not being very friendly."

"I'm not wasting another round," she said. "Next one goes in you."

He dropped to both knees, frowning. "Is this really necessary?"

"On your face," Randi ordered. "Hands out ahead of you."

He leaned into a pushup position, then lowered himself.

Randi heard an intake of breath from behind her.

"There's a gun in the back of his pants," Carla said quietly.

"You after our horses?" Randi asked. "That it?"

"You have four of them!" he erupted. "I only need one. I've been walking this stupid road through hillbilly country for weeks trying to get home. No one will help me."

Randi walked toward him, standing out of his reach. "Maybe I should just kill you and save the next folks the trouble."

"Maybe you should," he said. "You'd be doing me a favor at this point." He started to cry.

Randi walked around behind him, pointing her pistol at the middle of his back. "You even move and I'll shoot you in the spine," she warned. She leaned forward and snatched his pistol from his waistband. She thought he'd make a grab for her but he didn't. She'd been ready for it. He continued to lay face down in the dirt, crying. Randi's grandchildren watched him with silent fascination. They'd never seen an adult act that way.

"Carla and Sherry, you go on ahead," Randi said. "Take the pack-horse with you."

"What are you doing to do?" Carla asked.

Randi backed away from the man, shoving his pistol in the waist-band of her pants. "Do what I *said*. I'll catch up in a second." Randi moved closer to her horse and climbed on. She kept her pistol on him while the other horses put distance between them.

The man raised his head and looked at her. Snot strung from his nose. A mud of tears and dust blotched his face. "Is this where you kill me?"

She stared impassively at the pathetic creature.

"If you're going to give me a pep talk about how I can make it home, save it," he said. "I hope you die. Whoever those people on the horses are to you, I hope they die too. I hope you die last so you have to watch."

Randi cast a quick glance over her shoulder and saw that her family had reached a safe distance. She was not going to be sucked into his angry rant, nor was she going to waste a bullet on him if she didn't have to.

"Here's your pep talk—fuck you. And I don't think you're going to make it. I think you're going to mess with the wrong people and bleed to death in a ditch. That's what I think."

She turned her horse and galloped off. She only looked back once and saw him sitting there, his head in his hands, his body wracked by sobs. She could not bring herself to feel sorry for him. She knew his grief was for having failed to kill her and take her horse.

Galloping the horse was harder on her than it was on the horse. She could not recall the last time she'd done it. She imagined it was several pounds and two children ago. She was pleased that her family slowed as she rejoined them. She felt like she'd shaken a few vital organs from their moorings.

It was nearly full dark now and it was becoming difficult to see. They were in an interior valley of Rockdell Farms with no roads or homes in sight. Grazing land alternated with the stubble of feed corn. There were odd pieces of abandoned farm equipment scattered around the property, some of it so rusted it was unclear where the machine ended and the dirt began.

"There's something over there," Sherry said. "Carla wanted to go take a look but we wanted to wait until you were here."

"What is it?" Randi asked.

"Some kind of rock building," Carla said. "It looks like a beehive."

23

Randi

W HEN R ANDI AWOKE, she felt like she'd been beaten with a bat. Everything from her ankles to her neck was stiff and aching. Although she had expected to be sore from a day of horseback riding, it had far exceeded her expectation. She'd spent the night sleeping on the rock-strewn floor of the old lime kiln the kids had found last night. The folks at Rockdell Farms had used the kiln to make lime from limestone over a century ago. They packed the kiln with lime-stone and wood, then let it burn for several days so they could manu-facture lime for their farm.

It had been like sleeping in a cave, the ground damp and uneven. The conditions had not bothered the children, who fell asleep without even eating. Before long, even Carla and Sherry were asleep, the ride taking more of a toll on them than they'd admit. Randi had laid awake listening to the night. Her mind churned for a long time before she finally succumbed to sleep herself.

They had a breakfast of homemade strawberry preserves. They passed around a single spoon and each person scooped from the jar.

On an empty stomach, the sugar might give them a little short-lived energy, though it would not sustain them. Randi didn't think they had much farther to go, though yesterday had proven her navigation skills to be sub-par. She hoped she did better today.

When they had eaten their fill, they packed their few possessions back into feed sacks and tied them onto the pack horse. They saddled each horse and climbed up. Randi could tell that everyone was suffering. She perhaps worst of all. She could not make it back onto her horse at all. She was short, which already made it difficult, and her suffering legs could not lift her into the saddle. Her thighs felt as if they might perhaps be permanently damaged if such a thing was possible from simply riding a horse. She was ready to give up and walk when Carla finally rode alongside her, extending a hand. Randi took it and pulled herself up.

"Thanks," Randi said, mildly embarrassed.

"Which way?" Carla asked.

Randi nodded to where the farm road passed through a gap in the low hills. "That way. We'll find a road there that we can follow into the valley where Jim lives."

"Didn't you used to have a radio?" Sherry asked. "Can't you radio him to come get us?"

"It burned up in the fire," Randi said. "I didn't see any point in carrying it with us to your dad's house so I left it on the kitchen table."

Sherry looked glum. "Everything hurts. I'm not sure I can take another day of this."

"My second day of walking home from Richmond felt like this," Randi said. "I'd slept in the woods after walking all day. It was miserable. Just like now."

"I don't know how you did it," Carla said. "I would have given up."

"I already told you how I did it," Randi said. "I reminded myself of what I had waiting for me at home."

They rode in silence for a quarter-hour, the horses' feet scuffing on dirt the only sound. As they got closer to the gap, they began to see more cattle. The cows crowded around them and followed.

"I've never seen so many cows," Randi remarked.

"They look hungry," Carla said. "I hope they don't decide to eat us."

One of Sherry's daughters, riding contentedly in Carla's lap to this point, instantly became terrified. "Cow no eat me!" she cried. "Cow no eat me!"

"Shhh, honey, it's okay," Randi said. "Aunt Carla was just joking. Weren't you, Carla?"

Carla did her best to assure the little girl that it was a misunderstanding, though she didn't look so certain. The damage was done. The child would never again trust a cow.

When they reached the road, they found a tarpaper shack beside the gate they had to use to leave the farm. Randi had grown up around many houses like it, although most had been replaced by mobile homes now. There'd been entire neighborhoods of them, framed and sided of rough sawmill lumber then covered in the rolled tarpaper with red or brown brick patterns. The houses were never insulated and relied on coal fires in Warm Morning stoves to stay tolerable. This one had probably belonged to a tenant farmer at one time.

They stopped at the gate and Randi got off to open it. A scruffy man in a tank top and boxer shorts came staggering out of the house. He didn't appear to see them. He leaned against the round porch post, dropped his boxers to his ankles, and began urinating in the dirt.

"What the hell do you think you're doing?" Randi demanded.

Startled by the unexpected voice the old man jumped but did not —or could not—stop what he was doing. He squinted at them as if he had difficulty focusing.

"'Bout made me piss on myself," he grumbled.

"I don't give a damn if you piss on yourself," Randi said. "Do you not see that there are six ladies here?"

"All I see is six trespassers," the man said, finally relaxing enough to continue sprinkling his lawn. "You best be getting on your way because I got a gun."

"I can see that," Randi said. "It's old and wrinkled and it probably doesn't fire."

He took offense when Randi's daughters burst out laughing. He pulled his boxers back up indignantly and stared at Randi again. "For a second I thought you were my dead wife coming back to haunt me. You got her mouth."

Randi unfastened the gate and directed her family through, handing off her reins to Sherry so that she could lead her horse through. "We'll be on our way. You can go back about your business." The old man crooked a gnarled finger at her, a prompting to not run off so quickly. "Say, missy, you don't have a drink of anything, do you?"

"We might have some water," Randi said. "Not much. We could spare some."

The old man shook his head in irritation. "I don't need no damn water unless it's firewater," he said. "Liquor. Even a beer would do."

Randi shook her head. "Sorry. Fresh out."

The old man turned away. "Just as well, I guess. That shit got me fired last night anyway."

Randi shook her head at the old man, walked out, and shut the gate behind her.

24

Jim

AS SUMMER WAS TURNING into fall the various gardens in the valley were producing the last of their crops and Jim wanted nothing to go to waste. He had a substantial garden at his house. They had always enjoyed canning or freezing their produce, although this year it was likely to be canning or dehydrating. Even Gary had a garden, having inherited the one that Henry and his wife were raising at their home before they were killed. It had been slightly overgrown when Gary moved in, and his family resurrected it.

There were several homes in the valley that had been abandoned for various reasons. Some of the folks who lived in those houses had been killed by the released convict that had terrorized the community in the early days of the disaster. Sometimes Charlie Rakes had burned the home after the murder. Even in those cases where he burned the homes to the ground, sometimes the garden still remained, weed-choked and going rogue.

There were other houses that had been abandoned for unknown reasons. The people who lived there had simply left to go to work on the day of the terror attacks and had never come home, or left shortly afterward, attempting to reunite with family. Many of those homes had gardens, and while they were weedy and plundered by animals, there would still be vegetables that survived and could be harvested.

Jim still had the nagging feeling that he needed the permission of the community to harvest these gardens. Did he really need to do that? There was no committee or group overseeing such things and Jim didn't particularly want there to be. He was an anarchist at heart. He had never liked answering to people. Maybe that was what Ellen was seeing when she accused him of enjoying the state of the world. She was seeing the sense of freedom he was experiencing at no longer having to answer to anyone.

As far as getting any consensus on something like harvesting an abandoned garden, there were families in the valley that knew each other and regularly communicated. There were also several that stuck to themselves. It wasn't like a division existed, it was just a situation where people that hadn't associated with anyone before the disaster were continuing that pattern. Jim and his group didn't feel like they were trying to steal resources, they simply didn't want them going to waste. They didn't want to be sitting around the woodstove in the winter wishing they hadn't let those tomatoes fall to the ground and rot.

Jim figured at some point he needed to make an effort to get to know these other families. If they were going to live in this valley together, decisions one family made might impact the others. Like blowing up the road. Although he wasn't ready to take credit for it yet, his decision to blow up the road from town was a good example of that. He knew it was the right thing to do, yet how would he feel if someone else took such a major decision upon themselves?

In discussion with his group of friends and family—his *tribe* —someone came up with the idea of harvesting all those vegetables from the abandoned gardens, preserving the food through canning or dehydrating, and delivering some to each family in the valley. It would be a good icebreaker to open communication with those families who were still keeping to themselves. It would be a good way for

Jim to test the waters about his plan to close off the road at the other end of the valley, completely sealing them off from vehicle traffic.

They had pulled the hay wagon to two abandoned gardens already and found a variety of squash, pumpkins, tomatoes, peppers, beans, and some corn that had dried on the stalk. There were nearly a dozen of them working head down in the garden when Gary raised his head, a look of confusion on his face.

"Stop a second. You guys hear that?" he asked.

Everyone stopped what they were doing, always paranoid now that any new sound meant new trouble.

"I don't hear anything," Jim said.

"I hear it," Ellen said. "It sounds like horses."

Jim started to make a smart-ass comment until he heard it too. It was the clopping of hooves on pavement. He climbed out of the row of cherry tomatoes he'd been picking. "There," he said, pointing toward the road.

"How'd they get by Pete?" Ellen asked.

"They've come in the back way," Jim said. "Through Rockdell Farms. It's the only way to get in now and he can't see out that far."

Gary dug a pair of binoculars out of his daypack and raised them to his eyes. "Oh *shoot*." He still struggled with profanity.

"What is it?" Ellen asked.

"It's Randi."

"Randi?" Jim asked. "*Our* Randi?"

"Yeah. She's on horseback with a couple of young women and some children," Gary said. "This can't be good. That's a dangerous trip to make with children."

They grabbed their weapons and took off toward the road. Ellen followed with a Remington 870. The rest of the crew paused their labor and watched.

As soon as Jim and Gary were within earshot of the horses, they called to Randi, not wanting to startle her by charging toward her with guns. Both knew her well enough to know that she might open fire on them if she couldn't immediately identify who was running toward her.

Randi steered her horse to the open gate as the men reached it. She slid off the horse, groaning as she hit the ground, then gave each man a somber hug.

"What's going on?" Gary asked. "Is everything okay?"

Randi shook her head. She took a deep breath, gathering energy for what she had to say. "No. Everything is not okay. Everything pretty much sucks. My house got attacked. They killed my parents and one of my brothers."

Jim took in the group, studying each pained face. They told the story without words. He started three different curses, struggling to contain himself in front of the young children. "Do you know who did it?" he finally asked.

"We're pretty sure," Randi said. "We think it was a neighboring family. There'd been some bad blood over the years. I don't know why things broke loose all of a sudden."

Jim shook his head in disgust.

"Oh, Randi," Gary said. "I'm so sorry."

Randi maintained her composure. Each day made the callouses on her heart that much thicker. "We weren't home," she said. "Me, my girls, and one of my brothers had gone down the road looking for my ex-husband. My girls wanted to make sure their dad was okay. When we got back home, the house was on fire, and my parents and my other brother were dead."

"Where's your brother? The one who was with you?" Jim asked.

"He stayed behind," Randi said. "He wanted to make things right."

"I'm surprised you let him do that by himself," Jim said.

Randi twisted her mouth, still struggling with how she felt about that decision. "It's what I had to do. My main job was to get my family to safety. I just had to choke down the rest and leave it to Tommy."

Jim nodded. "I'm sorry you all had to see that."

"The little ones did see all of it. They were there. It's pretty much a miracle they made it," she said. "If they hadn't hidden in the coal bin, they would be dead too."

"They weren't with you?" Gary asked.

Randi shrugged. "It was too long a walk. They should have been fine with Mom and Dad. They said Mom hid them in the coal bin and told them not to leave. She left to help my dad and got herself killed," Randi said, letting that sink in.

"Do you want us to help you take care of the people who killed your parents?" Jim asked. "I can't speak for Gary, but I'd help."

"I appreciate that more than you can know," Randi said. "I'm going to let Tommy deal with it for now. I feel like I need to be here for my kids. I can't take a risk of getting killed for revenge. Yet."

"That's a wise decision," Gary said. "Even if it's not easy."

"I would like to find a place to stay over this way. You made an offer that I could hole up here if things got bad. That offer still good?"

Gary looked at Jim, not feeling like he could extend an offer since he was a guest here too. He liked the idea of Randi staying. They could use a nurse. Beyond that, she was tough as nails.

"Of course the offer is still good," Jim said. "We'd be glad to have you. We can find you a house to stay in like we did for Gary. If the people who own the house come back, we can deal with that at the time."

"Thank you," Randi said, taking Jim by the hand. "I would cry if I had any tears left."

25

Tommy

COPPERHEADS WERE the most common poisonous snake in this part of the Appalachian Mountains. Timber rattlers showed up, too, but they were more elusive. Anyone willing to comb the ridges and pull back a few rocks could easily find their nests, just as Tommy had done all day. For his efforts, he had a feed sack with a tangled mass of two dozen copperheads and another with seven timber rattlers.

Back at the remains of his home, he put three of the copperheads in a five-gallon bucket and securely fastened a lid on it. He took a nap, then ate a meal when he awoke. At dark, he headed out with his snakes, his guns, and a backpack with a few things he thought he might need.

At the Cross home, he was greeted by the dogs who were pleased at his arrival. He fed and petted them, then made his way to the outhouse at the edge of the yard. Many of the homes in this area didn't get public water until the 1970s, so quite a few outhouses were still standing. Like many of the families in coal country, they'd been unable to drill a well because mining had lowered the water table beyond the point where a private well was feasible. Until public water came through, the family hauled water each day from a spring down the road.

Even when they got indoor plumbing, the family never rushed to tear down the outhouse. They weren't the kind of people to take on any project they didn't *have* to do. Since there was no incentive to tear down their outhouse it was still standing nearly forty years after it was rendered obsolete. With the failure of power and then of public water, the outhouse was suddenly back in style. Families who would have turned up their noses at outhouses months ago were now aspiring to build one. All the Crosses had to do was remove forty years' worth of stored junk and it was ready to go. Its existence gave the Cross family an advantage that some other families didn't have. They weren't forced to squat in the woods like the folks who had torn down their outhouses in a rush to erase the memory of more primitive times.

As much as the thought disgusted him, Tommy had to work in the outhouse by *feel* to be sure that no one would see a light. He slipped into the dark chamber and pulled the door shut behind him. It smelled of rot, compost, and fresh excrement. He felt for the seat, his hand dragging along a wet, slimy board. He found a soft spongy substance that he couldn't immediately identify. It crumbled beneath his fingers. His mind raced to all of the nasty possibilities before he determined it was mushrooms growing within the rotting structure. A few inches further and he was pleased to find a modern plastic toilet seat complete with a lid. It was also wet and slimy. He preferred not to think about how it got that way.

Tommy picked up the five-gallon bucket, raised the toilet seat, and lowered the bucket through the hole. He wrapped a thin rope around the bucket several times then tied it around the hinge of the toilet seat so that the bucket hung flush against the bottom of the seat. He pried off the bucket lid and quickly closed the toilet lid before any snakes could find their way out. Once the seat was raised, the snakes should be clear to strike at anything within reach. He smiled at the thought of one of the Crosses kicking his way out of the outhouse, a copperhead latched to his backside.

Tommy backed out the door and eased into the woods like smoke on a windy night. He took a seat far from the house and waited for the lights to go out. He couldn't tell if they were using lanterns or candles but eventually, they were extinguished and the house went dark. There was no more talking and the sound of snoring cut through the otherwise peaceful night.

It was still warm enough that people slept with their windows open. The Crosses were the type of people who didn't have screens on their windows. That was because they were the type who often climbed in and out their windows or threw things from them. That could include pets, guests, and other family members.

An hour passed. Maybe two. He wanted to be sure that no one was awake. He rose stiffly and crossed the damp yard to the house. The dogs followed and sniffed him for more treats, not making a sound. He petted them with his free hand, the one not holding the sacks. They sniffed at the sacks, recoiling at the smell. They knew that smell and wanted no part of it.

The windowsill he chose was at head height. He held the two sacks over the sill and shook them until they were empty, then crept off into the blackness barely able to suppress a laugh. The family would never be sure of how many snakes there were. They would never know where the next one might show up. He hoped they'd all be bitten and die a miserable death, their skin swollen to the point of splitting, though he knew that was too much to hope for. This was only the first of the surprises he had in store for them. There would be more.

26

The Valley

DON SAT on the porch of his trailer eating a can of room temperature Lima beans. He was pondering his next cattle delivery to Wallace County. He couldn't deliver the cattle alone but he couldn't forgive Hodge for the way he'd acted on their last trip. Talking shit was one thing, even making threats was forgivable. Bringing the gun into the equation was a deal-breaker. Hodge was a full-time drunk completely dedicated to his profession. You couldn't expect a lot out of a drunk. Don knew that. Still, it was disappointing. They'd worked together for years, somehow finding a way to make it work.

He thought of all the people he might bring into his cattle scheme, ruling out most of them for one reason or another. It took a certain *mindset* for this line of work. It had to be someone who didn't question or dwell upon the morality of the situation. It took someone who was not as smart as he was. He didn't want to bring in anyone who might get ideas about cutting him out of the deal. The more he explored his options, the fewer he realized he had. He hoped he didn't end up having to go back to Hodge. That was truly a last resort.

When the can of beans was empty, he pitched it into the yard, aiming for a trash pile he'd started a few weeks ago. He stood up and hitched his pants, surveying the countryside. His trailer sat on a narrow lot at the edge of Rockdell Farms. There had once been a tenant house on this property though it had burned down about a dozen years ago. The owner of Rockdell Farms had put a trailer there and let Don live in it. The rent was deducted from his check each month. As a senior employee, he got better accommodations than most. The house his friend *...former friend...* Hodge lived in was a pure tumble-down piece of shit.

Don was pondering a trip to his outhouse. At least he called it his outhouse. He hadn't built the house part yet so the toilet simply consisted of a folding camping chair with a big hole cut out of the nylon seat. It wasn't very private but he didn't get many visitors. Besides, it was darn comfortable and the view was impressive.

His pondering on his bowels was interrupted by the sound of approaching vehicles. He recognized diesel engines and it reminded Don of life before the terror attacks when convoys of semi-trucks would show up to haul off hundreds of cattle en masse. There hadn't been any cattle sales in a while. Other than, of course, the ones that Don had conducted under the table.

He climbed down his porch steps and wandered down the grassy bank to the edge of the road, curiosity getting the best of him. In the distance, he could see a line of vehicles approaching. There was a tan Humvee with several green Humvees following tight behind it. Beyond that were a couple of dually trucks pulling gargantuan fifth-wheel campers.

"Son of a bitch," Don said. "Somebody seems to think they're coming to stay." He started to go back to his trailer and get a gun but there wasn't time. The vehicles would have passed by the time he got back. He walked out onto the center of the road and stood there, a human roadblock.

The tan Humvee slowed. Don squinted and tried to make out the driver. A reflection on the flat glass windshield prevented it. He was relieved when the vehicle stopped about thirty feet away. The passenger door opened and a man stepped out, his tall form familiar. Don's jaw nearly hit the ground.

"What the fuck are you doing here, Baxter?" Don growled.

The man in the safari jacket and Emergency Management Coordinator cap stared at Don. "The golf course has some vulnerabilities that will be difficult to overcome in the long term," he said. "It's too close to the interstate for one. It's also surrounded by Have Nots who maintain a grudge against the Haves living so well in their midst. I thought it prudent to establish a bug-out location, if you will. I'll consider Glenwall to be a Forward Operating Base from here on out."

Don frowned. "Run that by me again in English. What kind of location are you establishing?"

"A bug-out location. A safe retreat from the world," Baxter rephrased. "Is that clear enough?"

Don stiffened. "If that means you think you're moving in here then I've got some fucking news for you. That ain't happening. I run this farm now. You want cattle you go through me. You want a place to live, you turn your happy ass around and find a spot somewhere else." Don crossed his arms and stood defiantly.

Baxter smiled and turned around to share his amused look with his entourage. "These country folks are stubborn, aren't they?" he said. At the same time, he caught the eye of one of his security staff, formerly a Wallace County Deputy. Baxter nodded slightly at the man.

The deputy popped out of the roof hatch of the green Humvee. He threw up a suppressed Sig MPX and stitched a short burst of full auto into Don's chest before he could even uncross his arms. He staggered backward, high-stepping and jerking before collapsing onto the road. He was dead when he hit the ground, his blood volume dispersing among the falling leaves.

Baxter gave the deputy a thumbs-up and returned to the tan Humvee.

"Should I drag him out of the road?" the driver asked.

"No," Baxter replied after a moment of consideration. "They say hanging a dead coyote on your farm will keep the others away. Maybe his body will serve as a deterrent to anyone else coming through."

27

Wallace County

THERE HAD BEEN people begging at the gates of the golf course ever since resources began to get scarce. It was like the way that kids went trick-or-treating in nice neighborhoods because they thought they'd get more or better candy. Some people assumed that the folks at Glenwall were still enjoying prime rib with a nice wine from Vincent's Vineyard. Truth was, without the combined efforts of Baxter and the board of directors, who'd used their connections to bring in additional resources, the folks at Glenwall might have been worse off than the general community. The folks there dined out a lot and didn't keep large pantries for preparing dinner each night. They tended to shop for specific meals and consume most of what they purchased as part of that meal. They were a class with deep pockets and shallow pantries.

Soon after the terror attacks occurred, when Baxter was having organizational meetings to plan the county's disaster response, Valentine had offered his services to him. He'd approached Baxter after the meeting and explained that he was a security guard at the community college, and had a lot of experience with preparedness. Truthfully, his preparations were only focused on cool weapons and gear and not on the more practical concerns of food, water, and alternative energy sources. Valentine had the foresight to know he needed to pair himself with a group as soon as possible, one that had access to those things he'd overlooked.

He knew that if he could become part of the official local government response he would have access to a steady supply of food. What he hadn't counted on was Baxter selling out the county and pairing up with the Glenwall folks. He couldn't blame the man. While Baxter came from a different background than Valentine, he could just as easily see the writing on the wall. For all of those FEMA and DHS workshops that Baxter had attended, none of the promised disaster relief seemed to be coming. It would be up to people to save themselves.

After the attacks of 9/11, every agency at every level of the government prepared disaster plans and Continuity of Operations Plans, known as COOPs. They spelled out specific duties and who would carry them out. Those plans were adhered to for about three days then everything began to descend into chaos. It was around that fourth or fifth day that the folks from Glenwall approached Baxter and this plan fell into place.

Valentine brought a few things to the table with him. He knew a man in the shipping and logistics business from back home. He had access to acres of shipping containers on a lot not far off the interstate. Using cash obtained from the folks at Glenwall, Valentine had procured a dozen forty-foot containers. The container company used their rollback truck to arrange the containers around the perimeter of the clubhouse. While not completely bulletproof, the containers did provide both a way to store essential supplies and provide some additional ballistic protection. If they had to, the Glenwall folks could circle the wagons and pull everyone into the clubhouse if they fell under attack.

While they hadn't fallen under organized attack yet, they were constantly dealing with folks at the gate begging for food. Valentine had warned Baxter that the six-foot-tall decorative brick fence around the property provided no protection at all, but he'd yet to authorize Valentine to bolster their defenses. For now, folks showed up at the gate each day, begging that the wealthy do their part to help out.

"Do I fucking look wealthy?" Valentine asked the folks.

They would always look at him the same way. "Those folks in there got money. Look at those big houses. You know they got food in there," was the usual response.

"Get the hell out of here," Valentine would tell them. "There's nothing for you here."

If Baxter wasn't around, Valentine might even get a little rough to discourage them from coming back the next day. Baxter didn't like it.

"If the women and kids that live here see that, there will be complaints," he said. "We don't need complaints. We don't want to lose our meal ticket. Keep it civil."

Valentine agreed that they didn't want to lose their meal ticket though he got tired of dealing with the same thing every day. He thought a show of force would be the best solution for dealing with the beggars. On this particular day, he was in a bad mood because he'd wanted to go on the run to Russell County with Baxter. They were going to establish a camp and Valentine thought he should have been part of that. Baxter didn't know if they'd run into opposition over there and Valentine wanted to be in the fight if there was one.

Baxter had assured Valentine that he was being left in charge because he could be trusted to run things. Valentine didn't like missing out on the action. So far this entire Glenwall job had been little different than providing security at the college campus. Most days he felt like nothing more than a babysitter to the pampered and coddled. That brought out the worst in him.

The crowd outside the wall continued to grow despite Valentine's menacing presence. Folks chanted and sang, and the repetition was becoming an irritant to Valentine. He couldn't take it anymore. These folks needed to be discouraged.

"I need a break," he told the two other guards at the gate. "Can you guys handle this?"

"Sure," one of them said. "They know what that white line means."

The white line was literally the line in the sand. They'd told the protestors that if they crossed the line they'd be killed, and as of yet, no one had challenged that. They only sang and yelled, getting on Valentine's nerves.

Valentine hopped in a Humvee and drove to the house he'd been staying in with some of the other men. He'd stored a ton of his gear in the basement, hoping it would be safer than leaving it in his apartment. He shifted boxes around until he found the ones he was looking for. The label read *Tannerite*. The four boxes weighed ten pounds each, and it took him two trips to get them up the steps.

He followed the instructions, mixing the catalyst with the material and pouring it back in the containers the material had come in. When all the containers were full, he went back to the basement and found a cooler. He took it upstairs and packed all the containers into the white marine cooler. He carried it back to the golf cart and placed it in the back seat, unable to suppress his grin.

He zipped back to the main gate. Valentine waved at the other guards, urging them to get out of the way and let him through.

"Baxter is not going to be happy about you giving away food," one of them said. "It will only make things worse."

"You think I'm fucking stupid? I'm not giving away food," Valentine barked at them. "Now get that car out of the way!"

One of the guards reluctantly started the sheriff's department vehicle and moved it out of the way. Valentine hit the accelerator, heading straight for the crowd. They leapt out of the way, cursing and yelling.

About a hundred yards outside of the gate, Valentine stopped and dragged the cooler off the golf cart. By this time, the protestors and guards were both watching him, unsure of what was going on. He left the cooler sitting in the road while he drove back to the gate and shot through, then the other guard returned the patrol car to its position.

"What's that all about?"

"You'll see," Valentine replied to the inquisitive guard. He climbed up on top of a car hood and faced the crowd. "There's your fucking food. Take it and get the hell out of here."

The crowd raced off toward the cooler, shoving and tripping each other.

"Give me that rifle," Valentine told one of the men. It was a bolt-action with a scope.

"You can't shoot them," he said. "You gave them the food. You can't shoot them for taking it."

"I'm not going to shoot anyone," Valentine replied. He crossed his heart. "I promise."

He hesitantly handed the rifle over to Valentine, who laid it across the hood of one of the cars and sighted the scope on the cooler.

"You said you wouldn't shoot anyone," a guard reminded him.

"I'm not," Valentine replied, monitoring the racing mob through the scope. "I didn't say anything about not shooting the cooler though."

The guards looked at each other, frowning and trying to figure out why he would want to shoot the cooler. When the crowd reached the cooler, there was more shoving and fighting. There must have been twenty people who reached it at the same time. They pounded on each other, trying to get a hand on the cooler and drag it off. Valentine smiled. Then he pulled the trigger.

The boom of the .308 was loud in the quiet town, then the round hit the cooler and detonated the Tannerite. It was an explosive rifle target sold for recreational use. In small jars, it made a satisfying *BOOM* when you hit it. If you taped jars together, it detonated all of them. In quantity, such as the forty pounds packed into the cooler, it would blow apart bodies. The explosion shook the ground and shattered a nearby streetlight, wreaking havoc on the poor souls wrestling for the cooler.

"What the hell?" a guard shouted, yanking the rifle from Valentine's hand. His face was red with anger.

"I didn't shoot anyone," Valentine said.

"Baxter is going to be *pissed*," he said. "This is messed up."

"I bet we won't have any beggars at the gate tomorrow," Valentine said.

The other guards stared at the devastation. Some of the injured were running or walking away, leaning on others for support. Some writhed on the ground, stopping only as they bled out. Others lay in pieces, killed instantly for the promise of food.

"I always wanted to try that," Valentine said.

The guard whose rifle Valentine used, turned it on him. "I can't believe you did that!"

Valentine stared coldly at him. "Think carefully about where you're pointing that rifle, son. You may not be willing to pull the trigger but I'm more than willing to shove that damn thing in one end of you and pull it out the other. You think about that."

The man stared at Valentine for a long time, then dropped the gun. Valentine got back in the Humvee without a word and drove off.

28

The Valley

JIM SETTLED Randi's family into a house on a stretch of road between him and Gary. It was a white frame house that had belonged to an older couple, the Robinsons, who had been killed by the released convict that had wreaked havoc in the valley until Jim killed him. It appeared the couple had been beaten to death to obtain drugs since pills were found scattered all around the home when the bodies were discovered. The convict had gone through every bottle of pills in the house, dumping those that he had no use for into the floor.

The house was older, well-maintained, and neat. It had a well, there was a creek that passed through the backyard, and a spring nearby for drinking water. There was an overgrown garden and several fruit trees. Like most in the valley, the house had a woodstove that could help a family survive the coming winter.

It had been grim work burying bodies that had been left laying in the house for several days in summer heat. Jim had stopped by and left the windows open in that house whenever the weather permitted to try to purge the smell. He had anticipated there might be a day when the house was needed again. Despite a vague hope that Randi would rejoin them, he hadn't expected it and certainly not this soon. There was no denying, though, that having a nurse among them was a benefit.

On her first day in the house, Randi and her daughters were gathering up the old couple's belongings and storing them in the attic when they heard a knock on the door. Randi answered it with a gun in hand, finding Gary standing on the porch, an AR slung over his shoulder.

"Well good morning," Randi said.

Gary held up a thermos. "I brought you some coffee," he said. "I wasn't sure that you had any."

Randi's eyes lit up. "We don't. We've got some canned food and a few things that were here in the house. No coffee, though."

Gary handed the thermos over. "You can use the cup on the thermos. I've already had some this morning. Do your girls drink coffee?"

"Not if they don't know about it," Randi said. She gestured at the porch swing. "Have a seat."

Randi sat, unscrewed the cup off the thermos, and poured the cup full. She held it under her nose, letting the warm smell waft into her nostrils. "God, I've missed that." She took a sip.

"I have to admit I brought that as a bribe," Gary said.

Randi looked at him over the cup. "For what?"

"I'd like you to talk to my daughter Charlotte," he said.

"Have I ever met her?"

"Probably not," Gary said. "She lost her husband a few days ago. I don't know how much you've heard. We were basically run out of my neighborhood. It was an indefensible location and it became clear we would never survive staying there. All the preparation I put into the place was basically for nothing."

"I'm sorry that happened," Randi said. "I kind of know what it feels like to be run out of the place you dreamed about the entire time we were walking home. It's a sick feeling."

"It pisses you off. I kept telling myself that I was saving what was important—my family," Gary said. "The night before we came here we got hit by a group that had been antagonizing us and they killed my son-in-law. It was awful."

Randi didn't know what else to say.

"I'm sorry I'm going on about this," Gary sighed. "I know you lost family too."

"My parents and a brother," Randi acknowledged. "I've got another brother still out there."

"Well, the reason I came over is because I'd like you to take a look at Charlotte. She's been suffering a major depressive episode since he died. She has kids and she can't take care of them or herself. All she does is lie in the bed and cry or stare at the wall. It's like she wants to die."

"That's awful."

"We've had her on suicide watch since we got here," he said. "My wife and daughters have to stay with her constantly. They're afraid she's going to try something. Last night my wife was making her bed and found a steak knife under the mattress. We think she was going to try to kill herself with it."

"I'm sorry," Randi said. "What exactly do you want me to do?"

"I've got things I can trade for medication. I'd like an idea of what I might be able to give her in order to try to stabilize her mood. If I knew what medication I needed, I could start getting out and looking for it."

"There are common drugs like Zoloft and Wellbutrin that should be easy to find," Randi said. "Then it's a matter of keeping her stable until the drugs reach a therapeutic level in her system."

Gary nodded. "I can remember that, and I'll start putting out feelers for them. There may even be someone in the valley with those sitting around."

"Sometimes antidepressants were prescribed in conjunction with smoking cessation meds like Chantix," Randi said. "Ask about that too. There may be people who received other antidepressants that would work as well."

Randi took another sip of her coffee. Gary busied himself with the sling on his AR, flipping it one way, then the other. He was either nervous or wasn't finished.

"There something else?" Randi asked.

Gary looked at her, his eyes pleading. "Will you try to talk to her? We've all tried and none of us can reach her. Maybe a new face, a new approach, can do some good. We're about at the end of our rope. We've run out of things to try. I worry every night that we're going to find her dead in the morning."

"You start by looking for those meds I mentioned," Randi said. "Check with folks in the valley first. I'll go talk to her this afternoon."

Gary sighed with relief. "I appreciate that more than you could know."

"You and Jim got me home," Randi said. "I appreciate you all very much. I feel like we're practically family now."

"Jim's daughter says we're a tribe," Gary said.

"That could be true," Randi replied after a moment. "We're more than a family."

"Well, thank you," Gary said. "I'll tell my wife you're coming by, just in case I'm not there when you come."

"Tell her I will need to talk to Charlotte alone. It'll be easier to establish a therapeutic relationship if we can speak freely," Randi said. "Is that a problem?"

"I'll make sure it's not," Gary said.

29

The Valley

A DOG BARKED at Randi as she walked down the gravel drive to the house Gary was staying in. She didn't know if it was his family's dog or if it came with the house. It was always possible that the dog, like the rest of them, was here seeking refuge from the crumbling world. The dog walked beside her the entire length of the drive, not showing any aggression, though loudly announcing her presence. Everyone had to pull their weight and announcing folks was the dog's job.

Gary's daughter Sarah came out to greet her. The rhythmic squeaking of metal on metal drew Randi's attention and she saw three young girls on a swing set in the overgrown yard. It was not joyful play. There were no smiles. It was the swinging of bored, sad children. It tugged at Randi's heart.

"Those are Charlotte's babies," Sarah said. "We've tried to keep them busy and distracted. Jim's daughter Ariel has been playing with them, and the Weatherman girls from across the road come down here a lot."

"No replacement for a mother," Randi said.

"I know," Sarah said. "At that age, they want her every night and she ignores them. They cry for her and it's like she doesn't even hear them. It's enough to break your heart."

"Did Gary tell you I want a chance to evaluate her alone?" Randi said. "If you guys are in there, it can affect the dynamic of the assessment. I need to encourage her to respond to my questions."

Sarah burst out with a sarcastic laugh. "Good luck getting her to respond to anything. We've all tried. She's not snapping out of it."

Sarah glanced back at the house, making sure no one else was looking. "I know this sounds awful. It's just that this situation is bad enough without having to babysit her too."

Randi nodded. "I've already got your dad out looking for medication," she said. "Even if she won't talk to me, maybe she'll take the meds if we can find them and we can get her leveled out."

Sarah shrugged as if she weren't so sure, yet she led Randi into the house. It was a typical brick ranch from the 1970s, minus the shag carpeting and paneling. There were boxes stacked all over the place as the family tried to deal with reducing three households into a single, smaller house. The house was stuffy inside. The narrow windows didn't do much to release the heat building up in the house during the day. It was a reminder of how spoiled folks had become with air conditioning.

A woman greeted them in the hallway. It was Gary's wife, Debra, and Randi had never met her before. The two women exchanged awkward greetings, then Debra took Randi back while Sarah returned to the yard. Debra opened a door and led Randi into a smallish bedroom. The room smelled stale, of unwashed body and dank sheets. Despite the heat, a young woman lay in bed with blankets pulled up to her neck. She might have been attractive under other circumstances. Right now her hair was matted and her clothes rank. Her eyes were open and she stared blankly at the wall. Randi had a brief flash of the movie *The Exorcist*. She was Father Merrin meeting the possessed child, Regan.

"I apologize for her condition. We've tried to bathe her..." Debra shook her head. "She's dead weight. She won't do anything for herself."

"You don't have to explain anything to me," Randi said. "Just leave me alone with her and let us talk."

"I don't know how much talking you'll get done," Debra said. "If you're okay staying with her for a little while maybe I can take the kids down to the creek and let them play in the water for a few minutes? They need to get away from this house."

"That would be fine," Randi said, smiling. "They'll enjoy that."

"I'll be back in a few minutes, Charlotte," Debra called to Charlotte, who gave no response. Debra backed out the door and gently closed it behind her.

Randi went to the window and looked out at the kids on the swing set. Debra wasn't out there yet and they continued their glum swinging, the metal chains screeching with each arc. "You have beautiful children."

Charlotte had no reaction.

"How long has it been since you've held one of them?"

No answer.

"They need that at this age. They need the reassurance of being held. They need to know they can go out and experience things and still return to the safety of their mother. It's part of their social development."

Nothing.

"My grandchildren are around that age, and I can't go very long without holding them. I miss it too much. I'll have to bring them up here to play when we get settled."

Still no reaction. Randi was getting angry. This was a mother she was talking to, one who'd lost her bond to her children.

"Have you even looked at them lately?"

Again, nothing.

Randi went to the bed. She leaned forward and stroked Charlotte's hair. Charlotte didn't acknowledge the contact. Randi could hear the screeching chains in her head. Could picture the sad faces of those children. She grabbed a fistful of Charlotte's hair and violently pulled the girl from the bed and onto the floor.

Charlotte reached for Randi's hands, trying out of sheer reflex to pull them loose as she was dragged across the floor by her hair. Randi stopped in front of the window. She leaned down to Charlotte's ear. "You can stand up under your own power or I will lift you by the fucking hair," she hissed. "Do you understand me?"

There was no reaction. Randi started lifting by a fistful of hair and Charlotte gave in, scrambling to get her feet under her. She stood under her own power. Randi kept hold of her hair, shoving Charlotte toward the window.

"You look out there," Randi said through clenched teeth. "You see those fucking kids?"

No response.

Randi hauled back on Charlotte's hair again. "DO YOU SEE THEM?"

Charlotte made a whimper in the affirmative. Randi held her head in front of the window, making her watch. "Those kids lost *both* parents because you can't get your head out of your ass. They need you. No one else. You! You may feel like a sorry piece of shit right now, but you're the only mother they have."

Outside, Debra and Sarah rounded up the kids and began leading them off. Randi pushed Charlotte away from her. The young woman clattered against the wall, her face pressed against it. She slid down it starting to cry, smearing tears in a descending trail.

Randi leaned over, her hands on her knees, her head close to Charlotte's. "Those tears better be for your children because there are going to be *no more* for your husband. I hate that this happened to you but you need to get your shit together. I was with your dad and Jim in Richmond. That trip was a shit sandwich. No matter how bad things got we could only think of one thing—our children. It was the reason why we kept going every day. That's what good parents do. No matter how bad things get, you keep going. I know your dad didn't raise you to be like this."

Charlotte let out a loud sob and buried her face in her hands.

Randi stood upright and scoured the room. She saw a pair of sweat-pants and a t-shirt. She threw them onto Charlotte's sagged body. "Put these on."

When there was no reaction, Randi leaned forward again, resting her hands on her knees. "I am a nurse. I have dressed a lot of people in my day. I will dress you and I will not be gentle about it. You put on those clothes. We're going for a walk."

Randi went to the bed and sat down. When Charlotte didn't move, Randi got back up and went to the girl, grabbing her shirt and starting to pull it off.

"NOOOO!" Charlotte moaned. "I'll do it."

"Then do it!" Randi demanded.

Charlotte's crying tapered off and she turned her back to Randi, taking off the filthy clothes she'd been in for days and switching to those that Randi gave her. When she was done, Charlotte turned to her, wiping at a tear.

"Shoes!" Randi ordered, pointing at her feet.

Charlotte dropped to her knees and fished under the bed. She came out with a pair of flip-flops. She stood, scuffed one onto each foot, then stood in front of Randi as if presenting herself for inspec-tion. She even looked Randi in the face.

Randi patted the bed beside her. "Sit down here."

Charlotte obeyed, folding her hands in her lap and staring at them.

Randi put an arm around her. "Your dad and I are going to find you some medication. An anti-depressant. It will help you get through this. If we can find enough, you can take it for a couple of months and we'll see what happens. That's it—a couple of months. This is all on you. You have to pull yourself out of this."

Charlotte remained silent.

"Honestly, Charlotte, what you're doing is not fair to your family. It's not fair to your children. If you can't pull yourself out of this, the best thing you can do for everyone is to go off into the woods some-where and pull the damn plug on this life. At least then your family and your children can get on with their own lives instead of everything having to center around you. Seriously, you're just wasting everyone's time and energy."

This got Charlotte's attention. She raised her eyes to Randi's. There was neither anger nor judgment. She was simply processing Randi's words.

"Give it two weeks. If you still can't find your way back, you come tell me. I will give you the pills to do it with because I can't stand to see what you're doing to those kids. Nothing personal. I would rather watch you die than have to watch those kids die *inside*. Do we have a deal?"

Randi waited. "I need a nod or something."

Charlotte finally nodded.

Randi stood. "Then get your ass up. We're going to go watch those kids play in the creek."

Panic flashed in Charlotte's eyes and she opened her mouth to say something. Randi reached down and gently stroked Charlotte's hair. She leaned over and whispered into Charlotte's ear. "The creek is a long damn way to drag you, but try me and I'll do it. Your dad means a lot to me. I will not let you tear his family apart."

30

Tommy

ANOTHER TRICK that Tommy picked up from a striking coal miner was the construction of jack rocks. In Virginia, as in many other states who saw labor disputes, it was illegal to possess these ancient weapons. It was said that ninjas had once used the weapon, known as a caltrop, to deter pursuers. In modern times, it was used to flatten the tires of non-union coal trucks or of state police vehicles.

Though larger in size, it was identical in function to the jack rock used by children. No matter how it landed, there was always a point sticking up. For cars, striking miners would construct them of 16- or 20-penny nails. To stop a coal truck, they'd make them of railroad spikes. Men would gather in garages deep in the mountains and manufacture them during the coal strikes. They would drink beer or homemade liquor and tell hunting stories. They set up workstations with one man gathering the parts, one man welding, and other men sharpening the finished product. They were extremely effective, and illegal. To be caught with one meant a trip to jail.

In his father's barn, Tommy found a coffee can of 20 penny nails and had been inspired. He remembered purchasing the oversized spikes to build a horse shed out of sawmill lumber. While he didn't have a welder, there was a propane torch and some brazing rod in the barn. He made a jig out of some rocks on the ground to hold the nails in place while be joined them together.

He worked there for hours, brazing until the torch ran out of gas. He'd been able to make over thirty jack rocks. He held one up to the sky and touched a finger to the point. He suddenly felt the long nights catching up with him. He gathered the fruits of his labor and retreated to the dairy for a nap. It was still too bright outside to do anything right now.

Tommy's nap was fitful. He could not determine if it was the cold, hard substrate of his bed or the nightmares of his dead parents. He lay there in a state somewhere between sleep and wakefulness for a long time, unable to tell if he were awake, asleep, or dead. Then with a start, he sat bolt upright. He was in total blackness. He held his hand up in front of his face and could not see it.

No light shone through the cracks around the door. He felt around for his flashlight, then used that to find his pistol. He pushed open the door, stepping out of the cool building into the warm night. The stars were brilliant. His wristwatch had burned in the fire but he thought it was late. Late enough, anyway. He gathered a jar of meat chunks for the dogs and a few items of hardware from the barn, then set out through the woods.

The moon was bright enough that he didn't need the light at all. The trail had become familiar enough to him that he walked it as much from memory as from sight. When he reached the Cross house he settled into a recess of moon shadow and regarded the house. He wondered if anyone had been bitten by the presents he left. He couldn't hold back his smile. His hate for that family was the greatest passion he'd known in his life.

Satisfied that no one was awake, he approached the house. The dogs came to him, wagging their tails and sniffing at his hands. He opened the jar and hand-fed each of them several chunks, then stuffed the jar back in his pack. He went to the front porch. He knew from watching the house that the steps creaked and groaned so he didn't use them. The porch had no rails so he scooted up onto it, then crawled to the front door.

He pulled a sharp awl from his back pocket and pressed it against the soft wood of the door jamb. When he had a hole started, he removed a screw eye from his pocket and threaded it into the hole. When it became hard to turn, he put the awl through the eye and used that to apply leverage to the eye. He did the same thing on the opposite door jamb and then ran a piece of high-tensile fence wire through the eyes, putting several twists on each end to secure it.

He scooted back from the door and removed a folded towel from his pack. Inside were the jack rocks. He arranged them in a cluster in front of the door, in front of his tripwire. He shoved the towel back into his pack and then crept from the porch. The dogs were waiting on him and he emptied the jar onto the ground for them. He made two piles to hopefully keep them from snarling and fighting with each other.

He shouldered his pack and began to creep away from the porch. He heard a sound, a muffled thud he'd heard before but couldn't place. He turned back to the house, his hand on his pistol, and squinted, unable to see anything unusual in the moonlight. He heard the sound again.

It was above him.

He looked up in time to see a shape teetering on the edge of the roof, then dropping. He tried to move. He was not fast enough. It landed on him, knocking him to the ground. He hit his head on the ground hard and was stunned.

"Momma!" a voice screamed in his face.

It was Lisa Cross. He wanted to punch her, to fight, though his brain had been scrambled by the impact and he couldn't form a thought. A light clicked on between them and there she was, hovering over him, a pistol leveled at his face.

"Don't you fucking move," she snarled. "Momma!"

The front door opened and Oma Cross called out. "I'm coming! Hold on!"

A flashlight clicked on in the house, then came bobbing back toward the door. There was a cry of surprise and the light went flying when Oma's feet hit the tripwire. Oma's scream as she went down was abruptly cut off.

"Momma?" Lisa said again, this time with concern. She played her light across the porch and sucked in a breath when the light caught her mother. Oma lay on her belly in the cluster of jack rocks. She was attempting to get up. As she raised her face from the porch, they could both see a spike buried in the center of her forehead, another in her eye. Her mouth gaped but she was unable to speak. Each time she attempted to get up, her head sagged against the porch again. With each sag, the spike was pounded deeper into her brain.

Lisa turned back to Tommy. He grinned through his pain. She lashed out at him with the pistol and all went dark.

31

The Valley

BAXTER CHOSE a flat pasture beside a creek to set up their fallback camp. There was something about the site that drew him in. His group was not the first to feel that way. The same pasture had been a seasonal hunting camp for Native Americans for thousands of years. Where those tribes built wigwams, his group arranged modern campers. The purpose of both groups was similar—a desire to find a place with good water, plentiful food, and safety.

One of the Humvees pulled a generator mounted onto a trailer, while another pulled a trailer-mounted fuel tank. When those were positioned and unhooked, the group of men started raising a long white tent. With a table and chairs under it, it would serve as the command center, conference room, and dining hall.

Baxter had brought a dozen of his most trusted employees, with the exception of Valentine, who was running the show back at Glenwall in his absence. While he was certainly open to bringing more folks in the future, he couldn't pull all of his resources out of Glenwall yet without angering the folks paying the bills. He *was* an Emergency

Manager and he'd been trained in disaster preparedness, but he wasn't really a survivalist. He was more of a bureaucrat than anything else. The one thing his training had prepared him for was to identify what resources were critical early in the disaster and to cabbage them for his own purposes.

It had been good fortune that he'd ended up partnering with the folks of Glenwall. In the early stages of the disaster, he'd been at a public meeting and one of the residents of the golf course community had been in attendance. As Baxter was griping about a lack of operational facilities with adequate space, the man mentioned setting up at Glenwall. It became clear pretty quickly that it was to be a reciprocal agreement. One of those "you scratch my back and I'll scratch yours" deals. That was fine with Baxter. He had no family and no resources.

Once at Glenwall, he quickly set up strategic planning meetings with the Board of Directors of the golf course and found that he had tremendous resources on tap. One of those resources was money. Not only did these folks have overstuffed bank accounts, most of them kept lots of cash on hand for impulse purchases, travel, wagers, or whatever else the rich needed cash for.

In private meetings with those few very select, very powerful residents that were on the board, Baxter's training and their resources allowed them to hammer out a mutually beneficial arrangement. A man who owned a chain of grocery stores had five tractor-trailer loads of food brought in from one of his distribution centers and secured at the clubhouse. A man who owned several coal mines had two fuel tankers of diesel fuel brought in from one of his mine sites. A man in construction had brought in several sets of very powerful tower lights that operated off internal generators, and Baxter had access to several military surplus generators he'd obtained for the county. He brought them to Glenwall and was able to run power to the clubhouse so they could operate a central kitchen with meals for Glenwall residents.

Aware that lights, food, and fuel would make Glenwall a target, Baxter quickly pointed out that the group would need security beyond what the golf course normally provided. Baxter had been able to find a group of men with no families who were willing to come live in the maintenance facility at the golf course and provide security in exchange for food. Several of them were deputies who'd walked off the job. Others came from the county maintenance staff. A few more were regular folks Baxter knew from the local gun range where he shot skeet occasionally.

As far as the Board of Directors at Glenwall knew, Baxter and his crew were gone on a recon mission searching for more supplies. He'd left half of his security force, which would keep the residents from worrying about his absence. They didn't even have to take the campers from the golf course. They were county property and had been stored at a county maintenance facility. In the years following Hurricane Katrina, FEMA campers had been easy for local government to obtain for a fraction of their original cost. Baxter had made sure that Wallace County had picked up a few of the nicer ones, though he'd never expected he'd be living in one.

Baxter had imagined living a cushy life at the golf course community, holding a position of respect while this disaster played out. He figured that they'd have a few rough days and then things would start to get back to normal. During that time, he would gain credibility for keeping a cool head in a disaster. After a couple of weeks, he began to worry that this was a true cascading systems failure event. He'd read about them, assuming it was only a theoretical model. If that was the case, the model was proving accurate.

If the model continued to play out, being there in the middle of a small town on the interstate was a no-win scenario. Resources in town were already drying up, violence was increasing, the interstate would bring gangs and looters, and those remaining in town would have a much harder time surviving than those who got themselves out of town and found a secure location to hole up in. Baxter could see the writing on the wall and had been trying to think of such a place when Don and Hodge showed up. The more they talked, the more certain he was that he'd found his place.

He hadn't planned on doing much more than taking note of this location until the two cattle thieves mentioned that residents had blown up one of the roads leading into the valley. That forced his hand. His plan now was to develop this location into a fallback site fully stocked with supplies. He would leave a skeleton crew of men here. Part of their job would be to make sure the road into this end of the valley didn't get cut off. The rest of them would return to Glenwall with a load of cattle and never mention this valley. When the time came that they had to leave Glenwall for their own safety, they would pack up under cover of darkness and head to the valley.

With everything set up and with arrangements made for the crew that was remaining behind, Baxter called the rest of his men together and addressed them. "I don't mean to keep repeating myself, but it's critical that you don't go back and talk about what we're doing here. I'm setting this place up for the safety of all of us. If you tell anyone about it, you're compromising that safety. I take that so seriously that you only get one chance. You violate my trust, you're out. You can't live at Glenwall and you can't come here. You'll have to go back to your old life, whatever that was."

They nodded, looking at each other, assessing who might be the weak link in the arrangement. While Baxter was pausing for dramatic effect, the sound of singing unrolled down the road toward them. Baxter stared. The group spread apart a little and took a firmer grip on their weapons.

"I'll be damned," Baxter said. "It's the partner of the gentleman we left lying dead in the road. The local cattle thief."

Sure enough, Hodge was walking toward them with a step somewhere around the juncture of stroll and stagger. He walked directly to the gated pasture, let himself in, and approached the group.

"Evening, gentlemen," Hodge said.

Baxter nodded at him. "I take it you must live close by?"

Hodge nodded. "Yattaway." He gestured with his head.

"Where's your partner?" Baxter asked, wondering if he had seen Don flattened in the road.

"Fired me," Hodge replied. He was wobbly, his eyes not focusing well.

"That's a shame," Baxter said. He noticed a plastic bottle in Hodge's hand. "What is that?"

Hodge raised the bottle awkwardly. "Rubbing alcohol. All I got." Even drunk, Hodge wasn't going to mention his Lysol concentrate lest these men get ideas of stealing it from him. The Lysol was for real emergencies.

"That stuff will kill you," Baxter commented.

"It's why I'm here. Got any more of that good shit?"

Baxter shook his head. "We can get our own cattle now," he said. "Not sure we need you anymore. No offense."

Hodge stared at him. "So you're simply moving in and taking what you want? That the way this works?"

"I think so," Baxter said. "The cattle didn't belong to you either. We've got as much right to steal them as you do."

Hodge shrugged. He wasn't sure he agreed with that logic. What could he do about it, though? He mumbled something indecipherable and started to amble off.

One of Baxter's men came forward and said something to Baxter, who nodded emphatically. "Sir?" Baxter called after the drunk man. "Sir?"

Hodge stopped in an awkward, lurching maneuver. "What?" he asked, not even turning.

"We are in need of a decent storage facility," Baxter said. "Someplace clean, dry, and close to here. Like a shop building or barn with a concrete floor."

Hodge didn't reply for several moments.

"Sir?" Baxter prodded.

"Thinking."

Baxter didn't ask him again.

"What's in it for me?" he finally asked.

"I'll be coming back this way the day after tomorrow," Baxter said. "I'll bring you another bottle of the good stuff if you have the information I asked for."

Hodge lurched back into motion and continued on his way. "I'll have you a place."

As he staggered off, Hodge thought that getting liquor for information would be the easiest booze he'd ever earned. He wondered if other people might trade booze for information. With his part in the cattle operation done, he needed a new way to supplement his drunkenness.

32

Tommy

PAIN WOKE TOMMY. Nearly everything hurt. He expected that he would be tied up but he wasn't. He looked around. Enough light was coming in through the cracks that he could tell he was on the floor of the Cross's outhouse. He sat up and pushed against the door. It wouldn't budge. He pushed again, harder this time, and it still wouldn't move. He cursed against the pain and confusion.

He climbed up onto the toilet seat, making sure the lid was closed in case his bucket of snakes was still in there and looked through a crack. A band of yellow was running completely around the outhouse. At first he was confused, then he could see it was one of those heavy ratchet straps that truck drivers used to fasten their loads down. Tommy reached for his pocket. He could cut the strap with his knife and be out of there in no time.

The knife was not there.

He patted all of his pockets and found them empty. "That bitch," he muttered.

He jumped when an eye moved before a wide crack in front of him.

"You talking to me?" came a female voice.

"Let me out of here."

"No."

Tommy lashed out at the eye with his foot to no effect. He felt around, hoping for something he could use as a weapon, and found nothing. All his hand landed on was a damp roll of toilet paper.

"You're a real bastard," she said.

"You brought this on yourself," he said. "You killed my parents and my brother."

"Your brother started this," she said.

"You're lying," he said.

"My daddy died yesterday," she said. "He couldn't make water. He came out here to use the outhouse and a snake bit him on his privates. They swelled up and wouldn't nothing come through them. It was a bad way to die."

Tommy remained silent.

"My uncle got bit in the house," she continued. "A rattler got him when he set his feet out of the bed that morning. His body couldn't handle the stress. He had a heart attack not long after the bite. I'm assuming them snakes were your doing?"

"Sounds like we're about even," he said. "Maybe you should let me go."

"Momma and I finally caught all of those snakes," she said. "We were going to use them to kill you, but she's dead now. You going to tell me you didn't have anything to do with that either?"

"I admit it. I can't say I'm sorry about it."

Lisa laughed. "Oh, you'll be sorry all right."

She backed away and he didn't have to wait long to find out what she was doing. In a moment, snakes began raining down on him from overhead. He recoiled in fear but their ropy coolness was all over him —around his neck, on his arms, his bare feet. He could hear their hisses, see their rippling flesh in the narrow stripes of sunlight as they slithered overtop each other.

The first bite was on his finger, then another at his ankle. A sharp pain hit in his calf, then his bicep. He yelled and began kicking frantically at the door. There was another bite on his foot. He screamed at Lisa to let him out. While he didn't want to, he begged. He pleaded.

He could hear her laughing at him, at his pain. There was a bite on his thigh and he began to feel faint. His heart was racing. As terrified as he was, he had to sit down. He sat on a snake, felt it writhing beneath him. His head began spinning and he sagged over against the wall. His last sight was of that eye pressed to the crack only inches away, watching him, the curled lip beneath it. The smile.

33

Wallace County

IT WAS late evening when Baxter's group returned to Glenwall. As they neared the gate, the scene in the road was unavoidable.

"Stop the vehicle!" Baxter yelled.

"Sir, I'm not sure it's safe," the driver replied. "Do *not* get out."

Baxter stared at the blood-soaked pavement and the body parts littering the surface of the road. Sprays of blood splattered park benches, nearby cars, and a fire hydrant. He raised the microphone from the radio mounted in the vehicle. "Base, did we come under attack?"

"No sir," replied the guard.

"Then, what the hell happened?" Baxter screamed into the radio.

Silence.

"Sir, we probably should discuss that in person," the guard replied.

Baxter waved at the driver, who accelerated to the gate. The guard already had one of the cars pulled away from the gate and they drove straight through. Baxter jumped from the Humvee before it came to a complete stop and raced back to the nervous guards.

"What is *that*?" he asked, spitting his words in his rage and disgust.

They were all scared of Valentine, especially now.

"It was Valentine, sir," one of the guards said. "He took a cooler outside of the wall and told the protestors it was food. It was an explosive and he set it off when they tried to open the cooler."

Baxter stared in shock for a moment as if unable to process the words he was hearing, then he completely melted down. He screamed and stomped around. He kicked the quarter panel of the sheriff's department vehicle, pounded his fists on the hood. He even went as far as to punch a window though it didn't shatter.

He grabbed his injured hand and winced, closing his eyes. He breathed deeply, regaining his calm. His people had never seen him like this.

"I'm going home," Baxter said to his driver. "Get Valentine and get him to my place *now*."

"Do you need a ride, sir?"

Baxter shook his head. "I need to walk." He strode off, cradling his injured hand. His mind raced. For all he knew, the families of Glenwall were meeting right now, preparing to boot him and his men out of here. He had no idea what he'd do. His preparation had always been tied into his role with the county. He had no individual preparations. He wasn't even sure if the county had anything remaining at this point.

When he reached the house that he was bunking at, the Humvee was there and Valentine was waiting on the porch steps. Baxter had calmed down significantly on his walk and felt his rage returning.

When Valentine opened his mouth to say something Baxter hissed, "You shut the fuck up. I don't know what kind of closet psycho you are, but you've probably screwed our chances of remaining in this community."

Valentine hung his head and looked at the ground.

"The board members that run this place are practical," Baxter said. "They understand that violence may be required to keep them safe. What I saw out there," he stabbed a finger behind him toward the road, "was completely unnecessary. There's no excuse for that. How the hell am I going to explain it?"

"We were trying to send a message," Valentine said. "We felt threatened and felt a strong response was warranted."

"Are you being serious or are you just offering me something I can give the folks that live here?"

"I'm giving you an excuse," Valentine said. "To be honest, I don't feel the least bit bad about what I did. I'm tired of those people whining and complaining. They could be out looking for food. They could be hunting or fishing. They could be trading their labor at a farm in exchange for food, but they're not. They're here begging for handouts. I couldn't handle it anymore. I lost my shit."

Baxter sighed. "At least you're being honest."

Valentine looked his boss in the eye. "I'm being completely honest."

"Then I'll be honest too," Baxter said. "You can't stay here anymore."

Valentine flew to his feet. "WHAT? You can't throw me out of here. You all need me as much as I need you."

"Lower your voice and sit down!" Baxter ordered.

Valentine stared at him for a moment, then reluctantly sat down.

"You've got two options," Baxter offered. "You can leave or you can go help out at the Russell County location."

"I'll take Russell County," Valentine said without hesitation.

"It's rough," Baxter said. "It's only a field with some campers. There's a lot of work that has to be done."

"I'm fine with work," Valentine said.

"And I'm telling these folks here that I banished you," Baxter added. "You'll never be able to come back here again."

Valentine sighed. He wasn't happy about that though his options were limited. "Okay."

"Pack your shit and be ready to go tomorrow," Baxter said. "Don't come out of your house again tonight. I don't want anyone seeing you."

"What if there's trouble?" Valentine said.

"If there's trouble, you'll only make it worse," Baxter said. "Stay in your house."

"Okay," Valentine agreed. "I appreciate you keeping me on."

"You fucking better," Baxter said. "You pull a stunt like that again and you're gone. Do you understand me?"

Valentine nodded, then got up and left.

Baxter watched him go, hoping he wasn't making a mistake. A loose cannon like that could come back to haunt him. Right now, he was going to the clubhouse. He needed a drink and that's where they kept the good stuff.

34

The Valley

RANDI WAS SITTING on the porch of her new home cracking black walnuts. Several residents of the valley had offered to trade her home-canned food in exchange for jars of black walnut kernels that they could use in winter baking. With the limited resources at hand, she would gladly take what she could get.

She heard the clank of the gate chain being unfastened at the end of the road. When she looked up Lloyd was walking toward her, a paper bag in his hand and a broad grin on his face.

"Howdy there, good looking," he said.

She cocked an eyebrow at him. "You greet all the women that way?"

"Pretty much," he said. "I cast a wide net."

"What the hell you want?"

Lloyd frowned. "Ain't much of a conversationalist are you?"

"Nope. Pretty much anyone that knows me would agree."

"We'll need to work on that," he said. "I like a woman who chuckles at witticisms."

She raised a questioning eyebrow at him, not feeling a reply was warranted.

He raised the paper bag. "Brought you a present," he said, yanking the bag off to reveal a jar of purple liquid.

"What is it?" Randi asked. "Beet juice?"

"Hell no, woman, it ain't beet juice. It's blackberry moonshine." He unscrewed the lid and carefully held the jar under her nose.

She took a whiff and closed her eyes in appreciation. "Smells *good*."

"The best," he said. "My grandfather's recipe. I hope to start making it myself soon." He started to raise the jar to his lips and take a drink.

She cleared her throat. "What the hell are you doing?"

He paused. "Fixing to take a drink."

"Of my liquor?" she asked. "You have the nerve to bring me a gift and then take the first drink of it? That ain't right at all."

He sighed and handed the jar over. She smiled in satisfaction, then took a long sip from the jar. "Hmmm, that's some good stuff."

"Like I said, the best."

Randi could see him practically salivating for a drink, his fingers rubbing together. She intentionally took her time, taking another whiff of the contents and lingering over the mouth of the jar. She took another slow sip, her eyes on his.

"Oh, did you want some?" she asked innocently.

He shot out an arm. "Thought you'd never ask."

"I was considering not asking simply to toy with you."

"You're evil," Lloyd said, taking a sip from the jar.

"And you're a damn lush."

Lloyd recapped the jar and handed it over to her. "May I sit?"

"As long as it ain't too close or too long," she said.

He took a seat on the edge of the porch. She waved her fingers at him, urging him to move further away. "Really?" he asked.

She nodded and raised the hammer she'd been using to crack walnuts. He reluctantly complied, scooting about ten more inches away.

"This good?"

"It'll do," Randi said.

"What was the point of that?" he asked.

"Seeing if you could take orders from a woman. Simple test, and you passed."

"Finally, some progress."

"Don't let it go to your head," she said. "Jury is still out on you."

"Can I ask a favor?"

"You can ask anything," she said. "Whether you can handle the answer or not is another matter entirely."

He looked for the humor in her eyes, seeing none. "Somebody was a real dick to you once, weren't they?"

"Get to the point," she asked. "What do you want?" She wasn't interested in processing her emotional nuances with this man she barely knew.

He sighed and gave up on the small talk. "I wanted to see if I could borrow two of your horses tomorrow."

She regarded him. "Can you even ride a horse?"

"I *have* ridden a horse," he answered.

"Why do you need to borrow a horse?"

"I need two, actually," he said. "One for me, one for Buddy. We both lost folks and we want to visit them."

She softened. "Here's the deal. I love my family but they're driving me bat shit. If I lend you my horses, you have to take me with you."

Lloyd cracked a smile at that. "That's a deal. We'd be honored."

Randi chuckled. "We'll see. You may not feel so honored after you've had to spend a day with me. Some people find it challenging."

"You're stubborn and I'm hard-headed," he said. "That's about a perfect combination. Will 10 a.m. work?"

"I'll be ready."

35

Wallace County

THE GLENWALL GOLF course was located on the fringe of a beautiful little town that attracted families and retirees from around the nation. There were easily a thousand homes within a five-mile radius of the golf course. In most of those homes, if people didn't have some level of disaster preparedness they were now reaching the bottom of their pantries. Everyone had those old cans of soup or beans, those battered boxes of Jell-O, that orphan Pop-Tart that they couldn't remember the flavor of. That's what people had been eating for the last few weeks. For most, that was all gone now.

The Jell-O would have been served at room temperature, mixed with water of questionable purity. The old box of macaroni noodles had been soaked in lukewarm water until soft and eaten with whatever spices remained. As people ran out of food, most also ran out of ways to cook. Their gas grills were empty. Some burned broken furniture in backyard fire pits and cooked over that. Others broke up their ornamental trees and tried to cook on the smoky fires built of the green, unseasoned wood.

People had raided their candy drawers and ate the last lint-covered Jolly Ranchers and Starburst. They had eaten the stray french fries from under their car seats. They had sucked dry the packets of ketchup, salsa, and mustard they found in the junk drawer. They had brushed off and eaten the spilled cat food from the garage floor. Fat bullfrogs and goldfish were scooped from backyard ponds and cooked with enthusiasm.

Grocery stores had been looted of everything. The plate-glass windows of restaurants were broken and any contents taken. There were no more pets roaming around loose in neighborhoods. A few weeks ago, the idea of eating them was repugnant. Now, people tried to devise traps to catch them, praying they'd find a fat tabby in the morning.

Neighbor broke in on neighbor when the lack of food became unbearable. There were shootings every night and the cops no longer responded to the sound of gunshots in the little postcard community. People finally began to notice that not everyone in the community seemed to be suffering. Within the gates of Glenwall, life appeared to be a little better. There was limited power, which they used for cooking, and the sound of those generators carried a good distance in the quieter world. They also had the tower lights running at night, which shone like beacons over the dark community.

The tower lights had been intended to make it easier to guard the community at night. Those on duty could make certain that no unauthorized folks were wandering around. The lights were now having the opposite effect. They drew the desperate like porch lights drew moths. People outside the walls muttered with resentment. It smacked of elitism. The local government was certainly in on it, helping those with money weather the disaster using resources their tax dollars had paid for. In some ways, they were not far off.

As word spread of what Valentine had done outside of the front gates, the anger reached a fever pitch. Not only were the elite skimming off the cream of the community's resources, they had now killed several townspeople in what seemed like a cruel prank. There were several versions of the story floating around, though all seemed to have a thread of truth. The residents of Glenwall had baited starving citizens with food so that they could blow them up. They probably sat inside their gilded walls laughing while those poor folks bled to death in the trash-strewn streets.

No one should have been surprised when gunshots finally rang out within the brick walls of the Glenwall community. It was only a matter of time, really. Baxter was certainly not surprised. He sprang out of bed in the operations center. There was a flurry of traffic on the radio. He ran to the window and looked out. There were people rushing around with headlamps and firearms. Baxter knew those were his people responding to the shots.

There were more shots. People were coming out of their homes and gathering under the tower lights. There was the sound of shattering glass as shots raked across homes on the golf course. People screamed and ran outside. They should have been hiding in their basements. Instead, they seemed to have no idea of how to keep themselves safe. A resident running across the green with a child in his arms was dropped by a lucky shot somewhere in the darkness.

"Shit," Baxter said. He grabbed up a radio. "Kill those tower lights. Our people are sitting ducks."

One of his men bolted for the towers and they went dark a moment later. Baxter dropped onto the bed and zipped on his tactical boots. He'd been sleeping in his clothes lately, ready to bug out to the backup location in Russell County if he had to. He didn't carry a rifle on a daily basis, but he kept one handy. He threw on a plate carrier he'd gotten from the sheriff's department. It provided ballistic protection and held spare mags. He took up his Larue Tactical M4 from the corner and dropped the single-point sling over his head, dug a flashlight out of a pouch on the chest rig, and bolted from the room.

Baxter's team slept in a house near the clubhouse. By the time he got downstairs, everyone that was off-shift was dressed and scrambled. He strode out the open front door feeling awkward in the heavy vest. His guys were shining their lights over a body near the clubhouse. Baxter took off running, the rifle banging into his legs.

"What the hell happened?" he asked when he reached his team.

"It was a raid," one of the former deputies said, looking up at Baxter. The deputy pointed to the man standing closest to Baxter. "Check his weapon. Make sure he's safe."

"What?" Baxter asked.

The man closest to Baxter, an employee of the county water department, saw what the deputy was referring to. "Your finger, sir," he said. "You need to keep it out of the trigger guard."

Baxter looked down, saw that indeed his finger was laying on the trigger.

"Is the weapon safe?" the deputy asked.

Baxter held his weapon out and inspected the safety switch. "Yeah."

The water department man confirmed this and nodded at the deputy.

"So enough with the fucking weapons training," Baxter said. "What's going on?"

"I think it was locals. Not too terribly organized," the deputy said. "Someone set some tires on fire and sent them rolling onto the golf course. We sent two men in the direction they came from but they didn't find anything. I had a man on the roof of the clubhouse with night vision, and he said there were three men with baseball bats approaching the clubhouse from the back. I gave him the go-ahead to drop one of them. After those shots were fired, hell broke loose in all directions."

Baxter nodded.

"The others ran," the deputy confirmed. "We started taking fire from outside the wall. When we shot back, they booked."

Baxter looked around and verified that it was only men he trusted standing within earshot. "This was inevitable," he said. "Yesterday I saw a group of men playing golf. That completely sends the wrong message when you're surrounded by starving people. It's not only arrogant, it's stupid."

"Agreed, sir," the deputy said. "Not to mention the dumbass move that Valentine pulled with the explosive."

"We need to get ready to make a move," Baxter said. "All of you who worked tonight are going to need to pull special duty tomorrow. I'm going to tell folks that we found a warehouse to stash supplies in and that we need to get them out of sight in case there's another raid. We have two untouched semi-trailers of food and one tanker. I want those moved to the bug-out location in Russell County. I want a driver and someone riding shotgun in each truck."

"Do you want us to stay over there?" a man asked.

Baxter shook his head. "Not yet. I'll need you guys back here with those trucks. Just unhook and come back. We may have more to haul."

"Are you going to take everything?" asked the deputy.

"What do you mean by everything?" Baxter asked.

"I mean are you going to take *all* of the food that these people here have to live on?"

Baxter hesitated, trying to figure out how to say what he needed to say without sounding heartless. "Look, we can't save everyone here. I wish we could but we can't. There's no way we could organize these people to go with us. They'd want to take a bunch of crap and we don't have time for that. Besides, the more of them go, the shorter this food will hold out. I'm not taking everything. I'm only going to take what we can in the way of food, weapons, and fuel. It will give us a decent chance of surviving. If anyone isn't cool with that, this is the time to decide. You can stay here if you want."

He looked around his group. There were no dissenting voices. He couldn't read them well enough to know if that meant they were with him, though. Did he really have their hearts or were they waiting until his back was turned to take him out? It was hard to know.

"Good," he said. "I'm glad no one wanted to quit. We're a team and we need each other to get through this. From this point forward, your primary responsibility is the safety of each other. Glenwall residents come second."

36

The Valley

RANDI HAD three of her horses saddled and waiting when Buddy and Lloyd ambled down the driveway.

"Y'all are on time," she said. "I expected the musician to slow you down."

"I had to threaten him a little," Buddy replied. The older man appeared to be moving a little better now, his wounds healing. He was wearing a sparkly purple backpack that didn't go with the weapons he carried.

"Where'd you get that backpack?" Randi asked. "That's snazzy."

"Ariel," he said. "That sweet little thing made me a lunch and packed it in her own school backpack."

"When I asked where *my* lunch was, she told me to check the hog trough," Lloyd said.

"I like that little girl," Randi laughed.

Buddy grinned. "Me too."

"Got your .32?" Randi asked Lloyd.

Lloyd frowned. "Damn right I got my .32. I don't see how my pistol has become the joke of this whole valley. It's a perfectly respectable weapon."

"How does it make you feel that everyone in this valley, including the women, have a manlier gun than you?" Randi said. "And before you make any smart-ass comments about how manly your gun is, remember who you're talking to. My mouth can burn you like the sun through a magnifying glass."

Lloyd bit his tongue and said nothing.

"That's what I thought." Randi grabbed her Go Bag from the porch. She carried her pistol in her waistband and had the .22 rifle her brother had given her. She swung onto the saddle of her horse.

"You're making fun of my pistol and you're carrying a .22 rifle?" Lloyd asked snidely.

Randi cut him a look. "You get one warning," she said. "This is it. No smart comments or it's on."

Buddy laughed. "Gonna be a helluva day. I can tell already. Helluva day." He swung onto a horse and rested his Winchester .30-.30 across the saddle.

Lloyd tried to mount his horse while it edged away from him. He already had a foot in the stirrup so he had to hop on one foot to keep pace with it. Randi laughed.

"I'm trying," he said. "Damn horse."

"Lloyd's confused," Randi said. "Last horse he rode didn't move until he put the quarter in."

Lloyd finally had the horse trapped against the porch and was able to swing up on it.

"Let's go, Laurel and Hardy," Buddy said. "Time's a-wasting."

It took them nearly an hour of easy riding to reach Lloyd's childhood home. Randi and Buddy maintained a respectful distance while Lloyd paid his respects to his dead parents and went inside to check the house. He returned with a couple of pillowcases of items he wanted to take. He knotted them together and tossed them over the horse's neck.

They backtracked for a mile and headed north toward town. Each trip out of the valley was different from the one before it. It almost seemed that the cloud of desperation that had settled over the community had given way to apathy and an acceptance that it was futile to struggle. For most, death was coming. The time for preparation had passed, and those who had not made the effort were probably going to die.

They took the road toward town and paused to study it from the vantage afforded to them. There was very little movement. No cars were driving. A few lone folks walked about.

"I got no interest in going through there," Buddy said.

"You aren't tempted to see what town is like?" Lloyd asked.

"I ain't in no shape for a fight," Buddy said. "Someone might try to take the horses. Maybe even for food. Randi can take care of herself. I'm just not sure I'll be able to take care of me *and* you."

Lloyd was offended. "I can take care of myself."

Buddy laughed and Randi joined him.

"I don't get it," Lloyd said.

Buddy shook his head and nudged his horse forward.

They rode to the bottom of the hill, and instead of continuing on the road into town, they turned east along a creek. They followed a walking trail along the creek until they neared the cemetery where Buddy's daughter was buried. They rode their horses up the bank onto Main Street, turning into the cemetery gate about a quarter of a mile down the road.

Randi and Lloyd peeled off as they went through the iron gate. Buddy stopped his horse and turned around.

"What are you all doing?"

"I thought you'd like to be alone," Randi said.

"I'll be alone the rest of my life," Buddy said. "I'll take the company of friends while it's available to me."

They followed behind him until he reached an unmarked plot with a withered flower arrangement at its center.

"She was buried the day this all hit," Buddy said. "It ain't likely her marker will ever make it here."

"I'm sorry this happened," Randi said.

Buddy stared at the ground for a long time, his mind in a distant place, replaying an entire life. When he was done, he gave them a strained smile. "We can go now."

They cut through a silent neighborhood and an adjoining pasture, heading in the direction of home.

"Can I ask you guys a favor?" Randi asked.

The pair mumbled that she could.

"I need to go check on my brother," Randi said. "He didn't want to join us. I'd like to make sure he's okay. Maybe we can even talk him into coming back with us."

"I don't mind to go, but it seems like you'd be better off asking Jim," Lloyd said. "He's got a lot better guns than we do."

"Jim has a family," Buddy said. "She's asking us because we're single, which makes us expendable."

"Yes," Randi agreed.

"I will have you know that if I am killed, millions of banjo fans will mourn my loss," Lloyd said.

"There's no such thing as a banjo fan," Randi said. "People are just humoring you, same way they do a kid when he's got a bowl of spaghetti on his head. You think you're cute and so everyone goes along with it."

"Besides, think of all the people you've given haircuts to over the years. They'll probably rejoice at your passing," Buddy said. "All those kids with one missing ear."

Lloyd smiled at Randi. "Despite your verbal attacks on my person, despite you making fun of my pistol, despite your rebuffing of my romantic overtures, I will gladly go with you."

"Your romantic gestures are like your banjo playing," Buddy teased, "off-key and stumbling. I'll go with you too, Randi. We'll gladly help."

"It could be dangerous," she said.

"As they said in *Little Big Man*, it is a good day to die," Lloyd said.

"Speak for yourself, you old bastard," Randi cracked. "Dying ain't on the itinerary. Either way, I appreciate you two. Can we go tomorrow?"

37

Rockdell Farms

WITH THE RUBBING alcohol gone and all of his stash of store-bought liquor depleted, Hodge was in bad shape. He hadn't had a day without drinking since about age seventeen. He couldn't even remember the last time without a little nip to ease out the rough spots. The symptoms of withdrawal were beginning. He shook with delirium tremens. His body ached. He thought at any minute he'd throw up. It was time for emergency measures.

He retrieved his two bottles of concentrated Lysol disinfectant. Each diluted to make nine gallons of cleaning solution or, in his case, nine gallons of drinking solution. He'd learned about drinking Lysol the first time he'd been in detox. It was a tip shared among career alcoholics. That time he'd been picked up by the cops while staggering around town and nearly getting hit by cars numerous times. The police dropped him off at the local detox center and that was where he woke up the next morning. They'd fed him well, put some clean clothes on him, and gave him some nice medications so he didn't get in any hurry to rush off. It was better treatment than he was used to. Kind of like a spa for addicts.

He picked up a few tips from the old drunks on how to stay drunk when the money ran out, including drinking aftershave, rubbing alcohol, and Lysol. He'd only stayed in detox for the day, deciding that he preferred drinking to taking the Librium they gave for withdrawal symptoms.

He signed himself out and returned to the drinking life. He'd been in detox one time since then, picked up for the same reason, and found detox was no longer the same congenial place as it had once been. Usually populated by middle-aged drunks, the detox center was now full of kids addicted to pain pills. Apparently, drunks were a dying breed and Hodge decided he'd do his best to avoid detox after that.

He mixed the Lysol according to the instructions, having great difficulty with his shaking hands as he attempted to pour a measured amount of the concentrate into the empty gallon milk jug. When finally he had it, he filled the remainder of the jug with water and took a whiff of the mixture. It smelled of lemons and chemicals. He reminded himself this was not about the trip. It was about the destination. The destination was drunk.

He choked down a drink and heard a roaring sound in his head. He gagged a little and staggered to his worn-out recliner, the arms stained dark and threadbare. He sagged into the chair and stared at the wall at the framed pictures. There was an array of them, each displaying the sample photo that had come with the frame. He told people they were his family when in fact, he had no family left and no pictures of what family he'd once had. The pictures gave him comfort when he needed it. He'd named the folks in those pictures and assigned relationships to them within his meager family tree.

When the roaring in his head didn't stop, he regarded the clear milk jug on the chipped Formica countertop.

"That shit has killed me. My brain is shaking itself apart."

He got back to his feet and wandered outside, hoping that filling his lungs with fresh air might clear the roaring from his head. His porch was trash-strewn and rotting. He leaned carefully against the porch post, his eyes watering. He blinked several times and realized that the roaring was not the sound of an approaching aneurysm. It was the sound of approaching tractor-trailers.

He went back into the kitchen, grabbed the jug, and started back out the door. He knew the trucks had to be going to that camp those Wallace County men had set up. They had promised him booze and he needed it now. He would follow those trucks like a wolf stalking a wounded elk. He looked at the jug in his hand, wondering if he should take it or not, then deciding that he'd better. He might get thirsty.

He wove his way through his debris-filled yard. He looked long-ingly at his S10 pickup, wishing he could drive instead of having to walk. The truck had been sitting for ten years or so, since he got his fifth drunk driving conviction. The truck was now used for storing trash until he could haul it to the dump. The truck was full so he'd started a new pile in the yard about a year ago. Somehow hauling trash to the dump didn't seem all that important when he had all that empty yard.

As he walked toward the creek-side campsite those men had set up, he did indeed become thirsty and sipped from his jug. The taste wasn't so bad the second time. Perhaps it had damaged his taste buds. He tried to concentrate on the lemon taste, imagining that it was simply a chemical-infused lemonade. He could feel it working, filing off the hard edges of the day. Maybe things would be okay after all.

He started to sing as he sometimes did when was enjoying his first drinks of the day. He wasn't feeling it though. He was too anxious over getting the bottle he was promised. In fact, he was salivating merely thinking about it. The thought did cross his mind that the drooling might be a symptom of poisoning from drinking the Lysol. He'd seen a poisoned dog slobbering like that one time. What was he supposed to do? These were desperate times.

He'd had several nips from the jug by the time he reached the camp. Neither his vision nor his counting were very good, but he thought perhaps a half-dozen men were clustered there trying to assist with unhooking the trailer. He didn't see the tall fellow that seemed to be in charge.

No one noticed him approaching until he was right on them. When he *was* noticed, six weapons were immediately raised in his direction.

"Easy there," Hodge said, grinning. "I come in peace."

One man lowered his weapon. "Look who's back," he said to the others. "The town drunk."

The other men lowered their weapons and returned to work.

Hodge frowned. "Ain't no need for name-calling. That ain't neighborly, and it looks like we're neighbors now."

He chuckled. "What the fuck you want, old man? We're busy."

"That feller who was with you before, the boss man," Hodge said. "He with you?"

"He didn't come this trip."

"He might have sent it with you then," he said. "He was supposed to send me a little gift."

"I don't know anything about any gift."

"A bottle of liquor," Hodge explained, his voice rising a notch. "He said he'd send me a bottle of liquor. You all heard him. He promised."

He shrugged. "Sorry. Can't help you."

"Dammit!" Hodge said. "I told him I'd find you all a place to store your shit in exchange for a bottle. You sure you didn't keep it for yourself?"

Another man walked up. He wore a checked shirt, cowboy hat, and cowboy boots, and he carried a sidearm. "What you going on about?"

"Your bossman promised me a bottle of liquor if I found you a location to store your shit. I found you a location and I want my bottle of liquor." Hodge actually hadn't thought anything about a storage location. He was pretty sure he could come up with something on the fly. There were a lot of large barns in the valley.

"That's between you and him," the second man said. "I don't have time to fool with you. We've got work to do. Now get the hell out of here before I knock the shit out of you."

They returned to work, and Hodge stood there fuming at their dismissal of him. These men had probably stolen his liquor for themselves. Either way, they seemed to think it was funny to make a fool out of him like he was nobody. He'd been treated that way before and it ran all over him. He might be a drunk but he had feelings. He slid his hand down to his waistband and removed the pistol he was carrying. He centered it on the back of the man in the checked shirt.

"You fucker," Hodge spat.

He pulled the trigger, then kept pulling it, waving the barrel from man to man. Bodies fell and it meant nothing to him. Some of the men scrambled away, putting the truck between them and Hodge. He kept shooting what was in front of him until his head jerked violently and everything went dark.

38

Wallace County

BAXTER WAS SUMMONED to the private conference room at the Glenwall clubhouse around noon that day. He was greeted by his employers, the Board of Directors of Glenwall. The grocery store magnate was there, as were several coal company executives, and a man who owned a chain of car dealerships. Between these few men, they probably had enough money to buy every single home on the property. They were seated around an expansive burled walnut table and appeared to be in the midst of a discussion when Baxter arrived. He had the distinct feeling that the discussion had been about him. His gut twisted. This felt like a job interview, or perhaps a termination.

He wondered why men with this kind of money would live in a golf course community. The houses were practically on top of each other and the views only consisted of more houses that looked just like their own. Why wouldn't they buy a remote property or an estate in the country? A lakefront or mountaintop property? These men could have lived anywhere they wanted.

It was clear that living here wasn't about privacy. It was exactly the opposite. It was about being seen. People lived here so everyone would know how wealthy they were and so they would receive the deference they'd come to expect. Baxter had never liked men like that. In fact, he hated them.

"We'll get straight to the point," the grocery man said. "We have a list of concerns that we'd like to discuss with you." He was a CEO and obviously used to conducting business at meetings.

There was a chorus of nods around the table.

"What kind of concerns?" Baxter asked. These men owned him now, and they had questions. He better have some answers. He could always tell them to go to hell and walk out. Where would he be then? He would have to be careful. He may even have to grovel.

"First, what kind of shit happened at the front gate yesterday?" asked the car dealer. "I'm hearing all kinds of stories. My wife—hell, *all* the wives—are demanding answers."

Baxter sighed. "Can I have a seat?"

"No, dammit," the car man replied. "You can stay where you are. I want to know what happened."

Baxter clasped his hands behind his back. "I'm not a hundred percent sure. I was not here on-site when it happened. I was out securing resources for the benefit of the community."

"Are you going to answer the question or not?" the grocery man asked. "What happened at the gate?"

"I'm getting to that," Baxter said. "You all know that this place only had a single guard on duty each night before I came along. We had no choice but to recruit people to come in and assist with security. I had no way of doing background checks on them. It's not like we have a human resource department or any way to check references. I had one man who had been a security guard at the community college. I was able to confirm that. He knew a lot about emergency preparedness, and seemed like a good resource."

"I know about that one," the car dealer said. "My daughter said she'd heard about him before. Said he was always hassling the students at the college and behaving inappropriately."

Baxter shrugged. "How could I have known that? We needed bodies and he was a body."

The car dealer sat back in his chair, his mouth stretched tight, and didn't respond. He didn't approve of Baxter's response.

"Anyway, I think the guy was nuts or something. I'm still not sure how he did it. He rigged some kind of explosive and baited some protestors to a cooler. They thought it was food. When they surrounded it, he detonated the explosive with a rifle."

"Good Lord," the grocery man said. "How could someone do that? They were just hungry people!"

"I don't know," Baxter said. "Like I told you, I think he's nuts."

"That would be fucking obvious," the car dealer replied. "Where is this sick bastard now?"

"I guess, for lack of a better word, you could say I banished him."

"Banished?" the grocery guy asked, his voice tinged with sarcasm. "That's how you handle something like that?"

"What the hell was I supposed to do?" Baxter said, his voice rising. "You want him executed on the 9th hole? You want your families to see that? You want him hanging dead from a light pole? How would your wives respond to that?"

The car dealer cleared his throat. "Look—"

"Look at what!" Baxter erupted. "You think we can call the cops? You think they can put him in jail? We can't *do* that anymore. I knew he needed to leave and I sent him away. It was a judgment call."

The car dealer looked at him and fumed. He was not used to being talked to in such a manner.

The grocery man reviewed a yellow legal pad. "Let's move on," he said. "You tell us he's gone and we'll have to leave it at that for now. Onto last night. That breach was unacceptable. You gave us assurances that you had things under control. We took you at your word. I want to hear your plan for how you're going to keep our families safe or we're going to look at bringing in another security team. Some of us have connections in that department and have already made inquiries. We could have a new team here tomorrow."

Silent up to this point, one of the coalmen, Lester Hurt, nodded, and Baxter assumed him to be the one who had made inquiries. The coal business could be rough and these men were of a different cut than the grocery guy and the car dealer. They could be trouble for him.

Baxter couldn't have another team come in yet. There was no way he'd be able to pull off his plan of siphoning off resources if his authority was subordinate to another group. The residents here would not need him at all if they brought in another security director, and he'd find himself out on the street with nothing.

"My people have assessed the situation and determined that the security situation in the town has deteriorated quicker than expected," Baxter said. "We suspected this might happen. This community was built with a six-foot-tall fence around it that was designed to provide privacy, not security. I have men out now procuring the supplies to add barbed wire to the wall. We should have it ready in a day or two. There's a lot of fence and not a lot of manpower for doing such things. We can secure the perimeter with a little work."

"Are you sure you have enough men?" the car dealer asked. "Maybe we should look at adding additional forces."

"I'm working on getting more," Baxter lied. "We are trying to check these guys out a little more thoroughly. I don't want to bring in another guy like that college security guard. I don't want to have any more incidents like that."

"None of us do," the grocery man agreed. "I expect to see a significant change quickly. We cannot fuck around with this. This is the safety of our families."

"Give me a few days," Baxter said. "You'll see a change." The truth was, in a few days Baxter and his men would be gone. The residents here *would* definitely see a significant change, for the worse. They would lose their resources and their security.

One of the coalmen leaned forward in his chair and rested his arms on the table. "Look, we don't want to be pointing fingers so I'll throw it out there. Some folks are saying that supplies are moving out of here. Those supplies belong to our community. We paid for them.

The people around this table paid for them. I want to know if there's any truth to that."

To emphasize the seriousness of his point, he pulled a Glock from below the table and laid it in front of him, focusing his hard gaze on Baxter.

Lester cleared his throat and held up a handheld radio. "To be honest with you, Baxter, I'm pretty damned concerned about this. We dealt with a lot of theft in the mining business and I can't stand a thief. I've got a team available on the other end of this radio. If I'm not satisfied with your explanation, all I have to do is put in a call and you're out of here. We'll have a new security director by the end of the day and you'll be out there eating grubs and twigs."

Baxter's mind raced, yet he maintained his cool. The wrong answer, the wrong reaction, and he wouldn't be walking out of his room. He'd convinced himself that he was operating under the radar, but these were men who'd risen through the ranks by paying attention to details. He'd not been fooling anyone.

"I've had a project going," he finally said. "It's top secret. I didn't want any word of it getting out. I think you'll agree it's a worthwhile effort."

"Will this address our concerns about the missing supplies?" the grocery man asked.

"Without a doubt," Baxter said. "I need you all to take a short drive with me."

The board members at the table looked at each other.

"This some kind of bullshit?" one of the mining execs asked. "We don't have time for bullshit."

"No sir," Baxter replied. "In fact, I've invested significant time into a fallback plan. I think you'll be pleased. Give me thirty minutes to get the work crews here squared away and meet me at the maintenance building."

39

Wallace County

BAXTER STORMED into the house that Valentine was staying in with several of the other men. "Valentine!" he yelled. "Valentine!" There was no response and he went room-to-room continuing to call. He went into the kitchen, turned the corner, and was startled to nearly run into him.

"What the hell?" Baxter asked. "Why didn't you answer me?"

"I was in the basement packing my shit," Valentine replied. "Isn't that what I'm supposed to be doing since I'm being exiled?"

"There's been a change of plans."

Valentine raised an eyebrow.

"The *founding fathers* here at the golf course are accusing me of stealing from them," Baxter said.

"You are," Valentine replied.

"Dammit, I know that," Baxter said. "I don't want them to know that, though."

"What are you going to do?"

"They put me on the spot. I kind of pulled a story out of my ass,"

Baxter said. "I made up something about being concerned that we might be overrun and wanting to have a fallback position in case it happened."

"That's not far from the truth," Valentine said. "Except that you don't plan on taking them along."

"Right. That's another thing that they don't need to know," Baxter said.

"How is this my problem?" Valentine asked sarcastically.

"It's your problem because you're still here!" Baxter snapped. "As long as you choose to stick around and share in the rewards of our project, you can expect that you may have to share part of the burden."

Valentine stared flatly at him.

"I have to take them to Russell County and show them the fall-back location," Baxter said. "And you can't be there since I told them that I sent you packing."

"I thought I was supposed to head over there today?"

"You are. Here's what we're going to do. I'm transporting the Board of Directors in the Humvees. After we leave, I want you guys to hook a semi to a cattle trailer and bring it over. That will further add to the impression that we're using the Russell County location as a place to gather resources for the benefit of Glenwall. You can pack any shit you need to take into the cattle trailer under some tarps. I want you hid in the sleeper of that truck and I don't want you showing your face until those board members are gone. Got it?"

Valentine shrugged. "Do I have a choice?"

"No."

"Then I guess I better get packing and get my shit loaded," Valentine said.

Baxter started down the hall. "You've got twenty minutes. You better get cracking," he called back over his shoulder.

When the front door slammed Valentine stood in the kitchen and thought about the recent events in his life. He didn't like Baxter. It wasn't him in particular. It was more what he represented. Valentine thought of himself as a capable man and a hard worker. All of his career he'd worked for men like Baxter. He'd had to kiss their ass and laugh at their stupid jokes. He had to do the work while they got the credit. All that time, he knew that they were phonies. He knew that many of them could not do the things he did.

He was willing to play along to a point. For now, the smart move was to do what Baxter said. Valentine was sure he could survive on his own out there but this place had resources and staying with those resources was the smart play. He would continue running that play until a better one came along. He had a little loyalty to Baxter for keeping him around against the wishes of the board, very little. He knew Baxter only kept him around because he needed men like him. He needed someone to do the work that had to be done if things turned ugly.

Baxter certainly couldn't do those things. He wasn't only a phony, he was a coward. He could rant and yell, put on a good show, though that only worked on people who respected his title, his position. Baxter's position was meaningless now. It was as clear to Valentine as the nose on his face. He wondered if the others could see it as plainly.

40

The Valley

THERE WAS NO BETTER way to describe the societal structure of the valley at this point than to say that *tribes* had developed among the residents. The word had come up at various times and the accuracy of it became clearer every day. The folks associated with Jim had formed one tribe. They had come to realize that food resources were used more efficiently when they cooked as a group, so they'd all taken to eating at Jim's house with various members of the group contributing to each meal both in the form of labor and ingredients.

The Wimmers, who were more numerous than cedar trees in the valley, had formed a tribal group, taking their meals together. The Birds had aligned themselves with families closer to their end of the valley. It was not a divisive move. All of the tribes worked together and communicated with each other, but it was as if families now extended themselves beyond their blood borders. They expanded to include those who circled around them.

As a tribe or family group, Jim's people had developed a protocol of making sure someone at Jim's home knew if they were going to be out of touch for some reason. Whether they were hunting, gathering food, or going to visit someone, they left a message at Jim's house. Ellen had put an old corkboard on the porch for that very reason. If no one was home, a message could be tacked onto the board letting the others know of their plans.

As Buddy, Lloyd, and Randi rode past Jim's house on their way out of the valley, they stopped to leave a note. Randi grabbed a blank Rolodex card from the stack by the corkboard and scribbled a quick note that the three of them were going to check on her brother and would be back that night.

"Where are you going?" someone asked from the dark interior of the house.

It was Ariel, watching through the window screen as Randi wrote her note.

"You startled me," Randi said and heard a giggle of satisfaction.

"Where are you going?" Ariel repeated.

"Nunya," Randi said.

"Where's that?"

"Nunya business," Randi said.

"Does Daddy know you're leaving?"

"Your daddy is not the boss of me," Randi said.

"He's not the boss of me either," Ariel said. "I'm the boss of him."

Randi finished her note and stuck it to the board. "I'll see you later, Ariel. When I get back, we need to talk. I have a project you may be interested in. It's kind of an art project."

"A project?" Ariel asked. "I would love a project. Tell me now!"

"I can't," Randi said. "I have to go. We'll talk later."

"Okay," Ariel agreed glumly.

"Bye now," Randi said.

"Bye," Ariel said. "Bye, Buddy."

"Bye, sweetie," Buddy replied.

"Bye, Ariel," Lloyd said.

"Yeah right," Ariel replied, raising laughter in both Randi and Buddy.

They rode down the driveway and turned left toward the Rockdell

Farms end of the valley. Knowing that their valley was mostly safe, they remained on the road as they passed Randi's house and the Weatherman's house. As they passed Gary's house, Randi saw with some satisfaction that Charlotte was in the yard with her mother and sisters, watching her children play on the old swing set. She even raised her hand and waved at Randi.

"Think she was waving at me?" Lloyd asked.

Buddy and Randi both responded with laughter.

"I get no respect," Lloyd mumbled.

Beyond those houses, their plan was to cut across a pasture owned by Rockdell Farms, then across Route 80. They were still on the road, lost in the beauty of the day, when the eruption of gunfire startled them. The horses flinched and they reigned them in.

Buddy looked around them for a place to take cover but they were surrounded by open, treeless pasture. This particular section of road was fenced right up to the shoulder with no gates in sight.

Lloyd said, "There's a bridge up there. We can get into the creek and stand under the bridge until we figure out what's going on."

It was about a hundred yards to the bridge, though by the time they got there the gunfire had subsided.

"What do you think we should do?" Randi asked.

"Let's keep riding and see what we see," Buddy said. "If there's something going on, I'd rather be on the horse than on foot." He was riding off before they answered him.

They topped a rise and watched from a distance. Several men were scrambling around trying to care for men that had fallen. Even some of those providing care appeared to have been shot. There was cursing, crying, and a lot of blood.

"What the hell?" Buddy asked.

Randi nudged her horse to a gallop and was pounding toward the group.

"Randi!" Lloyd yelled. "What are you doing?"

The group of men heard the commotion and looked up. In their state of panic, all they knew was that there was yelling and someone was riding toward them. One went for a rifle and had it raised toward

Randi when she reached them. His finger was on the trigger, ready to fire. His adrenaline was high. He saw she was a woman and that was probably all that stayed his finger.

"Stop! Who are you?" he yelled.

She slung her leg over the horse without hesitation. "I'm a nurse. I can help."

She ran by him to where a man was pressing a PVC raincoat over a chest wound. She pulled the raincoat up and caught a spray of bright arterial blood. "You can't save him," she said.

The man holding the raincoat looked at her stunned but she had moved on. She went to another downed man. He was holding a bandanna over a shoulder wound. She removed the bandanna. Blood oozed.

"Raise up!" she ordered.

He complied and she helped him sit up. She felt the back of his shoulder and found the exit wound. He screamed when her finger pressed into it. "You'll be okay," she said.

The man who'd held the gun on her was at her side. "I think the rest are dead," he said.

She moved to the still bodies, felt for a pulse, and found three dead or dying from gunshot wounds to major organs.

"They're not all dead, but you can't save them," she said. "Who's he?" She pointed at another body at a distance.

"That's the bastard that did this," he spat. "I blew his fucking head off."

She could tell that there was no reason to check him out. He had a gaping head wound. It was nothing she wanted a closer look at. She'd seen too much death already.

"You've been shot."

"No shit," he said.

"Can I look?"

He studied her and decided that he might as well. He pulled up his shirt. He had taken a round to the lower right side. She examined it and he flinched from her touch.

"The bullet is still in there," she said. "It could have nicked an organ. If it did, you're probably going to die. If not, you should be okay with stitches and an antibiotic."

"You're a ray of sunshine, aren't you?" he said, gritting his teeth.

"I'm practical," she said. "You want the truth or bullshit?"

"The truth."

"The truth is we can probably get the bullet out of you back at my place. It seems to be close to the surface. You seem to be well-equipped here. Do you have antibiotics in your medical kit?" she asked. "If so, we'll need to take them. They'll increase your chances."

He nodded and went off to get the camp's medical kit. Randi noticed that the man pressing the raincoat to the chest wound of his friend had not abandoned his work. His friend was still conscious and blood ran from the edges of his mouth. Randi went to him.

"What's your name?" she asked the man holding the raincoat.

"Hunter," he said, looking her in the eye.

"What's your friend's name?" she asked.

"Anthony."

Randi leaned over and put a hand on Hunter's shoulder. "You are only prolonging your friend's death. We cannot save him. There is no ambulance coming. There are no emergency rooms. The longer you maintain pressure, the longer he suffers. You need to move your hands and let him go."

Hunter stared at her. He seemed to be in shock.

"Let him go," she said calmly.

Reluctantly, Hunter released the raincoat. Blood seeped from beneath it on all sides, soaking the ground, staining the knees of Hunter's pants. He did not take his eyes off Randi. She reached down and pulled the raincoat over Anthony's head.

"It's over," she told him.

The man returning with the antibiotics stiffened and raised his gun, cursing at the pain. He was pointing his weapon at Buddy and Lloyd, who were approaching the scene.

"Those are my friends," Randi said. "They're not going to hurt you."

He hesitantly lowered his gun.

"I need to get you three back to my friend's place," Randi said. "I can treat you there."

"You sure that's a good idea?" Buddy asked.

"I'm a nurse," Randi said. "The training kicked in. What was I supposed to do? I can't leave them here."

Buddy didn't look happy. "Jim ain't going to like it."

Randi looked around. The only vehicles there were the road tractors that had pulled the trailers in. "Can you drive?" she asked the man with the gun.

"I think so," he said. He seemed to be a little sluggish, perhaps from shock or blood loss.

"Let's get your people in one of these trucks," Randi said.

Buddy and Lloyd helped them load up and watched as the truck drove away. They regarded the scene around them.

"What the hell is this?" Lloyd asked.

"Looks like someone moved in on us," Buddy said. "We should have been watching this end of the valley closer. We don't know who these people are, and there could be more of them coming. They seem to have some resources available to them."

The two men took stock of the camp. They didn't know whether they should take the weapons from the fallen men though they weren't sure they wanted to leave them either. They ended up hiding them beneath some bushes a short distance from the camp. Continuing to dig around, they found radios, ammunition, and government-issue survival gear. Most interesting of all were the loads of food and supplies that had been brought on site. It was enough to hold perhaps hundreds of people for a good long time. Buddy and Lloyd hated to leave it behind though they felt like they should wait until it was clear who it belonged to. For now, they needed to get back to camp and let Jim know what they'd found.

41

Rockdell Farms

A CONVOY of four Humvees and a road tractor with a cattle trailer made its way down the road to Rockdell Farms. They'd broken the board of directors up over several vehicles so they could have an armed guard beside each driver. Baxter had hoped to ride in a Humvee with his men but Lester insisted on riding with him. It was the same guy who had been so adversarial and accusatory in the meeting. Baxter figured the guy didn't trust him and didn't want to let him out of his sight. He didn't have any ill intentions. His only plan was to let the board see the missing assets, explain that they were here for safekeeping, and then return the board to Glenwall. He had no intentions of actually abandoning those folks completely until he'd procured a few more items, including a tanker of fuel.

Lester sat back in the seat watching Baxter the whole time. He was reptilian in appearance, overweight, and clammy with oily skin. Despite his upscale casual clothes, it was clear that he was a man who'd done hard physical work in his life. He'd crawled around mines, worked late into the night on broken-down machines, bolted roofs, and shoveled the built-up coal from the base of conveyors. He'd gone toe-to-toe with federal inspectors and had once nearly beaten three striking miners to death with an ax handle for trying to vandalize his equipment. He'd come up the hard way and he wasn't easily impressed by the likes of John Baxter.

He stared at Baxter with his thick-lidded eyes as if he were trying to make him confess to something. It made Baxter uncomfortable, which he realized was clearly the intention. "You know, you don't fool me," he said, his stubby, calloused fingers folded neatly together.

Baxter was leaned forward, speaking with the driver, mostly to avoid having to engage with him. "Excuse me?"

"You don't fool me," he repeated. "I think it was a mistake to bring you into our community. I don't think you bring a damn thing to the table. The only reason you're there is that I was outvoted."

"I'm...sorry you feel that way," Baxter said.

"I doubt it," the man continued. "I think you're sorry that someone has you figured out."

"Whatever," Baxter said. "You'll see in a few minutes that we have an operation set up here. This is the collection point for the beef you've been eating and where we've kept supplies for safekeeping."

They drove past the empty house where Don, the man who'd told him about Rockdell Farms, had lived. Baxter stared out the window and noted the corpse that buzzards had dragged into the ditch. Tendons still laced the bones together and articulated the skeleton. Had Baxter not known what he was looking at, he would not have recognized the shredded and sunbaked flesh as a person. It looked more like deer after a week of warm weather, buzzards, and coyotes.

Baxter attempted to radio ahead and let his men at the camp know that they were coming with visitors, but there had been no response. Because there'd not been any regular radio communications between the camps, he assumed the men had grown lax about monitoring it. They were probably off doing something else.

When they neared the camp, Baxter immediately sat forward in his seat. He could sense that things were not right. The gate was open and there was no one in sight. Then he saw the buzzards, their beaks stained with gore. They hopped and hunched their backs, their wings rising and falling. They tore at the shapes on the ground, tugging at filaments of flesh and tendon. It was not until the lead vehicle was upon them that they reluctantly hopped away, then rose in flight. As he got closer, Baxter's suspicion was confirmed.

The buzzards were eating his men.

"Stop the car!" he ordered, fumbling with his door.

"Sir!" the guard bellowed. "We don't know if it's safe!"

Baxter was already out. He was wearing a holstered sidearm and had left his rifle in the vehicle. He was not reacting with a tactical or security mindset. It was purely out of horror and shock. He walked around waving his arms in the air and cursing, trying to process the sight before him. His lone guard was out of the vehicle now, holding his rifle at the ready and scanning the perimeter through his optic.

"What the hell is going on here?" Lester asked.

Baxter spun and found the coal man standing behind him. "How the hell should I know? I just got here, same as you." His voice held a sense of futility that bordered on hysteria. He was losing his shit. He appeared unhinged enough that Lester did not press him further, choosing to wander off and make his own assessment of the scene. He was made of tougher stock and was not as disturbed by death as Baxter.

The other vehicles pulled up and Baxter's guard directed the other guards and drivers. They all took weapons and established a perimeter. No one was sure what had happened yet, or if the threat was over. One of his team had a set of binoculars and glassed the hills.

"I recognize these men," the grocery man said, staring with disgust at the dead bodies nearest to the unhooked trailer. "These folks worked for us back at Glenwall. These are your men, Baxter."

The car dealer hesitated to come any closer, not wanting to see the dead bodies. The sight of murdered men was ghastly enough without the additional insult of buzzards picking at them. In his attempt to avoid the mass of bodies, the car dealer wandered upon Hodge's body lying some distance from the others. A chunk of skull was missing and brain tissue leaked from the cavity. He turned and loudly spewed vomit into the tall weeds beside the road.

Baxter walked toward the new body, recognizing the old man by smell before he got visual confirmation. "Son of a bitch!"

"You know him?" Lester asked.

"He's one of the locals we bought cattle from. I can't tell if we killed him or he was collateral damage in the gunfight."

The grocery man walked up to them, casting a wary eye at the surrounding hills, as if suddenly aware that they may be in danger. Unlike the coalman, he'd grown up in grocery stores, stockrooms, and back offices. It was a sheltered world compared to the coal business. "Have you had any trouble here before?"

"None," Baxter said. "There are families living back here along this road. We haven't had any dealings with them." His mind wandered to Don, the man they'd killed and run over when they set up this camp. Did he have family that had seen him killed? Had they come for revenge?

"Is everyone accounted for?" Baxter called to his guard. "I can't recall right now how many there were."

"We're missing some," the guard replied. "There's more blood too. They could have gone for help, tried to find an open hospital, or maybe even back to Glenwall. Or they could have been taken prisoner."

"Prisoner?" Lester asked as if he'd never heard such a ridiculous thing.

Baxter waved a hand in Lester's direction. "There's been no signs of hostility from the families in this valley. That's not likely."

They heard the sound of an approaching engine brake. The semi-truck with the larger cattle trailer had finally caught up with them. The truck couldn't negotiate the country roads as fast and had been a little behind the convoy of Humvees. The driver pulled up to the gate, waiting for instructions on where to park.

"Leave it out there in the road for now!" Baxter called to the driver.

"I don't know this county well," the grocery man said. "Where the hell are we?"

"Middle of Russell County," Baxter said. "We came across this valley while buying cattle. There was an opportunity to secure much-needed resources for the community so we took advantage of it. The more time we spent here, the more sense it made to try to cache some of the Glenwall resources here for safekeeping. To create a fallback location in case we had to bug out." He looked specifically at Lester when he said this and noted a smirk of disbelief on his face.

"Is there good water?" the grocery man asked.

"Several springs nearby," Baxter replied.

"Any big barns or anything?" he asked.

"We're told there are," Baxter replied. "We haven't secured any of them yet."

Lester and the groceryman exchanged glances. It was not lost on Baxter. He understood that he was still the outsider here, the hired help on the lowest rung of the ladder. If there were decisions being made, he had no reason to expect that he would be part of them.

"What are you all thinking?" Baxter asked anyway.

"I would guess that he's thinking we might should move all our folks over in this direction," Lester replied. "That's certainly what I'm thinking. We get a few more of these campers and set up a shelter in a large barn. We could winterize it and put in a few woodstoves for heat. It would be a hell of a lot safer than where we are now."

"That's what I'm thinking too," the grocery man agreed. "We don't have a sustainable plan for maintaining the golf course location. There are too many folks around us. In a place like this, we could grow crops, hunt, and raise livestock if this crisis continues."

Baxter shrugged. "There would be hurdles," he said. "Like the folks that live here. I'm not sure they would be welcoming to an entire subdivision of people suddenly showing up to share their resources."

"That didn't seem to concern you very much when you moved these campers in," Lester said. "I think the basic question is whether those folks could do anything about it or not. They might not like us moving here but do they have the guns and manpower to stop it?"

Baxter's mind was racing. He wanted to tell these men that this was *his* place and they weren't welcome. How could he make this place seem unattractive? How could he make them want to run back to Glenwall? He should have played up the violence aspect. He should have claimed that they sometimes came under random gunfire. It was too late now to throw something like that out.

He should never have brought them here. It was a stupid idea that rose out of panic. Now things were spinning out of control. He'd dreamed of forming his own group here. It would consist of men who didn't require coddling, who didn't come to him with stupid concerns and requests. He was tired of cowing to people. Had he blown it? He didn't see how he could fix this. The men were here now and they knew how to get here. They didn't need him anymore, the same way he hadn't needed Don and Hodge.

Baxter pulled his lips into a strained smile and looked at the Glenwall board of directors. "We can certainly talk about your ideas," he said in a conciliatory tone. "There are logistical issues we'd need to address."

"Fuck that!"

Baxter spun. Valentine faced them with an AK shouldered and pointed in their direction. Baxter opened his mouth to start berating him for not listening to orders. Valentine was supposed to be hiding. He was supposed to wait until they were all gone before coming out of the truck. While Baxter formed those words in his head, Valentine's finger began squeezing the trigger. Shots rang out.

"NOOOO!!!!" Baxter screamed

With practiced efficiency, Valentine dumped two rounds center-mass in each board member. In seconds the four members of the Glenwall board of directors lay dying on the ground.

Valentine lowered his AK, smoke still rising from the barrel. He smiled at Baxter. "That was some damn good shooting, if I do say so myself. That's why you run training drills. Practice makes perfect."

Baxter sagged to his knees, his head in his hands.

42

The Valley

"DAD! GARY! DAD!" Pete yelled into the radio.

Despite the routine nature of most days at his outpost, he had not given up on maintaining a daily watch. It was more than his job; it was his role in the tribe. He'd never in his life felt like he had so much of a purpose as he did now. Most days he saw nothing. Today, a tan Humvee was screaming down the road through the valley.

"What, Pete?" Jim responded. *"You okay?"*

"There's a tan Humvee flying down the road. He's in a hurry."

"Thanks, Pete. We'll get ready. Let me know what he does."

Pete knew his dad had to get everyone safe and didn't have time for small talk. Jim had been working on the chicken coop. Raccoons had been trying to get in and he needed to make sure they couldn't kill any more chickens. When he got the call from Pete, he went into red alert mode, running from the barn yelling at his family.

"Positions! Positions!"

Everyone in the family had drilled on this. At this command, Nana and Ariel were to retreat to the basement. Pops and Ellen were to take up defensive positions in the house, Ellen with a shotgun and Pops with a hunting rifle. Pete was to remain in his outpost and relay the movements of the visitors. Jim had a firing position between the house and the gate. From there he could interact with the visitors and determine their intentions. He could also engage them with his rifle if he couldn't charm them with his personality.

"House in position?" Jim asked into his radio.

"In position," Ellen replied.

Jim had borrowed the rural delivery mailboxes from some of the burned-out and empty homes in the valley. He'd dug postholes around his property and installed those mailboxes on their original posts in random locations. The mailboxes were weatherproof and made a convenient spot to cache spare ammo or other gear. As Jim ran for his earthen position, he stopped at one of his mailbox caches and retrieved a rolled-up chest rig with ten spare magazines for his M4.

He was dropping the rig over his neck when Pete came over the radio.

"They've stopped at our gate."

43

The Valley

WHEN GARY HEARD Pete's first transmission, he bunkered his family down. They'd run the same drill as Jim's family.

"What do you need me to do?" Charlotte asked.

Gary stared at her in surprise. They'd never made her do the drills because she'd been unresponsive to everything. This was the first time she'd ever asked to help with anything.

"Are you up to it?" he asked.

"I think so."

"Then you help watch the kids in the basement," he said. "I've got Will in the barn keeping watch, your mom and Karen will be here watching the road from the living room, you and Sara in the basement with the kids. Any questions?"

"Where will you go?" she asked.

"I'm going to take my long-range rifle and go high."

As everyone scrambled to get where they were supposed to be, Gary grabbed his Savage 110 and took off up the hill that rose between his home and Jim's. He was nearly at the top when Pete's second radio transmission came through.

"They've stopped at our gate."

Gary kept moving until he was in a position to see Jim's gate, where a tan Humvee sat idling. Gary shook out his shooting mat and dropped to the ground, unfolded the legs of the bipod, and settled the rifle. He'd dropped the Savage action into an MDT chassis. The caliber was .338 Lapua and it was a beast. He'd topped it off with a Schmidt Bender scope that had cost him more money than he'd ever admit to his wife.

Taking in the scene below him, Gary realized it would have been a good idea to have established a sniper's hide up here earlier and made a list of ranges to different landmarks. It was always faster than having to use the rangefinder on the fly when time was critical. As a matter of fact, he'd been doing that very thing at his house yesterday. He'd ranged distances to the barn, to the mailbox, to his own gate, and to other distinctive landmarks so that he could commit them to memory.

He slapped at the pouch on his rifle bag and confirmed what had just occurred to him. His rangefinder was still sitting on the kitchen counter. He cursed himself. Here he was perhaps needing to assist his friend and he didn't have a critical tool. He hadn't had many opportunities to train with this rifle, only having purchased it a few months back. All of the shooting he'd done had been performed using a laser rangefinder and a ballistic computer app on his phone.

Focus.

His scope had an MRAD reticle. He knew that a single unit, one MRAD, covered about three feet of height at one thousand yards. He stared through the scope at the Humvee. He saw a person get out of the passenger seat and run toward the gate. He immediately recognized Randi. She fumbled with the chain on the gate before realizing it was locked. She began yelling and Gary assumed she was yelling at Jim to let her in.

In the field of view, he could see other people in the vehicle. He had a friend who had a military Humvee and it seemed like the guy had once told him that his vehicle used a thirty-seven-inch tire. Gary lay the scale of his reticle on the tire. It was larger than a single MRAD so the distance had to be less than a thousand yards.

He turned his crosshairs on Randi. He felt odd about it, like it was a violation. It was also critical that he get a range on any targets in case he had to drop someone. He'd have to make sure that he never mentioned this to her or she'd probably kick his ass.

He thought he remembered her saying she was around five foot four inches tall. That was sixty-four inches. At nine hundred yards, an MRAD was thirty-two inches, or half the height of a five-foot four-inch woman. Gary placed the crosshair on what he judged to be the center of her body, between the waist and pelvis. The next MRAD line on his scope landed right on the crown of her head. It had to be nine hundred yards.

At least he hoped so.

He took the crosshair off Randi and calculated the other factors. Although there was no wind, he was shooting downhill. The stock of the rifle had a pouch with a transparent sleeve containing a ballistics table for the load he was shooting. He adjusted his comeups on the scope turrets, chambered a round, and settled in.

44

The Valley

"LET US IN!" Randi screamed. "I have wounded men."

Jim was not yet to the protection of his dug-in shooting position. He stopped close to it. This was Randi out there—his friend. Still, he hesitated. What the hell was she up to?

"Who are they?" he called.

She spread her hands in frustration. "What does it matter, Jim? They need help. I don't have the supplies at my house to help them."

"Where did you find them?" he demanded. "I am not letting strangers onto my property."

"Buddy, Lloyd, and I found them on the ride out of the valley," she said. "They've been shot, and they need help."

Jim couldn't do it. He could not turn into a hospital for every stray that came through here. He had stockpiled enough medical supplies to get his family through various scenarios. All of his calculations were based on a family of four. He'd already gone beyond that, treating people in his friends' families. He would run out of supplies if this continued.

"I can't do it," Jim said. "I don't have anything."

"Jim, I know you do," she said. "We can help these people."

He couldn't believe she was responding this way. She could be as cold as a hitman. He'd seen it with his own eyes. Here she was though, trying to get him to share his supplies with people he didn't know. Besides the depletion of his supplies, he couldn't let strangers become aware that he had gear and supplies. That could be a death sentence if word got out.

"Randi, come talk to me," Jim said.

"Open the gate."

"Not happening," he said. "You climb over and come talk to me for a minute. We'll sort this out."

Randi sagged and headed for the gate. "Damnit, Jim!"

"Hold it!" a man yelled, jumping out of the driver's seat. He had an AR raised and pointed at Randi.

"What the fuck?" Randi said. "I'm trying to help you. Put that away."

"You open this gate or I'm ramming through it!" he yelled at Jim. "I have two injured friends dying in there. They need assistance."

"You pass that gate and you'll all die," Jim replied calmly.

Jim's radio chirped. *"Dad, I don't think I can hit him from this far off,"* Pete said. *"I don't have a clear shot at this angle. I'm afraid I'll hit you or Randi."*

Jim raised his radio to his mouth. *"Do NOT shoot, Pete!"* he said. *"Do NOT!"*

He took a step toward Randi. "You open this gate now or the girl dies!"

Jim cursed. By opening the gate and saving his friend, he would possibly condemn his family to death. He couldn't do it. Randi was his friend but she'd screwed up big time and endangered them all.

He was trying to figure out his next move when a shot rang out. There was a fraction of a second where nothing happened, then the man holding the rifle on Randi suddenly dropped it. In fact, his entire arm below the elbow dropped to the ground with it in a spray of blood and tissue.

The man staggered back two steps, staring at the gushing stump below his right bicep. His mouth twisted in horror.

"*I didn't shoot!*" Pete screamed into the radio.

Jim knew at that point who must have fired the shot. He rushed toward the gate, rifle raised. Randi kicked the severed arm away from the AR and picked the rifle up. The man who'd held it had slumped to the ground, blood streaming from his arm and spraying his clothes.

"Tourniquet," he begged. "There's one in my pocket."

"You had one fucking chance," Randi hissed. She pulled the trigger and his head snapped back against the vehicle. She jerked the rifle back toward the vehicle. "Get out!" she ordered the men still inside.

Jim had climbed the gate and dropped over. He raised his rifle toward the vehicle. "How many?" he demanded.

"Two," she said. "One wounded."

Jim yanked open the back door and stepped out of the way, constantly keeping his rifle pointed at the strangers. "OUT!"

"Don't shoot us," said a voice. "We're not armed." It was Hunter, the man who'd had to let go of the raincoat and let his buddy die. He slid out, arms raised. Behind him was the man with the shoulder wound, cradling his damaged arm.

"I'm searching you men," Jim said. "Shoot them if they twitch, Randi."

"Got it."

He searched them, relieving them of their knives. The man with the shoulder injury had a sidearm in a holster, and Jim pocketed that. When he was done, he ordered them up against the vehicle. He and Randi both had their weapons trained on them. Jim pulled his radio from its pouch.

"Good shot, Gary," he said.

"*I was aiming for center mass,*" Gary said. "*I missed.*"

"That's okay," Jim said. "You still disarmed him."

"I can't believe you said that," Gary replied.

"You okay, Pete?"

"I'm good."

"You stay up there," Jim said. "Make sure your rifle is on safe."

"What do we do with them?" Randi asked. "Should I kill them? I realize I fucked up by bringing them here. I'm sorry."

Jim shook his head, suddenly mad again. "I don't get it, Randi. You know the deal. You know how important operational security is, then you do something like this?"

"As a friend and a mother, I can kill without thinking a damn thing about it," she said. "It's the nurse part that gives me trouble. It's a reflex to help people and I can't seem to control it. It's the years of training. You train to run toward trouble. I'm so sorry."

"I want the nurse here with us," Jim said. "We need your medical knowledge. That nurse better get her shit together though. You remember us talking about keeping our preparations private?"

Randi sighed. "Yes."

"You cannot compromise *any* of us for strangers!" he said. "We are your family. These people are the enemy. It has to be like that."

"So you want me to kill them since it was my screw-up?"

"You don't have to kill us," Hunter begged. "Please don't."

There was a burst of gunfire in the distance, further down the valley toward Rockdell Farms. It made Jim realize that there may yet be a use for these outsiders.

"Did you hear that?" Gary asked over the radio.

"I did," Jim replied.

"I'm getting back to my family," Gary said.

"Roger," Jim said. He eyed the men leaning against the vehicle. "Let's take these men to your house. You can patch them up and we can get to know each other."

"Buddy and Lloyd are riding by my place on horses," Gary said. *"Moving at a good clip."*

"See if you can get a hold of them," Jim said. "Have them meet us at Randi's house."

"Roger."

"Put these guys back in the vehicle?" Randi asked.

"Hell no," Jim said. "They ain't doing any more bleeding in my new Humvee. They can walk."

45

Rockdell Farms

AFTER A MOMENT, Baxter rose to his feet. He stalked toward Valentine and shoved him with both hands. "What the hell was that?" he yelled. He pushed him again. "What are you thinking?"

Valentine didn't answer. Baxter shoved him again. This time Valentine responded with a quick jab that knocked Baxter on his ass. He sat there stunned, trying to figure out what happened to him.

Valentine stood over him and pointed his finger at him. "You push me one more time and it will be the last time you ever push anybody." His tone left no room for misunderstanding.

Rubbing his chin, Baxter tried to process what was going on. Clearly, he'd underestimated Valentine. Maybe he'd underestimated the entire world outside of the sheltered confines of Wallace County.

"I'm sorry, Valentine. I'm sorry I put my hands on you. This is... not the way I planned this."

"Your plan was going to let all this slip through your fingers," Valentine said. "Those men were going to come back with their fami-

"Hell no," Jim said. "They ain't doing any more bleeding in my new Humvee. They can walk."

45

_____

Rockdell Farms

AFTER A MOMENT, Baxter rose to his feet. He stalked toward Valentine and shoved him with both hands. "What the hell was that?" he yelled. He pushed him again. "What are you thinking?"

Valentine didn't answer. Baxter shoved him again. This time Valentine responded with a quick jab that knocked Baxter on his ass. He sat there stunned, trying to figure out what happened to him.

Valentine stood over him and pointed his finger at him. "You push me one more time and it will be the last time you ever push anybody." His tone left no room for misunderstanding.

Rubbing his chin, Baxter tried to process what was going on. Clearly, he'd underestimated Valentine. Maybe he'd underestimated the entire world outside of the sheltered confines of Wallace County.

"I'm sorry, Valentine. I'm sorry I put my hands on you. This is... not the way I planned this."

"Your plan was going to let all this slip through your fingers," Valentine said. "Those men were going to come back with their families. They were going to replace us. Then you and I and all the rest of these men were going to be out on our asses."

"Maybe," Baxter replied. "But what the hell are we going to do now?" It was not a question. It was an accusation.

Valentine slung his AK over his shoulder. "I'm going to take a couple of these men and we're going to figure out where those shots came from. It might lead us to our missing men."

"I'm coming with you," Baxter said, staggering to his feet.

"Guess again," Valentine said. "You are hightailing it back to Glenwall."

"Are you kidding me? People will be all over us wanting to know where the board members are."

"You think so?" Valentine asked. "Their families *maybe*. I doubt they had time to tell very many people."

"What am I supposed to tell those family members? Am I supposed to keep doing my job like nothing happened?"

Valentine shook his head. "Can't do that. You've dicked around with this too long. We have to make it happen now. You leave those tower lights off tonight. After everyone is asleep, hook up to that fuel tanker. You load every truck and trailer with the food, weapons, and gear. Early tomorrow, you bring it all here and life starts over. Leave Glenwall to figure their own shit out."

Baxter grinned bitterly. "Just like the fucking Grinch stealing Christmas? Taking all of Whoville's goodies?"

"Exactly," Valentine agreed. "You better not grow a heart and double-cross me or I'll rip it out. Are we clear?"

"Yeah, we're clear," Baxter said. He rubbed his jaw. He couldn't remember the last time he'd been hit in the face. It hurt. "What about these bodies?" he asked, gesturing at the dead board members.

"Leave'em," Valentine said. "We'll deal with them later. It's not like they're going anywhere."

Valentine began shouting orders and in less than a minute, Baxter and his crew were headed back to Glenwall in the semi, leaving their Humvees behind. They would need every available man to drive the loaded vehicles back tomorrow. Valentine kept three men and they loaded in a single Humvee. They proceeded up the valley road, windows down and weapons ready. They were going to find their friends.

The camp was left abandoned and silent, the bodies of men scattered in all directions. The buzzards began to return, resuming their meal, and picking up where they left off. Several hopped toward the fresher kills. There was no use fighting when there were so many to choose from.

Lester, who'd so distrusted Baxter, lay face down in the dirt, his clothes soaked with the grocery man's blood. Valentine had been so pleased with his marksmanship that he hadn't even confirmed they were all dead.

The coalman opened one eye.

46

The Valley

GARY CROSSED the fence and was walking across the backyard of his house when he heard the sound of an engine. He paused, thinking perhaps Jim and Randi were driving to his house with the Humvee that had been at Jim's gate. Then he saw that it was a black Humvee and it was entering the valley from the Rockdell Farms side. He never had a chance to look for Buddy and Lloyd. He could only hope they heard the vehicle and got off the road.

He sprinted toward the house. He paused at the back door, knocking a special knock that let his family know it was him and would hopefully prevent his wife from vaporizing his head with a shotgun. She unlocked the door and let him in.

"Don't relax yet," he said. "There's another vehicle coming."

She went back to her position without a word.

He plucked his radio from the pouch on his belt. "Jim?"

"Jim here," came a reply.

"There's a black Humvee coming into the valley now," Gary said. "I'm at my house."

"Stay safe," Jim said. *"Let us know what you see."*

Gary pocketed his radio. He could hear Jim talking to Pete, confirming that he'd heard Gary's warning.

"I heard," Pete said. *"Not in my line of sight yet."*

Gary went to the front window and looked out at the road. He hoped Jim was able to hide the Humvee he'd confiscated from his visitors. The black Humvee continued winding its way along the road. When it got to his driveway, it slowed, then stopped, idling outside his gate.

Gary mumbled a curse. The horn honked a single long burst. Gary's mind raced. He didn't know what to do. He didn't want to break cover, nor did he want to provoke a confrontation. Maybe it was better to pretend like he had nothing to hide.

"I have to go out," he told Debra.

Her eyes got wide and she shook her head. "NO!"

"I *have* to," he said. "If I don't go, they may think we're hiding something. Who knows what kind of weapons they have or how many of them there are? I don't want to draw their attention down on us. The best thing to do is pretend like things are normal."

Will stood silently to the side. "I'm trusting you with my life, Will," Gary said. He picked up his Savage .338 and adjusted the turrets on the scope. "We ranged that gate earlier. The scope is adjusted to hit dead-on. If things go downhill, start shooting. I'll need cover fire to get away."

Will nodded and took the rifle. "Got you covered."

"Debra," Gary said to his wife, "radio Jim and tell him what's happening."

He kept his sidearm on in the exposed holster and walked out of the house. He waved at the Humvee both to catch their attention and to show that he was not carrying a rifle and jogged casually toward them, closing the distance. The driver killed the engine. He slowed to a walk as the heavy passenger door of the vehicle was pushed opened and a large man got out.

When he reached the gate, Gary stood close to it. He did not cross it nor unlock it. He found himself facing a tall, bald man in black military fatigues. He carried an AK-47. He was wearing some kind of badge that Gary couldn't read over the distance. He nodded at Gary.

"I'm looking for some buddies of mine," he said without introduction. "They would have been in a vehicle like this one but tan. You see them?"

He was all business. The fact that he was kind of overweight in the current state of society also said a lot. He obviously had connections to resources. Most people were having to tighten their belts to keep from losing their pants these days.

"I haven't seen any vehicle traffic through here at all," Gary replied. "It's been days since I noticed anyone come by and then it was only a tractor."

The man studied Gary hard—cop look—trying to determine if he was telling the truth. Gary knew he wasn't a good liar. He didn't have any expectation that he could fool anyone. All that mattered was how the man reacted. Would he sense that Gary was lying and challenge him on it or would he sense that Gary was lying and go on about his business?

"I heard a shot," he said. "Was it you?"

Gary shook his head. "There's a lot of shooting goes on back here. This is the country. People hunt. I heard shooting earlier too." Gary looked the other man in the eye. *Was that you shooting earlier? What were you shooting?*

The man didn't bite. "I thought I heard a couple of rifle shots."

"Probably a deer hunter," Gary said.

He studied Gary, then his eyes moved to the house. "You live here with your family?"

Gary saw no reason to lie about that. "Yeah."

"You getting by?" he asked.

Gary nodded to that. "Things are tight, but yeah," he said, not offering any more.

He looked off down the road. "There a lot of people live down through here?"

"Yeah," Gary replied. It was an exaggeration. Since the man didn't know how many people lived there it probably meant he wasn't a local. It also meant he didn't have any business being back there.

"Be seeing you," he said, getting back into his vehicle.

Gary backed away from the gate. He watched to see if the vehicle would continue into the valley or if it would return the way it came. He was disappointed to see it continue into the valley. He was also concerned with the way that the man said he would *be seeing him*. With that was the implication that they were not going anywhere. They would be back at some point and he would have to deal with them again.

47

The Valley

RANDI'S HOUSE was a short walk from Jim's driveway. When they got there, the radio call came through from Gary.

"We've got a second Humvee," he said on the radio.

"Shit! You're going to have to look after these guys for a second," Jim told Randi. "I've got to move that vehicle we left in the road."

"The tractor shed behind my house is empty," Randi said. "You can put it there."

Jim ran back for the vehicle. Randi kept her prisoners a safe distance ahead of her, a rifle on them the entire time, safety off. When they reached the tractor shed, Jim was racing down the driveway in the heavy vehicle.

The two prisoners stood in the door of the tractor shed watching him approach.

"You better be backing up," Randi told them. "He doesn't yield to pedestrians."

They heeded Randi's advice just in time to avoid being flattened. Jim nosed the machine as far into the shed as he could get it. He flung the door open, got out, and slid the tall shed doors closed on their steel tracks. With the door closed, the level of illumination dropped to what ambient light crept in through cracks, holes, and the dusty windows.

"You men sit down and keep quiet," Jim said. "Not a fucking word or I slit your throats."

The men were tired, scared, and weak enough at this point that they did not protest. Jim ran to the door and watched through the cracks. He could hear the vehicle approaching.

"I hope Buddy and Lloyd are somewhere safe," Randi said.

"Don't worry about them," Jim said. "They're resourceful."

"Did you close the gate when you came through?" Randi asked.

"Shit," Jim said. "I forgot. I was in a hurry. Where are your kids and grandkids?"

"They're hiding out in the basement for now."

The black Humvee stopped at the entrance to Randi's driveway. The horn honked.

"Are you going out?" Randi asked.

"No way," Jim said. "They want us, they have to come get us."

The vehicle honked again. Jim held his breath. If they wanted to come to the house the gate was wide open and they could drive right in. There was nothing stopping them. They could drive right to the shed. They could drive right to the house.

Then the vehicle accelerated away and was gone. Jim let out his breath and turned back to the prisoners. "I'm going to assume those guys were with you. Who are you people and what are you doing in my valley?"

The one with the shoulder wound was pale and his head bobbed a little. If they were going to provide medical attention, he needed it soon. The other man appeared to be uninjured but very scared.

"What's your name?" Jim asked the uninjured man.

"He told me his name was Hunter," Randi said when there was no response.

Jim stood in front of him, looking him in the eye. His fear was palpable. "Who are you people?" There was nothing conversational about the tone of Jim's voice. It held nothing but the promise of bad things.

His hand trembling as he wiped the sweat from his forehead, he replied, "We're regular guys. We're not here to hurt anybody."

"What are you doing here?"

"We came for cattle."

Jim was startled by a sound from outside. He started to swing his pistol away from his captive, then recognized the sound as the crunch of gravel under hooves.

"It's Buddy!" Randi said.

Jim went to the door, pushed it slightly open. Buddy and Lloyd were leading their horses and breathing hard, their faces red.

"We didn't expect you to be here," Buddy said. "We had to get off the road and hide when we heard that vehicle coming. Once it was gone, we decided to bolt for the nearest shelter."

"Tie your horses up behind the shed and get in here," Jim said. "I'm still not sure it's safe to be in the open."

Jim started back into the shed and his radio chirped.

"Dad?" It was Pete.

"Here," Jim said. "What's going on?"

"They're at the end of the driveway, Dad. They can't get through. They're sitting there with the engine running."

"Ellen, are you listening?" Jim asked.

"Here," she said.

"Don't engage these guys," he said. "They went away when we didn't come outside. I'm at Randi's. If they get out of the vehicle, let me know immediately and I'll be there. Otherwise, stay inside."

"Got it," Ellen said.

"Got it," Pete said.

Buddy and Lloyd returned from tying up their horses and slipped through the corrugated steel door. Jim pulled it shut behind them. They all stared at the men on the ground.

"I thought there was three of them," Buddy said.

"There were definitely three of them when she left," Lloyd said.

"One got ornery," Randi said.

"Gary disarmed him," Jim added.

"I wish you'd quit saying that," Randi said with disgust.

Jim shrugged.

"Excuse me for changing the subject but what was that stunt you pulled back there, Randi? You shouldn't have done that," Lloyd said. "You're lucky they didn't shoot your ass. You didn't know those people. You weren't under any obligation to help them."

Randi frowned at him. "I've already had a lecture, thank you," she said. "I won't do it again. You all don't understand. The nurse in me *did* feel obligated."

"Tell that nurse she's a dumbass," Lloyd said.

Randi gave him a look that said things were about to get serious.

"This is not the time," Jim said.

"Jim, you should see the setup these guys have," Buddy said. "They've got shipping containers of gear, semi-trailers of food, and a bunch of campers with generators. They moved in right under our noses and we didn't even see it. We left a big hole in our defenses and they drove right through it."

The information didn't sit well with Jim. He had planned on blowing that road, but they'd had trouble scraping together the supplies. He should have done something, even if it was simply felling trees in the road. If he kept screwing around someone was going to get killed. They needed to be more decisive. They needed to figure things out and take action.

Jim looked at Hunter. "Is this true?"

He looked back at Jim and nodded slowly.

"Sounds like you plan on staying a while."

"I don't know," Hunter said. "I guess. Maybe."

Jim holstered his pistol and leaned over, his hands on his knees. "Let's start with a simple question. Where did you come from?"

"Wallace County. The Glenwall golf course," Hunter said, a tremor in his voice.

"Why did you come here?"

"We bought cattle off a man. We figured out where he was getting them from and my boss decided to set up a camp over here.

He didn't want to have to go through a middleman to get cattle. When he got over here, he decided it seemed like a safe place to stay."

Jim knew those men loading cattle that day had been up to something. Despite what the cattle thieves' intentions had been, they had brought these other men into their valley. They had endangered the lives of everyone in the valley.

"So who are *you*, Hunter? What did you do before shit fell apart?" Jim asked.

"I worked for Wallace County. On the road crew. Mostly a backhoe operator."

"How did you become affiliated with this group?"

"When things got bad, the people living on the golf course wanted to hire private security. They paid the county's Emergency Management Coordinator to find people for them."

Jim nodded in the direction of the other man. "All of you are county employees?"

"No. There's some campus security, some deputies, people from the county maintenance shop. None of us had any place to go. They promised us food and a roof over our heads if we came to work for them."

"Sounds like a good deal," Jim said. "So why did you all bring so much gear over here if you have such a cozy setup over there in Wallace County?"

"Our boss, Baxter, is concerned that Glenwall isn't safe," Hunter said. "He says that eventually the hungry people in the community will overrun it and take our supplies."

"Baxter?"

"Yeah," Hunter said. "He's the Emergency Management Coordinator. We work for him."

"Baxter decided you needed to have a backup plan?"

"Basically."

"So the backup plan is to move all the folks from Glenwall golf course into *my* valley?" Jim asked. "That's a lot of people. That would take an enormous effort."

Hunter shook his head. "No. Just those of us that work for him. That's all that was coming."

"Those supplies out there, they belong to you all, or did you steal them from the golf course?"

Hunter hesitated, then replied, "We stole them."

Jim straightened out and let out a low whistle. "Stealing from the hand that feeds you. That takes some balls. Baxter the Badass, huh?"

Hunter didn't respond.

Jim went back to the door and stared out, checking the road. "Did it not occur to you, Hunter, that there were already people living here?"

Hunter shrugged. "We have a lot of guns. We weren't worried."

Now Jim was worried. He didn't like the sound of that. "How many men work for Baxter?"

"Maybe two dozen," Hunter admitted. "A few less now."

Jim looked at his friends. There was an entire world contained in that look. All in the room had seen the look before and knew what it foretold. Jim met Randi's eyes. Her lips tightened and she looked away. He met Buddy's and he nodded a grim nod. Lloyd shrugged as if he didn't know what to do.

Randi's horse blankets lay over a wooden sawhorse. Jim took one and folded it into quarters, drew his Beretta, then wrapped the blanket around his hand.

"What are you doing?" Hunter asked fearfully.

"If I let you go, I'll only have to fight you later," Jim said. "Some of my people may get hurt. I have a rule about that, something my grandfather told me when I was a kid."

Hunter looked around frantically. "Don't let him do this," he begged, locking eyes with Randi.

Her eyes filled with tears.

"Do you need to go outside?" Jim asked her.

She put her balled fist to her mouth and shook her head.

"You don't need to do this!" the man pleaded. "You can't!"

Jim raised the Beretta to the back of Hunter's head, dropped the safety, and pulled the trigger. While the sound was still loud in the confines of the metal shed, the blanket hopefully muffled it enough that it wouldn't carry to the other Humvee. Hunter fell forward, arching, clawing, kicking, then was still. Jim watched with a sick feeling in his gut. Headshots weren't always instant. You never knew how the brain would react to a slug. It was ugly work.

Jim unwrapped his hand, then cycled the action since the blanket had inhibited the movement of the slide after that shot. He looked at the other man. He was pale from blood loss and perhaps going into shock. He had no response to his friend's death nor to his own impending death. Jim raised the gun and did it again. This time the man fell forward and was gone instantly.

Jim looked around the room. Buddy was staring impassively at the bodies. Lloyd was shaking his head. Randi was crying.

"Do you understand why I had to do this?" he asked her. "I had to."

"It's my fault," Randi said. "I shouldn't have brought them here. Their deaths are on me."

"Maybe you shouldn't have," Jim agreed. "but if you hadn't, we wouldn't have known what was happening."

"That's why I made myself watch," she said. "I'll remember next time. So I'll think first."

"I'm glad to hear that," Jim said. "Their deaths are not on you, though. They came to our valley. They made this decision."

Lloyd moved over to hug Randi and she let him.

48

Wallace County

WHEN THE SEMI returned to the golf course, the guards manning it moved the cars out of the way to allow Baxter through.

Baxter climbed from the vehicle and explained to his men what had happened. He told them that the plan had been expedited and this would be their last night at Glenwall. He gave them instructions for what he wanted done when their shift on the gate ended and then he got back in the truck.

They parked the semi at the maintenance shop and Baxter called together all of his men who weren't performing a critical task at the moment. He repeated the story of what had transpired at the camp in Russell County.

"I need you men to go to your rooms and pack all of your personal gear. Do not load anything in a vehicle until after dark. We can't allow the residents to see us bugging out. Anything you want to take needs to be packed and ready for transport. Are we understood?"

He looked around the maintenance shop and all of the workers nodded. It struck Baxter that his force was not as big as he recalled it being. He had perhaps a dozen men remaining, not counting those who were dead or in Russell County.

"We're pulling an all-nighter. Once it's dark, I need all hands loading gear," Baxter continued. "We're not bothering with the food that's already offloaded into the community center. The residents can keep that. Anything in the trailers is going with us. We're also taking the fuel tanker. Anything you can think of that we might need gets loaded tonight. I figure that we won't be welcome back after tonight so there won't be any returning to pick up things we forgot."

Some of the group smiled at that comment. Baxter had mixed feelings about that reaction. These were the kind of men that he needed working for him, but the fact that they took pleasure in the misfortune of others revealed something of their character. He was certainly not in a place to be pointing fingers. His character was clearly questionable as well.

With everyone on board with the plan and having assignments to take care of, Baxter retreated to the house he shared with some of the other guys. He had his own gear to square away and was going to work on a list of things he wanted to get that night. As he'd told his men, they needed to be thorough. There would be no coming back. There were things he wanted to make sure were not missed.

There were other men working in the house doing the same thing. Baxter had a supply of military duffel bags and he began throwing items into them. He still had a tiny house outside of town and he wondered for a moment how it was faring. Had people broken in? Was someone living there? He might have to swing by and check on it when he left town. What did it matter? It was a relic of an old life. An old world.

He grabbed the corner of a sheet and started rolling his bedding up, cramming it into a duffle bag. He heard the front door open and close. There was conversation and someone turned some music on. He hoped the guys were focusing and doing what he told them. Maybe the music kept them motivated.

He hoped his guys remembered not to be carrying their gear outside yet. He didn't want to draw undue attention. He heard a sound from downstairs that he didn't recognize. He paused for a second then went back to work. He had a lot to do. He continued trying to fit his bedding into the mouth of the bag. It didn't want to go. He was shoving with all his might when he heard the sound again. It sounded like a cough.

"Going somewhere?"

Baxter spun, then froze in his tracks. He couldn't believe his eyes. His legs went weak and he sat down on the bed. Lester stood in front of him, a fat automatic in his hand. Behind him was another man of about the same age. He carried a similar automatic with a long cylindrical attachment on the front.

"You're dead," Baxter said. "I saw you get shot. I saw your dead body on the ground."

Lester stepped into the room. "I did get shot. But as you can see, I'm not dead."

"That's great. How?" Baxter asked. He was questioning his sanity. Had the whole thing been a setup? Had it been a show put on for his benefit? "Are the others alive?"

"No," Lester replied. "They made the mistake of trusting your sorry ass. Richard back here was the chief of security for my mining operations. He set me up with some body armor before we left. I'm lucky that fucker was a good shot. Had he missed the ceramic plate, we wouldn't be having this conversation."

"I didn't mean for that to happen," Baxter said. "You saw that right? You heard me yelling at him."

"I believe that," Lester said. "Still, that doesn't change the basic facts of the situation."

"What facts?"

"That you were planning on stealing all our food and supplies."

Baxter started to protest but Lester pointed the gun at him. "Save it. Don't waste your breath on me. You'll have a chance to plead your case."

"I will?" Baxter asked hopefully.

Lester grinned. "Definitely."

It was not a reassuring expression.

Richard came into the room and secured Baxter's hands with sturdy zip ties. Baxter held out hope that his men might be aware of what was going on and try to rescue him as they left the house. It wasn't to be. As they walked down the hall he passed three men dead of gunshot wounds.

"I didn't hear a thing," Baxter mumbled.

"Smith and Wesson .22 with a suppressor and subsonic loads," Richard said. "It's pretty damn quiet."

They led Baxter out the front door and across the green to the clubhouse. He noticed that the decorative cherry trees that lined the drive looked unusual. He squinted against the sun and saw that most of his men were now zip-tied to those trees.

"Shit."

"Don't get your hopes up because a few of them are missing," Lester said. "No one escaped. If they're missing, that means we had to kill them before they got this far."

Baxter swallowed hard. In short order, he was tied to a tree as well.

"Richard, go ring the bell for happy hour," Lester instructed, pointing out its location to the other man. He leaned toward Baxter. "Don't let the word *happy hour* confuse you. I don't think it will be *your* happiest hour. I could be wrong, though."

Richard walked to the brass bell and shook the white rope for nearly a minute. Assuming it to be an emergency or something of importance, people began to stream out of their homes.

"Everyone come this way!" Lester shouted. "We need to have a community meeting."

It took about five minutes for the residents to assemble. It was a long five minutes for Baxter. He felt the eyes of the residents upon him, questioning why he was tied to a tree. He was used to them looking to him for answers. These were different looks: accusing, distrustful, angry, and suspicious.

When every family was present, Lester called for silence.

"We have something important to discuss," he began. "The first order of business is that I need to inform you I am the only remaining member of the board of directors. Mr. Baxter over there saw to that. To summarize what has taken place, Mr. Baxter and his employees have been stealing our food and supplies. They've been transporting them to an off-site location with a plan to move there and use our supplies to start their own community. When the board of directors became aware of this and confronted Mr. Baxter, they were shot and killed."

There were gasps and some outbursts of sobbing. Lester tore open his jacket, revealing his body armor. "You can see from the holes in my vest that I was a target. I wore this because I did not trust Mr. Baxter. I could not convince my fellow board members. They believed his lies and it cost them their lives."

Baxter was getting a lot of angry looks now. "No, it's not like—" he tried to interject.

"I will have Richard gag you if you don't shut up, Baxter," Lester said. "I've heard enough of your lies."

There were murmurs of agreement from the crowd. Their fervor elevated Baxter's fear.

"The reason I've called you all together is that we need to make a decision as to the fate of these men," Lester said. "They conspired together to steal the food from your mouths and your children's mouths. They intended to leave us here to our own devices with no food, no supplies, and no weapons. What would be a suitable punishment for such a thing?"

There was a chorus of suggestions.

Lester raised his hands to quell the shouting. "I have a suggestion if you are willing to entertain it. You are welcome to take my suggestion or you may go home, close your door, and not take part."

"What's your suggestion?" someone shouted.

"I'm glad you asked that," Lester said with a smile. He spoke into a radio.

From behind the clubhouse came several golf carts. The backs of the golf carts were packed with dozens of golf bags containing hundreds of heavy wood and steel clubs. The golf carts stopped in front of the crowd. Lester made a sweeping gesture toward the carts,

an offering to the crowd. The glow of awareness and understanding spread across the assembly like a ray of sunlight moving across a pasture.

With a variety of expressions on the assembled faces, the people began to come forward. Everyone took a club. Not a single person left to go home. The golf carts pulled out of the way and Baxter faced the crowd. There were men, women, children, and grandmothers. Some smiled in anticipation. Others wore a mask of grim anger. Without a word from Lester, the crowd surged forward.

Baxter screamed.

49

The Valley

THE BLACK HUMVEE cruised the length of the valley. Pete and Gary's warnings on the radio had hopefully reached all of the families in the valley, making them aware of the presence of the strangers. Either way, Valentine and his crew did not see a soul. They drove until they ran into the section of road that Jim had blown up.

"I guess it's safe to say that our men didn't drive out this way," Valentine said. "So either they drove out the other way or they're dead and their vehicle is hidden somewhere in this valley."

The driver idled in the road, parked at the edge of the demolished asphalt. "What do you want to do?"

"Turn around," Valentine said. "I'm not sure we have enough men to go house-to-house doing a search. Let's go back and secure our camp for now. We'll come up with something."

"The other men will be back soon enough," another of the team suggested. "We could wait until they get here. That's a bigger show of force."

Except for the Humvee that went missing with them, those men weren't of that much value. If they were injured, as the blood indicated, they might be nothing more than a burden if Valentine did find them. They might be able to eat and consume resources while unable to work. He didn't need that.

"The fewer mouths, the longer the food will last," Valentine said.

They drove back to their camp as slowly as their first pass through the valley. They didn't see a single soul outside moving around, although the presence of dogs and penned livestock seemed to indicate that people lived here. There was even a trickle of smoke from one chimney.

"This isn't a bad little spot," Parker commented. He had once been a sheriff's deputy. When the county government changed hands after the last election, he'd been let go. He was working at a sock factory when the terror attacks occurred.

"I was thinking the same thing," Valentine said.

"You cut off both roads into this place and it would be like a castle surrounded by a moat," Parker said. "You'd still have foot traffic to worry about though you could set up security against that."

"There would be a lot of families to take on," Valentine said. "I'm sure they wouldn't give up their homes without a fight."

"You wouldn't have to take them all at once," Parker said. "That's not how I'd do it. I'd start at one end and work my way through the valley, dealing with one family at a time. Take one house, occupy it, then take the next. In a week or two, you'd have the entire valley."

"You take enough of them, the rest may pack their shit and run off," Valentine said, nodding.

"Except we might need their shit," Parker replied. "So they probably can't take it. I'm not sure we could allow that."

"Good point," Valentine said.

He stared out the window at the houses they passed. The people who lived in those houses probably lived in them because they liked being out in the country. Valentine hadn't ever lived off to himself like this. As a child, he'd lived in the crowded coal camps where the houses butted up against each other and had tiny yards. As an adult, he'd always lived in cramped trailer parks or in cheap little apartments on the edge of town. This kind of space seemed nice. He could learn to like this. It gave a man some breathing room.

He wondered if this was how warlords started out, finding themselves in a unique position to take advantage of an opportunity. He could own this valley. They could control the cattle and livestock. That made him wonder if it was better to physically take the valley and drive everyone out or if it was better to terrorize the valley until everyone agreed to work for him.

He certainly didn't know anything about raising cattle. He'd have to think about this. He could be the lord and they could be the serfs. He'd never thought like this before, but the mind had the luxury of wandering when everything was going your way. When you got on a winning streak in life it was hard not to wonder how far that streak might take you.

A new job could have you wondering if you could one day be running the company. A profitable business dealing could have you wondering what it would be like to be a billionaire. A winning twenty-dollar lottery ticket could have you wondering what a four hundred and twenty million dollar lottery ticket would be like. It was human nature to dream and aspire. When the course of one's life is altered and skewed by circumstance, those dreams and aspirations can become twisted, sending a man in a trajectory that he'd never imagined.

That was what was happening to Valentine now. His life had gone in a completely unexpected direction and the world was opening up to him in completely unforeseen ways.

The grand visions ended with the return to camp and the grim work that awaited. There was never a shortage of flies in cattle pastures and they now coated the dead bodies, which had grown stiff from their encrustation of gore. Fluids had seeped and dried in the sun, gluing them to the long pasture grasses. Buzzards had strung out entrails and punctured vile cavities that released noxious and inescapable odors.

"What the hell are we going to do with this?" Valentine asked, standing with the three men he'd retained. "That's a lot of damn graves."

"I grew up on a farm," Grayson said. He was a scrawny heavy equipment operator that had worked for the county. "When we had a cow die, we tied them to the tractor and dragged them off to a sinkhole at the far corner of the farm. Wasn't worth the trouble to bury a cow. In a few days, the buzzards and coyotes would do away with everything but the bones."

Valentine looked at Grayson with a frown on his face.

He shrugged. "Sorry," he said. "Just an idea."

"Reckon I'd rather do that than dig graves," Parker agreed. "There's rope in one of those containers. We could tie them to the pintle hitch on that Humvee and pull them off somewhere they won't contaminate the water."

"These were our friends," Valentine said. "Our coworkers."

"Somehow I doubt they'll be complaining," Grayson said.

"Then fuck it. Let's get it done," Valentine said. "After that, I want you guys to grab some rest. I'll keep watch. Tonight I'll need you guys out on recon. We need to know what we're dealing with in this valley."

"Do we have any of the night vision devices?" Parker asked.

"I don't think so," Valentine said. "There were only a couple and I think the guards at the golf course were using them. We should have them tomorrow. I don't want to wait that long. I'd like to take that first house tomorrow."

"The one where we talked to that guy?" Grayson asked.

Valentine nodded. "Just one guy with a family."

"Did you notice his pistol?" Parker asked.

"I saw he had one," Valentine said. "I had the AK on him so I wasn't too worried."

"That's not what I meant," Parker said. "He had a Glock in a top-end retention holster."

"I didn't notice," Valentine said.

"It might not mean anything," Parker said. "Or it might mean that he knows guns and is well-armed."

"Your concern is noted," Valentine said. "Now get these fucking bodies out of here before the buzzards come back."

50

The Valley

JIM, Buddy, and Lloyd wrapped the bodies of the executed men in a sheet of dirty black plastic and tied them shut with baling twine. They didn't want to take a chance on any of Randi's family finding them, so they put them in the Humvee along with the man Gary had shot with the .338 for Jim to dispose of later.

"We need to scramble," Jim said. "Things are as critical as they've ever been for us. We need someone from every family. Have them at my house in one hour. We need to make some plans."

"Can I call them on the radio?" Randi asked.

"No." He turned to Buddy and Lloyd. "Could you guys hit each house on horseback? We don't know what kind of scanning technology these guys might have. They could be listening to our transmissions. We need to be careful what we say from this point forward."

"That's too slow," Randi said.

"Then go to my house and get the tractor," Jim said. "It's got a full tank of heating oil. Just make it quick. Make sure they know it's an emergency."

Buddy and Lloyd slid the shed door open and headed out. In a moment they were trotting across the field toward Jim's house.

"Randi, take your family to my house," Jim said. "Tell my wife that I'm going to be sending some of Gary's people there. His house is closest to this mess and I don't want those grandkids in harm's way."

"Got it," Randi said. "I appreciate it. And again, I'm sorry about bringing those guys to your house. It was a reaction."

"It's done," Jim said, holding up a hand. "But I do need you to talk to Pete while you're there. Tell him what's happening and to minimize radio transmissions."

"Then what?"

"Wait at my house until the other families get there," he said. "I've got to get Gary up to speed and then I'll come over."

51

The Valley

AFTER SPEAKING with Gary and his family, Jim walked the fields back toward his house. Gary and Will remained behind to keep an eye out for any suspicious activity. Debra, Gary's daughters, and his grandchildren all followed Jim. Debra carried a grandchild in one arm and had a rifle slung over her shoulder. Jim was carrying a child piggyback, the little girl using his pack as a seat. He carried his M4 at the ready, his adrenaline simmering. Each of Gary's daughters was armed, even Charlotte, who would not have been trusted with a firearm mere days ago. She'd been showing significant improvement. No one knew what Randi had done to break through to her but it appeared to have worked.

At Randi's house, they added her family to the entourage. They threw a few clothes, some food, and some blankets into a bag. It occurred to Jim that this would be a large group to protect if gunfire broke out. Daylight could give a false sense of comfort. Jim chose to go with that and hope for the best on the short walk.

When he reached his home, Jim found his backyard crowded

with representatives from nearly every family in the valley. Certainly all of the folks he'd interacted with since he'd gotten home had someone here. They sat on all manner of lawn chair, stump, camp stool, and overturned bucket. There were greetings as he came into the backyard, but he declined all questions until he had Gary's grandchildren in the house. Jim's daughter Ariel and Gary's daughter Karen took all of the kids to Ariel's room to play. Everyone else was outside except for Pete, who continued to man his post on the hill.

Jim stood so that he could be heard by everyone. "I won't waste a lot of time because we have stuff we need to do. It will be dark soon and we need to get some things in place. Some of you probably know that I blew up the road between here and town."

There was some murmuring and Jim knew that not all of it was supportive of his decision, which was why he'd kept it low-key.

"I did it because I was concerned about strangers coming through here," Jim said. "I've been out there in the world and seen how ugly things are. Gary and Randi have too. Most of you have not been outside this community."

"My mother would string you up if she knew you did that," one of the Wimmer men said. "She's pissed. She wants to know how her sisters are going to get here for Thanksgiving."

"*If* they're alive, they're not coming for Thanksgiving," Jim said. "I'd put money on it."

"I'll let you tell her that," the man said.

Jim sighed. "I planned on blowing the road at the other end of the valley. I had trouble getting supplies together though."

There was louder murmuring this time.

"You realize that leaves us with no road out of the valley in an emergency?" It was Mrs. Bird. Jim couldn't remember her first name.

"I preferred to look at it as leaving no way in for those with bad intentions," Jim said. "We could always get out if we needed to. There are farm roads and logging roads, and most of those aren't on maps. Either way, it doesn't matter. It's too late now."

"Wait, wait, wait," Thomas Weatherman said. "What's that mean?"

"We were too lax in our security," Jim said. "We were comfortable and complacent. We haven't had the ends of the valley under surveillance. Armed men moved in at the edge of Rockdell Farms. They basically control that end of the valley now. They have a large camp with supplies and military vehicles. There are more coming, and they don't intend to leave."

"Well, if you hadn't blown the damn road up, we'd have a way out of here," one of the Wimmers said.

"And go where?" Jim asked. "Your life is here. Your family is here and has been for two centuries. All the stuff you need to survive is here. Are you going to be pushed out?"

The man stared at the ground and shook his head in frustration.

"How do you know all of this?" Weatherman asked.

"There was a shooting at their camp earlier and we had the opportunity to speak to some of the men from the camp," Jim replied. "They were injured. They told us everything."

"You the cause of that shooting at their camp?" Weatherman asked.

"No," Jim said. "We don't know who shot whom, only that there was a gunfight and some bodies. I didn't see the scene. The injured men succumbed to gunshot wounds."

It was not a complete lie. Jim wasn't sure that his group could handle the entire truth. He wasn't going to mention who inflicted the gunshot wounds. Some of them thought he was too quick to pull the trigger already. They didn't understand. They hadn't had his grandfather to explain to them some of the basic laws of human nature and violence. While his mother hadn't wanted Jim to hear them either, those bits of wisdom had saved his life several times over the last months. You didn't leave an enemy alive to fight a second time. If you fought him, you finished it.

With no questions, Jim continued.

"My guess, as I understand human nature, is when it gets cold these folks will start to look at our homes and wonder why they shouldn't simply take them. They'll be tired of living in campers. They'll come to think of this valley as *their* valley and they'll decide *we* have to go. In my opinion, the only way to deter that is to not let them get a firm foothold. We try to run them out. If they don't run, we kill them."

The group was silent while this settled in.

"Look, I don't know you well, but I don't want to be forced out of my home." It was Mack Bird. Jim had hung out with him a couple of times over the years, shooting at the Birds' backyard range. "Without fuel, most of us aren't going to be able to get very far and we won't be able to take our stuff. If we try to run, we won't make it through the winter."

"Ain't there someone we can call?" asked another Wimmer. "Ain't there still cops in town?"

"You're welcome to try," Jim said. "Your phone isn't working and I doubt you'll find anyone interested in coming out to help us. People are on their own. *We're* on our own. This is our battle to win or lose."

"Bullets fly both ways," Buddy said. "There's a chance we'll lose people if we turn this into a war. I'm with Jim. I think we defend what's ours, I want you all to understand the risk. If you choose to participate and someone gets hurt, don't come back blaming Jim for it. If you go into this, go in with your eyes open."

"Thanks, Buddy," Jim said.

"What do we need to do?" Mack asked. "Where do we start?"

"I think we need folks from every family on watch tonight. This isn't a watch against an imaginary enemy. There are real people here and they could come for any of us tonight," Jim said. "We need a manned and heavily armed outpost near Henry's farm where Gary here is staying, and the Weathermans' home. It has a long sightline and it's the first spot they'd hit if they come along the road. It needs to be a secure, dug-in emplacement."

"It's probably a good idea if no one is out walking around tonight," Thomas said. "I'd hate to shoot someone by accident on their moonlight stroll."

"If anyone doesn't want to be part of this we need to know now," Mack said. "It's important we know who has our back and who doesn't. If anyone is not participating, they should identify themselves now."

Jim and Mack watched the group and not a single hand rose. Jim hoped that it was an accurate count and there weren't folks out there too afraid to raise a hand.

"We've only got a couple of hours before dark," Jim said. "We need to get that outpost dug and stocked, and I'm going to need a few extra men to station at Gary's house."

52

The Valley

WITH EVERYONE RUSHING OFF to perform their assignments, Ellen fell into the role of hosting the people sheltering at her house. Fortunately, Ariel took naturally to that role, which gave Ellen time to ready weapons and ammunition in case they were needed. Nana was pitching in with the kids, while Pops was going around supervising. Ellen made coffee for a thermal carafe. She expected it was going to be that kind of night. They were not yet low enough on coffee that she felt like she couldn't share it freely.

Randi had asked about helping at Gary's house but Jim had told her he'd prefer she stay and help protect his home. She hadn't argued with him. She was still embarrassed over bringing those men to his home earlier. She wanted to be better at this. She knew that he had too much to do to spend his time arguing with her. Still, it burned her up that she felt like he'd dismissed her to *stay back with the womenfolk* like this was a Western. She tried to keep herself busy and not think about it. It wasn't working. She didn't have the kind of mind that could be switched off for convenience.

She found Charlotte sitting on the floor, knees pulled up, watching her children play with Ariel.

"How are you holding up?" Randi asked.

"I guess I'm functioning," Charlotte said.

"That's all anybody expects," Randi said. "No one is asking that you pretend like it didn't happen."

Charlotte leaned closer and lowered her voice. "I still feel messed up inside. Like something is damaged. Your entire life you learn how to interpret what happens around you. Then something like this happens and all that gets screwed up. I don't know how to respond to what's going on around me. Things don't make sense the way they should."

"In some ways a broken heart is like a broken leg," Randi said. "It takes a long time to heal, and it may never be the same again. You learn to live with it. Everyone I know who has suffered a bad loss says that's what happens eventually."

"How did you know I wouldn't kill myself after you threatened me?" Charlotte asked. "That was kind of a bold move."

"I wasn't really threatening you," Randi said.

"Sounded like a threat to me."

"I was *challenging* you," Randi said. "I knew there was a fighter in there. I was trying to provoke that fighter. Trying to make your instinct kick in and take over since nothing else was working."

"Still seems like a risky play to me," Charlotte said.

"I'm not a believer in medications for every condition," Randi said. "I think it leads to people placing the responsibility for their wellbeing on the meds and not back on themselves. That approach wouldn't have worked with everyone. It worked with you because of who you were before this happened."

Charlotte was silent for a moment, watching her children. "Why are you here, Randi? Why aren't you out there with them? You're a fighter."

"That's a good question," Randi said. "I'd rather be out there."

"Just go then," Charlotte said. "You don't strike me as the kind who needs a man's permission to do things."

"It's not about permission," Randi said. "I screwed up today by bringing those men here. I could have compromised everything. I'm not going to sneak out to be part of the action and make people worry about me. This is where I'm supposed to be tonight so I'll stay here. I have to trust that there's a reason. The reason could even be that it gave you and me time to have this talk."

Charlotte smiled. "I'm glad you're here."

53

The Valley

VALENTINE TRADED his weapon for something that would function better in the dark. He had a Saiga 12 shotgun he'd had for several years and a chest rig with ten spare magazines for it. The magazines were bulky and the buckshot loads made them heavy. In the tool trailer he found a hacksaw and shortened the weapon into a short-barreled shotgun. A few months back, a weapon like the SBS would have required filing paperwork with the BATFE and waiting half a year to get it back.

"ATF wait time has been reduced to five minutes," Valentine announced as the barrel dropped off and he shouldered the weapon. He couldn't hold back a smile. The Saiga 12 was a devastating weapon.

He was pissed that they didn't have night vision. One of the deputies had secured several sets for patrolling Glenwall in the dark, and they were in use every night. The plan had been to bring them over in the big move, which hadn't taken place yet. They did have some extremely bright tactical flashlights which could be weapon-mounted. There was some moonlight, so they would go dark and try to use the moonlight to navigate the terrain. Their primary plan was only reconnaissance tonight anyway. They wanted to peep in some windows and see what they were dealing with. They wanted to get a count of the *enemy*. If they had the opportunity to take someone out and improve their odds for future encounters, that would be an added bonus.

Those called into action prepared packs with food rations, spare ammo, and binoculars. They strapped on their guns, knives, and first aid kits, then blackened their faces with soot from the fire. They drank energy drinks from the trailer of food and swallowed convenience store speed from their personal stashes. When they were physically, psychologically, and logistically prepared, Valentine briefed them on their assignments.

"Adam, you're going to be on guard duty here," Valentine said. "Keep an eye out for anyone who might try to approach the camp."

"Got it," said Adam, the youngest and least experienced of the team.

"Grayson and Parker, I want you guys on that house closest to us. Do a sneak and peek. Try to get a number on occupants. Note any weapons you see."

"Got it," Parker answered. "It would be easier with night vision."

"Everything would," Valentine said.

"Where are you heading, boss?" Grayson asked.

Valentine liked the sound of that word. He liked that they were using it with him instead of Baxter. "I'm going to go deeper. There are several houses beyond that first one. I'm going to try to do the same with them. Sneak and peek. Get a count on folks. Everyone understand their assignments?"

All said that they did.

"Good," he said. "Be careful. Don't be stupid and don't fucking shoot each other."

54

The Valley

THEY DIDN'T HAVE time for the dug-in emplacement that Jim wanted so they improvised. They found an ancient oak that had fallen during a high wind. They banked earth against the base of it and it gave them a fairly bulletproof position as long as their heads were lowered. Jim was going to trade out with Gary. He and Will would man Gary's house along with Buddy.

Gary with his .338 Lapua would be more effective at the oak tree outpost. Initially, Jim had planned on manning that position with Gary, until Mack Bird had talked him out of it. Jim asked him why he wanted to man that station.

"I hunt coyotes," Mack said. "I have an AR-10 with an ATN thermal scope."

Jim couldn't hold back a grin. "You guys will make an excellent team."

While Gary didn't have a thermal scope, he did have an inexpensive Gen 1 Armasight night vision device that could operate as a monocular or be added onto a regular scope to give it night vision capabilities. Some people were disappointed in the low optical quality of such a setup. Still, any advantage in the dark was an advantage over total blackness.

Gary had several boxes of infrared light sticks in his gear. As it got dark, they used a laser rangefinder to place the sticks as markers at various distances within their sightline. They marked one hundred yards, two hundred yards, and five hundred yards. With his night vision, Gary would be able to see those light sticks in the dark although their illumination would not be visible to the naked eye. Using the rangefinder at night with its bright red laser would tip off a target that they were being ranged. The light sticks were a passive method that would allow Gary and Mack to more accurately estimate distances if they had to engage long-range targets.

Will had suggested they each tape one to their bicep with electrical tape so that they could identify "friendlies" if they had to leave the house and move around outside. Jim nixed that idea in case the trespassers had night vision. He didn't want a glowing target on his arm.

They had to use the radio for this operation even though Jim had been a little paranoid about too much radio traffic. He was concerned the men may have scanners that would pick up their conversations. In the end, they found it necessary to use the radios as a timesaver while trying to remain aware that their conversations might be monitored. They would simply have to be careful about what they said.

The sun fell and the day reached that point where the blackness of night snuck up on them. People throughout the valley were hustling to get the last drops of caffeine into their bodies and to get into position for a long night. Ellen and Debra used blankets, quilts, and sleeping bags to arrange a massive slumber party at their house. Pops strapped on a headlamp and appointed himself to read bedtime stories.

Lloyd would be on watch there all night. He would spend the night in Pete's outpost while the boy hopefully got some well-deserved rest. Jim only had one night-vision device and he had it with him, so Lloyd would be watching for anything that might be visible with the naked eye. It wasn't ideal.

Thomas Weatherman and his wife were going to stay awake and patrol their own property with their dogs. Jim insisted that everyone try to maintain an awareness of where other people would be that night and to make sure any shots were aimed for clear targets with solid backstops.

Jim had at one point thought he would position himself on the roof of Gary's house for a better vantage point, but he could not escape the concern that folks with access to surplus Humvees might also have access to night vision devices. He decided to sit in the house, which would make things look more normal to someone conducting recon and would provide him with some concealment.

Gary and Mack had settled into their hide. They each had a thermal mug of coffee and several packs of Jim's Sports Beans, caffeinated jelly beans. They were both gun lovers and had plenty to talk about as they scanned the darkness.

A coyote sang out and more joined it. It would be a long night.

55

The Valley

THE THREE MEN from the Rockdell camp worked their way down the paved road into the valley, each mentally preparing himself for the night.

Valentine had no fear, only anticipation. He loved shit like this. It made him wish he'd been able to become a real cop and not a security guard at a community college.

Parker was wary. As a deputy, he'd gone into danger many times in his career. This was different. He didn't have the legal and moral authority that accompanied him on those previous experiences. This was new territory for him.

Grayson didn't say a lot for fear his voice would tremble. He was consumed with fear. He was in a strange place participating in unfamiliar activities in total darkness. He kept stumbling over stuff. He'd turned on a flashlight earlier only to be cursed at that he would ruin everyone's night vision and make himself into a target. He'd lived in town his entire life and was not accustomed to the sounds of the night. He only wanted to make it out of here alive. If he did, he would consider returning to the safety of Glenwall despite what Baxter said.

"When we get to where we can see that house, we'll split up," Valentine said. "You two split off the road. One of you will watch the front and the other will watch the back."

"What if we can't see anything?" Grayson asked. "What if they're all in bed?"

"Then you keep watching until morning. You got somewhere else you need to be?" Valentine asked. "I need intel. We need to know what we're up against. Don't come back with nothing."

"Where are you going again?" Grayson asked.

"I'm going to see if any of the other houses on down the road are lit up," Valentine said. "Then I'll come back and meet up with you guys."

After another quarter-mile of walking, they rounded a bend in the road and crossed a low bridge.

"I think the house was up there," Parker said.

On the hill ahead of them, nearly six hundred yards in the distance, Gary went on alert.

"I've got movement on my night vision," Gary said. "Coming up the road."

"What do you see?" Mack asked.

"Can't tell much. They're grouped up and I'm only using starlight. I'm not gonna hit the IR illuminator in case they have night vision too."

"Give me a second," Mack said. He shifted his rifle, punched some buttons on his scope, and peered at the display. "Got 'em. Crystal clear."

"What do you see?"

"Three men. Looks like they have packs and rifles. I don't see any night vision goggles. I'm guessing they're the bad guys."

"You think I should try my IR spotlight?" Gary asked.

"I don't see any optics," Mack said. "Go for it."

Gary had an add-on IR spotlight mounted to his weapon that

could flood the area with infrared light and improve the image quality of his night vision device. He reached forward and activated it. Warm green light flooded the display of his night vision scope. "That's a lot better," he said. "I've got a shot now."

"Me too," Mack said.

"Should we take them out?" Gary asked. "We should probably let Jim know so he doesn't panic when he hears the shooting."

"Get him on the horn," Mack said. "I'm not taking my eyes off these guys."

"Jim, you there?" Gary asked into the radio.

"Jim here," came a reply.

"We've got three armed men on the road. They're coming in our direction. We can make out packs and guns," Gary said. "Both Mack and I have a shot."

"Give me a range," Mack said.

Gary looked for his IR light sticks. "Just this side of the four hundred yard marker."

"They're splitting up now," Mack said. "We need to do this."

"Take them," Jim whispered.

"I've got the middle man," Mack said. "You take right."

"Count it down," Gary said. "On one."

"Three...two...one."

Mack pulled the trigger and the 7.62x51 boomed in the darkness. At the same time, Gary pulled the trigger, his .338 Lapua emitting a deep boom. Two men dropped.

"Got a runner!" Mack said. He shifted position, tracking the fleeing man, a ghostly white visage on the display of the thermal scope. Mack banged out three more rounds, the reports ringing off the hills and echoing down the valley.

"You get him?" Gary said. "I lost him in the weeds."

Mack hesitated. "I can't tell. I can't see him. I don't know if I dropped him or if he found cover."

"Tell me something!" Jim said over the radio.

Gary thumbed his radio. "Two down and not moving. One unaccounted for."

"Gary, you get down here to your house," Jim said. *"You, Will, and I are going to look for the missing man. Mack, you stay up there on over-watch. Use the thermal but do not shoot. If you see a target, relay the position to us."*

"Got it," Gary said.

56

The Valley

IT WAS darkness and dumb luck that saved Valentine's life. Moments before the shots rang out, Valentine and his men had crossed a concrete bridge. When he heard the shots and the wet smack of rounds hitting meat, he knew what had happened. He'd shot enough deer in his life to know that sound. Instinct kicked in and he was running before the other men's bodies even hit the ground.

He charged through the deep weeds and across the field. More shots rang out and he could hear the thud of the impacts hitting the dirt behind him, then his feet were pedaling air. He threw his hands out and landed hard on wet rocks. Pain shot through his body. He rolled over onto his side and cold water soaked into his clothes.

Another shot rang out. He scrambled to his knees. His pack had soaked up water and it dumped out on his back. He felt his chest. His Saiga 12 was still there, the sling thrown across his neck. What little moonlight there was reflected off a creek, and he was at the rocky edge. He took off at a jog, stumbling every other step.

He didn't know where he was going but he knew he couldn't stay where he was. Whoever they were dealing with had some kind of advanced optics. The men beside him were taken out with kill shots in the pitch black of night. That was not amateur shit, nor was it luck.

The bank smoothed from rocks to mud and he increased his pace. He actually felt like he was putting some distance between him and the shooters when he found himself on his ass again.

"Fuck!" he hissed.

Several strands of barbed wire were stretched taut over the creek and he'd been clotheslined. At first, he thought it was some cruel booby trap laid out just for this situation, then he recalled that this was cattle country. Barbed wire fences were everywhere.

He was totally disoriented. He'd entered woods and lost sight of the night sky. Less moonlight was reaching him. He could barely see his hand in front of his face. He felt around for the strand of wire and followed it up the bank. He stood there in the darkness and listened. He could feel a raw wound down his neck, burning from his sweat. He was breathing hard and the sound of it filled his ears. He'd be lucky if they didn't track him down purely from the noise of his heaving lungs.

He heard no footsteps and saw no flashlights. He kept a hand on the fence and followed it a little further. There was a trail along it and the walking was decent. Much better than the creek bank. He heard a laugh and froze.

It couldn't be the people pursuing him. He assumed those to be men. This was not a man's laugh. It was a child's.

He crept along the wire and detected a glow in the distance. The farther he walked, the more the glow evolved into a square of window. The interior of the house was lit by candles and lanterns.

He moved closer and could see several women standing around. One woman was speaking into a radio. The rest of the women were listening. The clatter of a wooden door startled him and he froze. A flashlight cut through the darkness again. The same laugh rang out. A woman holding a child's hand was walking from what must have been the outhouse. They returned to the house and went inside.

Valentine watched and saw no men. Was this where the locals left their women while they looked for him?

That was a mistake.

The Valley

JIM RELAYED the situation to the women staying at his home.

"*You listening, Lloyd?*" Jim asked over the radio.

"*That would be a yes,*" Lloyd replied.

"*Pull back to the house. We need to circle the wagons. I don't want anyone out where they may be confused for the man we're looking for.*"

"*Got it,*" Lloyd said. "*You girls don't shoot me. I'm on my way.*"

"No promises," Randi muttered.

"Jim, have you checked the bodies of the people that were shot?" Ellen asked.

"*Yes,*" Jim replied.

"They armed?"

"*Heavily.*"

Ellen looked at the other women, saw the concern in their eyes. "You guys be careful," she said. "Keep us informed every step of the way."

"*Will do,*" Jim said. "*We're going to comb this property and then work*

*our way back toward their camp at Rockdell Farms. We figure the guy
probably retreated to his camp. We'll let you know what we find. Jim out."*

Ellen set the radio on the counter. "I don't want to take any
chances. Let's get the kids down in the basement. It's below ground
and there's no chance of stray rounds coming through the walls. You
ladies brought guns, right?"

"I have a rifle," Debra said.

"I have a pistol," Randi said.

"I have a pistol too," Charlotte said.

"What about your daughters, Randi?" Ellen asked.

"They know how to shoot but they don't have weapons," Randi
replied. "We lost most of what we owned in the fire."

"Once we get the children in the basement, we'll put the older
girls down there to watch after them. The rest of us will arm up and
keep an eye on this place."

"We need to lower the lights," Debra said.

"The basement is light-tight," Ellen said. "There's plastic over the
windows. Let's move them all down there with the kids."

"Ellen, do you have another gun I can use?" Randi asked.

"Did you have something particular in mind?"

"You have a shotgun? I'd like to set up outside. I can't stand the
thought that there might be someone creeping around outside and us
not know about it."

"I've got a Remington 870 you can use," Ellen said. "It's pump-
action."

"Is there one I can use?" Charlotte asked.

Ellen looked at Debra, who looked at Charlotte and then Randi.
Randi nodded. "She needs this. I think she's ready. She wants to
help."

"Then I've got another shotgun you can use," Ellen said. "It's a
Remington 1100. It's an automatic so there's no pump to work. Just
snap off the safety and start pulling the trigger."

Charlotte smiled. "Thanks, Ellen."

Ellen returned her smile. "Let's get these kids situated and we'll
get down to business."

58

The Valley

LLOYD CRAWLED out of the tangle of Pete's outpost. It was clearly built for a younger man with its low clearance and maze of tangled logs. When he made it out, he straightened his stiff back and stretched for a moment. He'd brought a banjo with him because that's what banjo players do. He slung it over his shoulder and took up his rifle for his trip back to the house. With word from Jim that they assumed the strangers to be heading in the other direction, Lloyd wasn't too concerned and let his guard down. He was not a tactical-minded person anyway, preferring to describe himself as a lover and not a fighter. He'd made the mistake of saying that in front of Randi once and she'd laughed until she cried.

His eyes were well-adjusted to the darkness at this point. In the distance, he could see Jim's home and the warm light emanating from its windows. The shortest trail from the outpost to the house was not the easiest. It was straight down the steepest part of the hill and made old knees ache. Lloyd preferred the easier, indirect route. It was smooth dirt and took several switchbacks down through the wood, by the creek, and then back up to the house.

The trail was easy to walk in the dark. With his banjo over his back, Lloyd imagined himself as a musician of the 1930s walking home from a barn dance. He'd kept his distance from the liquor jar that night though he knew that had he been playing a barn dance he'd be weaving his way home for certain. He pictured himself playing with the likes of Uncle Dave Macon and his Fruit Jar Drinkers or Gid Tanner and his Skillet Lickers. They were only about fifteen miles from the home of the Carter Family at Hiltons, Virginia. Lloyd knew he wouldn't be a good fit with those folks. They didn't approve of drinking and didn't allow it around them. He sure loved their music though.

He began humming "Dixie Darling." Before long, the words formed on his lips and he was singing it into the darkness as he walked. While he sang quietly, it was the loudest of the night sounds.

He was confused when the shadow of a tree split as he passed. It took him too long to recognize it wasn't merely the play of shadows. It was the movement of a man. By the time he realized this, the butt of a gun smashed into his head, stunning him. He fell, the banjo ringing out in the night as it struck the ground.

A man stood over him and punched him hard in the face. With his head pressed against the ground, it couldn't snap back and disperse the energy of the blow. Lloyd was disoriented. A strong man yanked him back to his feet and shoved him against a tree. His hands were pulled back around the trunk of the tree and flex cuffs were zipped onto his wrists. Valentine punched him in the stomach. Lloyd sucked in air, choked, then vomited.

A hand grabbed his hair as he threw up, wrenching his head back. "You're going to tell me everything I want to know."

Unable to breathe, Lloyd couldn't answer.

"Who are you people?"

Lloyd still didn't answer.

"How many of you are there?" He released Lloyd's head and it sagged down against his chest. "Are you the people who killed my men?"

"I don't know what you're talking about," Lloyd croaked.

"You tell me what I want to know or it's gonna suck to be you."

Lloyd could see that his attacker was huge. Still, he would not disclose anything if he had a choice. "Fuck you!"

Valentine chuckled. "There was a joke when I was a kid—ask me how my grandmother plays the piano."

Lloyd remained silent.

Valentine fired out a foot, catching Lloyd in the groin. He grunted, then threw up again.

"Ask me how my grandmother plays the piano," he repeated.

"How does your...your grandmother play the...piano?" Lloyd choked out.

"She doesn't," Valentine said. "She doesn't have any fingers." He yanked a heavy tactical knife from its sheath. He pinned Lloyd's pinky against the tree, placing the blade over the knuckle. Without warning, he tapped the blade hard with the butt of his shotgun. The joint separated and the pinky dropped into the thick moss at the base of the tree.

Lloyd screamed.

The sound carried through the night. In Jim's yard, his two new Great Pyrenees pups, bartered from Thomas Weatherman, perked up at the sound and began growling. Beside them, Randi and Ellen stood, chills running down their spines.

59

Rockdell Farms

"JUST LIKE OLD TIMES," Jim said. "Walking through the dark toward some kind of trouble. Didn't we get this out of our systems coming home from Richmond?"

"I hoped we did," Gary said. "I was hoping for a future that was more like *The Waltons* than *The Walking Dead*."

The two were creeping through the dark toward the camp on Rockdell Farms. Buddy and Lloyd explained to Jim earlier where it was located and Jim knew the exact spot. He'd driven by it hundreds of times. They left Mack on watch at the observation post with his thermal scope. Will and Buddy remained at Gary's house keeping an eye on things. They'd both wanted to come with Jim and Gary but Jim felt it was important to keep another line of defense in case Mack picked up something on the thermal.

When they neared Rockdell Farms, Jim tugged on Gary's sleeve and pointed to a low hill. "If we get up there we should be able to get a good view of their camp. With your night-vision we can get the lay of the land."

They climbed through the strands of high tensile fencing and tried to hike quietly through the tall grass. When they crested the hill, they dropped to a knee, hoping to keep themselves from being silhouetted against the sky.

"Looks like night vision won't be necessary," Gary said.

"I know. Can you believe that guy?" Jim said.

About seventy-five yards below them, a younger man sat on a camp chair. He had a roaring fire going beside him and was sipping coffee, a rifle across his lap.

"You think he's a decoy?" Gary asked.

Jim shook his head. "No, probably just an idiot."

"What do we do with him? I'm not sure I want to take him out like this. It'd be like shooting fish in a barrel."

"I'd like to ask him some questions," Jim said. "Maybe I can verify some of the information we got from the other men."

"What do you want me to do?" Gary asked.

"Stay up here. Keep watch. Let me know if there's anything I need to be concerned about."

"Got it," Gary said, settling onto his stomach. He flipped out the bipod on his rifle and took a comfortable position where he could watch the scene through his scope.

Jim retreated back the way they came, then swung in a wide circle to approach the camp. His plan was to come up on him from behind and give him no choice but to drop his weapon. Jim moved slowly and methodically, carefully placing his feet and trying not to brush against anything that would make noise.

When he reached the camp he ducked beneath a semi-trailer, flattened himself against a camper, and listened. There was no sound other than the crackling of the fire. He crept around that camper and behind another, still concealed from the man at the fire. He had his short-barreled rifle at a high ready position, both eyes open, the red dot sight visible through one.

He skirted the camper and ducked behind a pickup truck. Reflected firelight flickered off the windows of the cab. Hoping the cab would shield him from view, he rose up and peered through the cab, seeing that the man was still where he expected him to be. If Jim went around the bed of the truck and took five steps, he would be upon him. The guy would have no choice but to drop his weapon and surrender.

He breathed and calmed himself. He crouched and took a few steps toward the end of the pickup truck. He paused at the taillight, sighted through his weapon. When he turned this corner, there would be no stopping. He oozed around the corner and took a short step, then another, the reticle of his optic centered on the back of the guy in the camp chair. He took another step and struck his shin on the trailer hitch extending from the receiver. There was a loud *clunk*.

His heart sank. If he had a nickel for every time he'd tripped over a truck hitch... He lost the element of surprise.

"FREEZE!" he yelled.

The man in the camp chair was already spinning on him, pulling his rifle up. He dropped from the chair to the ground, ignoring Jim's command. He was going to shoot. Jim threw himself to the side.

The man fired a single shot. It was high and punched a hole in a camper. He was looking for Jim, his eyes having trouble adjusting to the darkness after staring at the fire. Jim had no trouble acquiring his target. His glowing crosshairs swung across the man. The guy's knees were pulled up causing Jim to have to shoot high.

He pushed on the forward handgrip which activated the bump fire mechanism. A five-shot burst stitched the guy across the chest and neck. He jerked and his rifle flew to the side. Jim crawled backward to the concealment of the truck bed. He rose to his feet, scanning his surroundings. His ears rang from the shots though he saw no movement.

He keyed his radio. "You see anything, Gary?"

"*No,*" he replied. "*You good?*"

"No leaks," Jim said.

"*You want me to come down there?*"

"Yeah," Jim said. "Let's get a quick look around."

When Gary reached him, Jim was snooping around the place and trying to get a count on who was living there. It was difficult, taking into account that some of them had been killed already. One thing became clear. By whatever means these men had obtained them, they had access to some significant resources. Not only were they able to get food and gear, they had access to fuel for transporting that gear. That in itself was even more surprising than the trailer loads of food.

Gary was huffing and puffing when he reached the camp. He'd been jogging along the road. He found a bottle of water in a cooler and helped himself. They stayed clear of the fire, not wanting to suffer the same fate as the guy they'd been forced to kill.

Jim's radio chirped. *"Everyone okay?"* It was Mack Bird.

"We're fine," Jim said. "One bad guy down."

"He the one we're looking for?"

"I don't think so," Jim said. "I think he was a sentry."

"So we've still got one out there."

"And no fucking clue where he is," Will piped in from his own radio.

"Jim?" It was a woman's voice.

"Ellen?" Jim asked.

"Yes," she replied. *"I think there's someone outside the house."*

"Get everyone into the basement," Jim said. "Secure the house. No one goes outside."

"Almost everyone is in the basement. Some of us are upstairs with weapons. We've killed the lights," she said. *"We heard someone cry out in the dark. We think it was Lloyd."*

"Shit! We'll be there as fast as we can," Jim said.

"One more thing," Ellen said. *"Randi went after him."*

Jim sighed a curse. He felt like throwing his radio. That girl could get herself in more trouble. He admired her guts while he hoped she didn't get herself killed.

"Are there keys in that truck?" Jim asked.

Gary opened the door and checked. "Yeah."

"Get in," he said.

Gary slid into the driver's seat, Jim into the passenger side. Jim keyed the mike on his radio. "Mack, Buddy, Will—you guys get down to the road. We're coming to get you in a truck. Don't shoot."

Gary cranked the truck and the diesel engine roared to life. He punched the accelerator, spraying sod out behind them. He shot between the gateposts and skewed onto the roadway, speeding into the night.

60

The Valley

WHEN THE LIGHTS went off in the house, Randi slipped off into the darkness. While she didn't know the area well, she knew the path from the house to Jim's cave, to the various farm structures, and to the creek. The cry that she and Ellen heard sounded like it came from somewhere between the house and the cave.

She wandered in that direction, staying to the path. Around her, the moonlight reflected off the dewy grass, crickets chirped, and peepers chanted. Her shoes grew damp, which was something she hated. The farther she got from the house, the more her nerves went on edge. Whomever the men were looking for could be behind any tree. He could have a gun on her right now.

She questioned why she was even out here. Who did she think she was? It certainly wasn't because of any particular attraction to Lloyd. Still, he was a member of the group and it's what you did when one of you was in danger. He was part of the tribe. She realized, though, that she'd never convince Lloyd that she didn't do it out of love for him. He'd never shut up about it.

If he were even still alive.

She soon discovered that he was, learning it in a manner that gave her chills. She could hear stifled sobbing. Whimpering. She wondered what had been done to him. She crept on. Step. Step. Step.

"Everyone imagines they're the hardass that won't crack."

The words came from a man she hadn't seen at first. He was perhaps twenty feet in front of her. His clothing was dark and she could barely make him out. Her eyes began to decipher the shapes around her. Several feet beyond the man was a sagging form bound to a tree.

"Everyone thinks they can hold out and not tell their secrets," Valentine continued. "Once the cutting starts everyone gives in."

"There's nothing to tell," Lloyd choked out. "I'm here staying with my friends. We're trying to get by, same as everyone else."

"I don't give a damn who you are," Valentine said. "I'm interested in how many of you there are. I'm interested in resources. I want to know about food, guns, and tools. I'm counting to ten and then I'm cutting you again. You better start talking."

"Noooo!"

Randi braced the barrel of the shotgun against a tree. She was concerned about the way he was standing. His back was to her. Depending on how the shot spread, some might miss him and hit Lloyd. That would be one more thing she'd never hear the end of. She needed to get a better angle but the ground here was littered with twigs from the maples overhead. If she walked off-trail, one would snap beneath her feet and she'd be caught.

"DON'T FUCKING MOVE!" she ordered, feeling like she was out of options.

Valentine dodged instantly to the side, spinning away from Lloyd. She couldn't follow his movement in the dark and she was afraid to shoot blindly for fear she'd hit her friend. She saw a burst of flame, heard an explosion, and shotgun pellets shredded the bark off nearby trees. Her instinct for self-preservation kicked in and she pulled back behind the tree, trying to make herself as narrow as possible. There was a burst of more gunfire, more rounds fired than she could keep up with, and more pellets buried themselves into the tree where she stood. She flinched and cried when chunks of bark sprayed against her face.

She heard the rattle of what she thought must be the man reloading the shotgun. Unsure of when another opportunity might occur, she leaned around the tree to see if she could locate him and put an end to this. She gasped when Valentine was suddenly in front of her grabbing at the barrel of the gun. He locked his fingers around it and she pulled the trigger.

BOOM!

It was too late. He'd diverted the barrel away from himself. She started to pull the trigger again. She hesitated, trying to figure out where Lloyd was in relation to her barrel.

Then he had both hands on the barrel and shoved the shotgun back at her. The butt caught her in the stomach and knocked the breath from her. Randi lost her grip on the stock. She couldn't get her finger out of the trigger guard fast enough. Her finger was caught and snapped like a breadstick. She fell over backward, the pain taking her breath.

There was enough light to see Valentine standing over her with the gun in his hand. She could see the glint from his teeth as he smiled and raised the gun over his head like a club. He was going to crush her skull.

In a reflex born of growing up with brothers, she raised her foot and lashed out at his groin, shoving as hard as she could. He grunted and staggered back, falling against a tree. She reached for her waistband, for the automatic she'd tucked in there. It was gone. She felt around in the leaves but her hand didn't fall upon it. She rolled onto her hands and knees, crawling, trying to find the shotgun Valentine had dropped when she kicked him.

Her hand brushed the barrel and she pulled it to her. Realizing what she was up to, Valentine lunged at her, stomping down hard onto her back. There was a dull snap inside her. Randi screamed and fell flat on her face. He reached down and grabbed her by the hair, pulling her to her feet. The kick to her back had left her too stunned to scream. She couldn't breathe well. She thought he'd broken a rib. Then his forearm locked around her neck and raised her off the ground.

She grabbed for his arm and kicked wildly but couldn't draw a breath, couldn't utter a sound. She tried to aim her kicks backward at his groin, couldn't land anything solid. She could see in the direction of the house, could see the movement of lights through the trees. She tried to elbow him. She couldn't muster the strength. Couldn't focus. Couldn't breathe.

Randi was dying.

Then there was a massive bellow in her ears, the scream of a bull. Valentine dropped Randi and she fell to the ground. She rolled onto her back. She needed to crawl away. She couldn't think clearly enough to do so. She saw flashing lights, another shadow behind the large man. A glint of steel. Valentine tried to move but the shadow clung to him, holding onto his back, plunging the knife into him dozens—perhaps hundreds—of times.

Valentine fell onto his face and the shadow was on him. Randi could hear the grunts of exertion. There was a guttural scream, not of fear—of anger. Rage. Hate. It was the banshee wail of a demon clawing its way from the core of a person. The knife raised and raised again, punching into Valentine. He no longer moved but the knife didn't stop. The sound of it filled Randi's ears. The puddle it was creating in his flesh. The splash of the clutching fist plunging into that puddle again and again.

"HERE!" came a voice from the dark.

"Oh my God!" said a man's voice.

There were hands on Randi. A light hit the fallen man, the shadow still releasing its fury on him. In the stark white light, she saw a bloody knife, an arm bloody to the elbow. She saw a face splashed with blood, a snarl cut across the face. She saw eyes filled with fire.

Charlotte.

61

The Valley

"RANDI WE NEED YOUR HELP," a woman said. "We need you to wake up."

She was on the couch in Jim's living room. There was a cold compress on her head. She jerked awake, a reaction to having passed out while she thought her life was in danger.

"Lloyd needs help," Ellen said.

Randi tried to rise. She was unsteady and hands supported her from all sides. She took a step and sucked in a hard breath. "I think I have broken ribs."

The hands didn't let up. They led her to Lloyd, laid out on the floor, a bandaged hand elevated. The dressing seeped fresh red blood.

"It's still bleeding," Randi said.

"I know," Ellen said. "That's what we need help with. We tried stitching it but we can't get the skin together."

Randi shook her head. "Amputations. Sometimes you have to

resect the bone and tissue to give you enough skin to close the wound. You'll have to cauterize."

Ellen grimaced. "How?"

"Do you have any pain meds?" Randi asked.

"Some," Ellen replied. "Leftovers from various medical procedures over the years."

"Give him two of whatever you got," Randi said. "It's going to hurt. Heat a piece of steel red hot with a propane torch. Press the fingers against it."

"I don't know if I can do that," Ellen said.

"I'll help," Randi said. "It's got to be done."

Ellen went to the back of the house and returned with two pills. Randi studied them, then gave them to Lloyd. She held a bottle of water and helped him wash them down.

"Tell Jim to get a propane torch and a thin piece of steel. An old butcher knife or something would be perfect," Randi said.

Ellen went to the door, then came back. "Jim's getting something."

"Charlotte?" Randi asked.

Ellen nodded outside. "She's outside with the neighbors and her mother."

"She okay?"

"They had to pull her off him. She didn't want to quit stabbing him. Gary had to get up in her face and scream at her before she came out of it. She was someplace dark and far away."

"She was probably picturing the man who killed her husband," Randi said. "This man was the personification of everything that was wrong in her life."

"Not anymore."

Jim burst through the door with the items they needed.

"Get people in here to hold him," Randi said. "This is going to be hard to watch."

Jim rounded up several folks while Randi heated the butcher knife blade with the propane torch.

"Make sure that basement door is closed," Randi said. "He's going to scream."

"It's closed," Ellen said.

"Lloyd," Randi whispered.

He only mumbled in response. She pinned his hand down.

"Help me hold it," she said. "The knife has to stay there for a moment."

Other hands joined her in holding Lloyd. She pressed the knife firmly to the stumps of his two missing fingers.

Lloyd's eyes flew open and he tried to scream but couldn't get the air. He bucked and tried to jerk his hand away. They held him tight. Buddy turned his head away and squeezed his eyes shut, unable to watch. Mercifully, Lloyd passed out. The sickening smell of burning flesh filled the room.

In a few seconds, Randi pulled the knife back and examined the charred stubs. Judging them satisfactory, she released his hand. "Keep him drugged up. Don't bandage it yet. I need my ribs taped. Then I have to lie down."

62

The Valley

It didn't take Jim much deliberation to conclude the residents of the valley should seize the spoils of their battle with the Glenwall folks. If they didn't, someone else would. Worse yet, others from that same Wallace County group may return and use those supplies to continue establishing a foothold in the valley. Jim was determined to prevent that, even if more blood had to be spilled.

The folks in his *tribe* worked together to inventory the food and supplies from the camp at Rockdell Farms. They were divided evenly between each household with Jim and Buddy personally delivering them. For families like Randi's, who'd not come with much in the way of supplies, it was a life-altering bounty. Besides emergency rations, there were bulk groceries, personal hygiene items, and medical supplies.

The travel trailers and all of the support vehicles from the camp were brought into the valley for safekeeping. The fuel tanker was driven to a central location and all residents with a need for diesel fuel now had a windfall. Diesel pickups, tractors, and construction equipment could be operated for a few months longer. They could farm and haul supplies.

There was no more discussion about blowing up the road on the Rockdell Farms end of the valley. All residents were now in agreement that the existence of the road was not a liability, it put all their lives at risk. The next vehicle to enter the valley could bring raiders, a gang, or any number of lowlifes looking to take those things that the people of the valley fought so hard to hang onto.

As it turned out, one of the Wimmers had worked in construction. He *may* have brought home some blasting caps from work one day to use with some old, weeping explosive that Mr. Wimmer had on the farm. As a group, they planted the charges under a bridge and detonated them. The bridge fragmented and dropped into the water. While not a certain guarantee against more trespassers, it was a step in the right direction.

Additional steps would have to be taken in the way of security. Permanent observation posts were being established at vantage points with helpful lines of sight, to be manned daily, and they intended to work on establishing a network of paid informants in the surrounding communities. With the gear they'd obtained from the trailers and the liquor that Lloyd hoped to be soon making, they would have plenty of goods that could be traded for information.

After several days of medicated stupor, Lloyd awoke in his bed at Buddy's house with the old man watching over him. It was the same way Lloyd had watched over the old man after he'd been attacked by coyotes.

"I've got good news and bad news," Buddy said.

Lloyd looked at him groggily, trying to focus. "Oh shit," Lloyd said. "This is payback time."

"The bad news is that you can't play the banjo. The good news is that you never really could anyway."

Lloyd cracked a weak smile.

"It's fortuitous that you were a student of the three-finger style popularized by Earl Scruggs. Of course, he had all his fingers and only choose to use three," Buddy said.

"I assume it's also good fortune that I prefer the four-string over the five-string," Lloyd said. "That's one less string to worry about."

Lloyd was not the only one with healing to do. Randi had broken several ribs in her scrape with Valentine. For several weeks she couldn't do much other than sit around. To pass the time, she worked with Ariel on the art project she'd mentioned to her earlier. They didn't tell anyone what they were doing. Each day they'd spend a few hours together in the barn. Afterward, they'd cover their project with an old pink bed sheet and come back to the house.

When Randi finally felt well enough to get around, she finished the trip she'd set out on with Buddy and Lloyd. The three of them, along with Charlotte, took the day-long trip to Randi's home and back. Randi could tell that her brother had not been there in some time. His gear was there and that seemed to tell the story. She assumed him to be dead and she could only hope that he'd taken some of the Crosses with him. She was not going to pay the Crosses a visit and check. She was calling an end to that battle, for now anyway. She needed some peace and some healing. She needed some time to mourn.

63

The Valley

THE DAY after her trip to her old home, Randi and Ariel gathered their tribe for an outing. They brought together Jim's family, Gary's family, Lloyd, and Buddy. They would not tell anyone what they were doing, only that they were going on a picnic and would have to walk for several miles. The children would ride on horseback with one being utilized as a packhorse. Despite it being a picnic, everyone carried their preferred weapons.

Randi asked Jim to borrow one of his large backpacking packs. She and Ariel packed their project into it, then closed it up without revealing it to anyone.

They followed the creek, then the road, and eventually found themselves at the edge of town. Ariel didn't know exactly which way to go, so Randi took over, leading them to the cemetery.

"I ain't so sure about this," Buddy said.

Ariel took his hand and tugged on it. "You have to come, Mr. Buddy. You *have* to."

Torn, he relented. He smiled at her. "Whatever you say, sweetie."

Randi led the way, with Ariel behind her tugging Buddy. The rest of the crew followed behind, still unsure as to what was going on. Randi led them to the smooth plot of unmarked dirt that marked the final resting place of Buddy's daughter.

Buddy paused and took his hat off, staggered by the wave of memories. The rest of the men took their hats off as well, out of respect. They all gathered around Buddy, patting his back and offering their support.

"What's this all about, Ariel?" Ellen asked, feeling a little uncomfortable.

Ariel grinned. "Randi, let's show them."

Randi unslung her pack and lowered it to the ground. She unbuckled the lid of the pack and opened the drawstring that sealed the top, reached inside, and withdrew a thick slab of wood, roughly two feet wide and three feet high. She handed it to Ariel.

Ariel worked to maneuver the bulky item. She propped it against herself, standing in front of Buddy. He stared at the object, the deeply carved and surprisingly delicate lettering:

Here Lies
  Rachel Baisden
  Beloved Daughter

A SOB ERUPTED from Buddy and he put his hand over his mouth, staring at the slab of wood. Ariel blushed, embarrassed by the attention her surprise had garnered. She wasn't sure if she'd done the right thing or not. Buddy went to her, wrapping his arms gently around her and hugging her.

"I wanted to make you something," Ariel said. "Randi said you would like this."

"I do like it," he said. "I love it more than I have words to tell you."

Buddy looked over at Randi then, catching her eye. Randi lost it, breaking into tears. Buddy stood and hugged her too.

It wasn't long before everyone except for the confused children was crying. They cried not just for Buddy, but for all that each of them had lost. For Lloyd's parents, for Charlotte's husband, for the people of the valley.

Randi pulled an entrenching tool from her pack and they used it to set the marker on the grave. While she and Jim dug, Lloyd moved his banjo from his back to a proper playing position. The missing fingers were on his picking hand and not his fretting hand. The digits were still very painful and he kept thick bandages on them to protect them. Still, with the three fingers he had, he played.

"A banjo player named Ola Belle Reed wrote a little song about the hard life of mountain folks," Lloyd said. "It was called 'I've Endured.' I've always been partial to it."

Lloyd eased into the song the way people slip into a hot bathtub. The music swelled around them. When he began to sing, it became the words of a prayer that echoed in the heads of everyone.

How much could one endure?

Made in the USA
Columbia, SC
03 June 2024

36511099R00157